"I realize I gave up my rights to Sam's upbringing when I left England. But your father is gone now, and I would like to have a part in my son's life."

Instead of disputing this, her face cleared and she smiled. "I think that's wonderful." Before Luke could take comfort from Bobbie's encouraging tone, she continued. "But you can do it best by taking over Father's firm." She waved at the blueprints spread across the wide desk. "Doesn't it make perfect sense for you to take over this project right here in London?" Her voice rose, gaining momentum. "That way, you'll be nearby for Sam." She gave a slight gasp, her eyes growing rounder. "Perhaps that was why Father never changed his will! He realized how wrong he'd been to take Sam away from you—and wanted to atone for that."

Luke made a sound of disbelief. "You can imagine anything you'd like, but I know he would be turning over in his grave right now if he thought I'd be taking over Sam's upbringing!" He stood. "No, I'll get any other job before working for this firm again."

Books by Ruth Axtell Morren

Love Inspired Historical

Hearts in the Highlands
A Man Most Worthy
To Be a Mother
  "A Family of Her Own"
A Gentleman's Homecoming

Steeple Hill Single Title

Winter Is Past
Wild Rose
Lilac Spring
Dawn in My Heart
The Healing Season
The Rogue's Redemption
The Making of a Gentleman
A Bride of Honor

RUTH AXTELL MORREN

wrote her first story when she was twelve—a spy thriller—
and knew she wanted to be a writer. There were many detours
along the way. She studied comparative literature at Smith
College, taught English in the Canary Islands and worked in
international development in Miami, Florida, where she met
her future husband.

She gained her first recognition as a writer when her second manuscript became a finalist in the Romance Writers
of America Golden Heart Contest in 1994. Ruth has been
writing for Steeple Hill Books since 2002, and her second
novel, *Wild Rose* (2004), was selected as a Booklist Top 10
Christian Novel in 2005.

Ruth and her family divide their time between the
down-east coast of Maine and the Netherlands. Ruth
loves hearing from readers. You can contact her through
her website, www.ruthaxtellmorren.com or her blog,
www.ruthaxtellmorren.blogspot.com.

RUTH AXTELL MORREN

A Gentleman's Homecoming

Steeple
Hill®

Published by Steeple Hill Books™

STEEPLE HILL BOOKS

Steeple
Hill®

Recycling programs
for this product may
not exist in your area.

ISBN-13: 978-0-373-82859-3

A GENTLEMAN'S HOMECOMING

www.SteepleHill.com

Printed in U.S.A.

And I will restore to you the years
that the locust hath eaten, the cankerworm,
and the caterpillar, and the palmerworm…
—*Joel* 2:25

To Mom,
Thanks for all you've been to me.

Chapter One

Sydenham, October 1888

"Aunt Bobbie, I don't understand why I have to be here."

Roberta Gardner gazed at her thirteen-year-old nephew, Sam, who sat half hidden behind the tall potted palm at the bay window. He swung a leg impatiently over the edge of the window seat, the other folded under him. One shoelace was untied.

Bobbie could well understand her nephew's outward display of indifference, even hostility, toward his father. After all, since he was five, Sam had scarcely seen the man. Though neither had spoken of it, she knew both she and Sam harbored the secret fear that his father would come and take him away.

Bobbie drew a deep breath. Her heartbeat quickened as it did each time she thought about being face-to-face with Luke, the man she'd been secretly in love with since she was fourteen. "Your father is arriving at any moment. Of course you must be here to greet him."

The thought of seeing her former brother-in-law had

Bobbie so on edge it was all she could manage to re-assure her nephew.

What would it be like to see Luke Travis after six years?

"He isn't my father."

Her nephew's insistence only deepened Bobbie's worry. How she hoped Sam wouldn't reject his father outright. She had so longed and prayed for this day, when Luke would come back to his only child and be the father that time and circumstances had denied him.

Sam's square chin, so much like Luke's, jutted forward. "Grandfather was the only father I ever had." At the mention of his grandfather, his young voice quavered.

Bobbie's father had been gone only a week now, and still she could scarcely believe it. As soon as her thoughts alighted on her father, her throat tightened and tears filled her eyes. How could he be gone? She had bid him goodbye that morning expecting to see him that evening at the dinner table and now he was gone.

How were they to continue? Would Luke step into the gap and fill the emptiness that permeated their lives?

She didn't allow herself to hope. It was a miracle he'd even replied to her telegram informing him of her father's death.

She removed Luke's telegram from her pocket now. She'd received it the day after the funeral, but she'd read it at least a dozen times since then. She smoothed out the wrinkles and scanned the brief words.

Arriving London twenty-first Will call following
day Condolences Luke Travis

Bobbie traced the letters of the cable. In the nature of telegrams the words were curt and abbreviated. She couldn't help thinking the worst.

The last time Luke had been home to Sydenham had been for his wife Irene's funeral. Her older sister. Was England forever to hold bereavement for him? Since then Bobbie hadn't heard a word from him, although she sent him quarterly reports through his solicitor's office on his son's progress.

But the telegram in Bobbie's hand was tangible evidence that Luke was indeed returning home.

She glanced at Sam, whose nose pressed against the pane of glass. Despite his antagonism, he'd been on the watch for his father since morning. How much he needed a father now, whether he realized it or not.

Bobbie sighed, staring out the rain-spattered window. Would her meeting with Luke be as painful as the last? They had exchanged bitter words over Sam's future then. Would Sam's well-being draw them together now, or push them further apart?

She surely needed a friend now…someone to lean on and to help share the load. Would—could—Luke be that friend? She scarcely dared hope.

The chilly spring rain fell steadily through the bare limbs of the elm trees lining the wide, unpaved street and dripped down Luke's black umbrella. The tips of the branches showed the buds that would soon unfurl into leaves. Bright spots of purple and yellow crocuses dotted the grass and peeped under the dark hedges along the street, their colorful petals braving the steady drip of rain.

Luke breathed in the damp air. The scent of new life and promise that spring had always held for him as a boy growing up in England. But for the last half dozen years, it only reminded him afresh of Irene's death.

As Luke drew closer to his in-laws' house, his thoughts returned to what had been uppermost in his mind throughout his journey from America, his apprehension growing with each step.

What would transpire when he saw Sammy? His son would be thirteen. Luke had little idea of who he was. He'd broken with Sammy as surely as his wife had broken with him—though in Luke's case, the rupture hadn't been his intention.

The last time he'd seen his son, at Irene's funeral, Sammy had been a shy, frightened seven-year-old clinging to his young aunt Bobbie's hand. Luke wouldn't even know him now, nor Sammy him.

Had he made the greatest mistake of his life by relinquishing his only child to his wife's family? What had started out as a practical arrangement, given the constraints of his profession, had ended by his signing away all custodial rights to the Gardners. His father-in-law had made sure of it.

And now Mr. Gardner was gone. It seemed unimaginable that this dominating, larger-than-life gentleman was no longer among them. Luke had fully expected his late father-in-law to live well into his eighties or even nineties, ruling them all with his iron fist. But death had a finality that made a person reassess all that seemed important in life.

It was long past time for Luke to discover who his only son was.

Unsure of his reception in the Gardner household, Luke stopped at the redbrick villa in the prosperous London suburb where his late wife had grown up and where his son had spent the last eleven years of his life.

It was an imposing three-story house with a wide, front-facing gable and side wing. The ground floor was partially hidden by a tall, thick yew hedge.

Suddenly, Luke wanted to turn tail and run, like a young schoolboy afraid to face the bully in the yard.

He gave a mirthless laugh. He who built bridges and tunnels for a living quaked at the ghosts from the past?

By staying away from Sydenham, Luke thought he'd put it all behind him. Except that he had a son...a reminder that the past lived on.

Samuel Luke Travis was the sole reason Luke had returned to England this time. That and the fact that his father-in-law was no longer a hindrance to a relationship with his son.

With a decisive movement, Luke swung open the low, wrought-iron gate and strode down the slick, wet flagstones to the front door.

But the memories kept flashing before him.

The first time he'd visited this house, he'd been down from Oxford for the day, a shy young man, hoping to make a good impression on the parents of the loveliest young lady he'd ever met.

And it filled him with apprehension to know her father was a civil engineer, the very field he was studying.

But Irene, the beautiful nineteen-year-old girl of his dreams, had laughed aside his fears at meeting the eminent professional. "Papa will take to you and you can work in his firm. We can get a house in London. It will be splendid!"

Yes, splendid it had turned out...for the first year at least, before the dissatisfaction and recriminations had started. Regret bit deep into Luke, like an acid whose burn lingers long after it has been washed away.

No, he wouldn't go down that road again. He was here to pay his respects to the Gardner family, see his son and settle his future before leaving again.

The dark, polished wood door opened soon after Luke had let the brass knocker fall, almost as if someone had been watching for him.

A petite young maid took his card. He didn't recognize her from his last visit. Otherwise, everything looked unchanged in the wide, dimly lit hallway he was left to wait in. He removed his top hat and closed his umbrella, setting it against a stand full of furled ones.

Even the smell of the house was the same…heavy wooden furniture, potpourri and the faint odor of fine tobacco, from the evening cigar Mr. Gardner used to smoke.

Used to. Luke expected Robert Gardner to come striding out of his study, cigar in one hand, his other outstretched, the expression in his piercing blue eyes half genial, half accusatory.

His late father-in-law had only been in his early sixties, Luke calculated. What would happen to the engineering firm now? Surely he'd groomed a successor. Luke found it hard to picture Mr. Gardner relinquishing any of his control to another. He shook his head. It wasn't his concern anymore.

A few moments later the maid reappeared from the room she'd entered, which Luke knew was the front parlor. "This way, Mr. Travis."

Stepping through the doorway was like stepping back in time. Nothing had changed in the long room facing the street, from the large-patterned flower wallpaper to the dark, heavy furniture, the backs and arms covered in lacy antimacassars. A coal fire radiated heat from the black-marble fireplace shielded by the embroidered fire screen at the near end of the room. Porcelain figurines, wax flowers under glass domes, and other bric-a-brac filled every tabletop and cabinet. Potted ferns and palms crowded a bay window at the opposite end of the room.

His gaze swept across the clutter, expecting to see the elegant Mrs. Gardner, his former mother-in-law, presiding in one of the armchairs. Instead, the only person present was his young sister-in-law.

She was seated in an armchair by the window, looking pale and solemn in her deep mourning, her dark hair swept back in a knot, her eyes staring at him through her wire-rimmed glasses. She looked just as she'd looked the last time he'd been here, only then it had been in mourning for her older sister Irene.

Her hands folded in her lap, her slim shoulders straight, Bobbie struck him as too composed. Her father's death must have devastated her. Luke felt a wave of compassion for his sister-in-law.

He'd always felt a little sorry for Bobbie, the youngest in a family of strong individuals who seemed to overshadow her. The first time he'd met her, she'd impressed him as a refreshingly unspoiled and down-to-earth young girl with a keen sense of the absurd evident in her twinkling blue eyes.

Since then, he'd come to realize, Roberta Gardner was just as much a Gardner as the rest of them. When his son's future was at stake, his sister-in-law had stood staunchly by her father's side, evincing the same Gardner determination.

Perhaps it was appropriate, after all, that she was the late Robert Gardner's namesake. Unlike Irene, Bobbie resembled him physically, with her dark brown hair and slate blue eyes. Six years ago, Luke had realized how much of her father's character she had inherited as well.

Bobbie swallowed, her eyes riveted on the man standing just inside the doorway. Should she stand or remain seated? But she remained paralyzed in her chair.

A second later, he spotted her and began walking toward her, his steps muffled by the thick carpet.

Lean, but with a wiry strength, his face tanned by the hours he spent outdoors as a civil engineer, he strode across the room with that purposeful step of his, giving her little chance to arrange her features. Arrange her features? Who had coined such a ridiculous phrase, as if one could move things about? Relax her eyebrows, keep her eyes from expressing too much of anything, smile or not—her lips felt frozen in a stiff line, which ruled out that alternative.

She prayed that her features didn't betray her true emotions—terror, anticipation, the greatest relief a person could ever know. *He'd returned.* That was all that mattered at the moment.

And now Luke was standing before her, his hand held out. "Hello, Bobbie." His tone was low, his features grave as his eyes scanned her face.

What did he see? A twenty-eight-year-old spinster, a maiden aunt living at home, raising her nephew? The plain younger sister of his dazzlingly beautiful late wife?

She swallowed, unable to look away from him. At thirty-six, his face had lost all the boyishness, which had given his expression an endearingly vulnerable quality to it at times.

It was all hard planes now, until you came to those pale green eyes, the color of jade, below tawny eyebrows. His light brown hair was longer than before, a bit damp and tousled about the edges.

That fact finally brought her to her senses. She stuck out her own hand and felt it immediately engulfed by his firm grip. "Hello, Luke." His skin felt cold. "Oh, how chilled you must be. It's so beastly raw outside." She stood, her heart thumping against her ribcage. She felt as she always had in his presence, like the stammering fourteen-year-old in awe of her older sister's beau.

"If…if you'd let us know when you were arriving, we'd have sent someone to meet you." She was speaking too quickly, so she paused and took a breath, releasing her hand from his and motioning toward the fireplace.

"No need. I caught the fly and decided to walk the last few blocks—" He broke off, looking past her.

Of course…he had seen Sam. The boy stood by the window seat, his large blue eyes wide, staring at his father.

"Hello, Sammy."

At the baby name the boy's lower lip thrust out. When he made no move, Bobbie said quietly, "Sam, come and say hello to your father."

For a second, Bobbie wasn't sure he'd obey. But then, without a word, her nephew stepped forward, his jaw knotted, his eyes hard. "Hello."

Luke reached out a hand. When Sam made no move to extend his, his father let his own fall back by his side. "I'm sorry about Grandfather."

Sam looked down.

Although Sam resembled his mother in his fair coloring and blue eyes, his personality reminded Bobbie much more of herself at that age. Painfully sensitive and vulnerable. The boy's blond hair, ruthlessly brushed this morning, already had several strands falling over his forehead, and his tie hung askew. He was wearing long trousers for the first time—a gray suit with black trim purchased for the funeral—and looked so much like a young gentleman, it made Bobbie's heart ache. Where was the little boy who'd come to look on her as his only mother?

Her nephew's discomfort made Bobbie forget her own nerves. Squaring her shoulders, she turned to Luke with a hesitant smile. "Why don't we sit by the fire? I'll ring for some tea."

His glance lingered on his son, but when Sam only stared back, Luke nodded and followed Bobbie to the armchair she indicated.

"Thank you. I came as soon as I received word."

After yanking on the bell pull, Bobbie sat down on the settee across from Luke. "I wasn't quite sure where to locate you, but your solicitor had…an address. You were in America?" She didn't feel able to ask more. He seemed a stranger. His attention was clearly on Sam, with what looked like both awe and longing in his eyes. She felt a pang, realizing how much of the boy's childhood he had missed.

He seemed to drag his attention from his son with effort. "Yes. I just finished a project out in Kansas City, a railway bridge."

She nodded, her curiosity immediately sparked. But she hesitated to ask anything more, so she looked down at her own hands, wondering what to say next.

"How did it happen?"

Her glance flickered back up to his. "Father?"

He nodded.

"He collapsed in his office. His secretary discovered him." She found it hard to continue. "It was his heart."

"I'm sorry," he said quietly. "Your mother—?"

Bobbie knotted her hands together. "Not well. She is taking it very hard. I'm sorry she isn't able to receive you today."

"I understand. Please give her my sympathy."

She nodded, pressing her lips together, feeling as if she were talking to a polite stranger. A part of her ached to express her true grief to him, but she didn't think he would understand. He and her father had not gotten along.

"It must have been a terrible shock to her. Your father was such an…energetic man."

He had hesitated, as if finding a proper word to describe her father's sometimes overbearing nature. The two had clashed soon after Luke had gone to work in her father's firm. "Yes, he was." She smoothed down her black crepe skirt as she formed her reply. "It came as a shock to all of us." She fell silent, unable to speak, her throat constricting again.

"I'm sorry," he repeated.

She nodded, trying to swallow. Thankfully, he remained silent, giving her time to compose herself. When she felt able, she continued. "We're still trying to grasp the reality of his absence."

"Yes, I can imagine. I find it hard to believe myself, and I hadn't seen him in some years."

Was he thinking of that last occasion, Irene's funeral? Father had not been at his best then, so shattered by his favorite daughter's sudden death. It had embittered her father to a degree that not even Irene's past behavior had managed to do.

Luke's green eyes studied her, as if beginning to look

beneath the surface. "You are not having to shoulder everything yourself, I hope?"

She winced, his gentle tone threatening to disarm her. He knew how helpless her mother could be in a crisis—real or imagined. She gave a half shrug, once again not trusting herself to speak. If only he knew how much she'd had to assume in the past week.

He shook his head, a slight smile playing around his lips. "I find it hard to believe you are the head of the family now. I still think of you as—" he gestured to Sam "—his age."

She couldn't help returning his smile. Relief washed through her that perhaps Luke no longer remembered the acrimony of their last meeting. "I was, when I first met you."

He shook his head. "So you were. And I recall you were quite displeased about having to attend such a tedious adult function as one of your sister's garden parties."

"You were the only person with any sense of humor there." She looked toward Sam to include him. The boy seemed to be listening to their conversation, although he remained at the far end of the room. Maybe this would be a beginning, however small, of bridging the gap between the two.

She continued. "Your father had found me down back by the sycamore tree. I'd already snagged my stockings climbing up in my best party frock."

Sam made no reply, but his eyes showed his interest.

At that moment, the tea cart was rolled in. As Bobbie poured, Luke stood and took a turn about the room. He stopped by the window seat and said something to his son. Bobbie couldn't hear Sam's reply but could tell it was brief.

Luke soon returned to his seat and took the cup she handed to him.

Before she could serve Sam, her nephew came up to her. "May I be excused, please?"

"Don't you want any tea, dear? Are you unwell?"

Sam shook his head. His mouth had that set look, when he was determined to do things his own way—a look he was beginning to assume more and more as he entered adolescence. "I just don't wish any tea, thank you."

Bobbie glanced helplessly between Luke and Sam, but Luke's gaze was fixed on his son. "Very well. Bid your father farewell."

The boy turned to him. "Good day, sir."

If Luke thought it strange to be addressed so formally, he made no sign. "Goodbye, Sammy—Sam," he quickly amended. "It was nice to see you." His tone remained gentle, as if he were unruffled by the boy's cold tone.

When Sam had left the room, Bobbie dared to look at Luke. His son had not once called him "Father." Had he noticed?

He met her gaze. "I'm a complete stranger to him."

"I'm sorry. He…he is taking things very hard."

"Of course." His fine lips pressed together. "Robert was the only father he knew."

She nodded sadly. "He was very good with him."

"I'm glad of that at least." There was a hard edge to his words.

They sipped their tea in silence a few moments. "He looks very much like Irene."

Bobbie started at the words. "Yes, at first glance perhaps." She could feel her cheeks redden. "But I find him looking more and more like you as he matures."

"He's grown so much." He gave what seemed an embarrassed laugh. "Clearly, he is no longer a 'Sammy.'"

Bobbie longed to say or do something to encourage Luke, but she didn't know what. "I—I'm sorry Sam seems so distant," she finally repeated. "He hasn't seen you in so long. It must be a shock for him."

His glance flickered away. "Undoubtedly." He sighed, setting down his cup. "Perhaps I shouldn't have come. After all, I gave up any parental rights when I left him in your care."

His words sounded almost accusatory. Did he blame her for Sam's estrangement? "You know that is not what I wished."

His green eyes regarded her levelly. "Isn't it?"

"Of course not." She set down her own cup, afraid her shaking hands would cause a spill. "I expected you to write to him, at least…so he wouldn't feel abandoned by…" She almost said "both his parents." She hurried on. "And visit—oh, I don't know, whenever your work permitted." He could have found work in the United Kingdom if he'd wished to, instead of going off to America to build bridges and railroads.

They stared at each other, and already she felt at an impasse. Were they going to be at odds again, just like the last time, over Sam?

"I abided by what you and your father wished, that Sam know this as his home, his family… You didn't want him sent away to school, the only practical place I could have had him." He swallowed, as if the next words were difficult. "I didn't want him to be pulled in two directions. I wanted him to have a real home.

Goodness knows, he'd known little of one before." He looked away.

She knew they were both thinking of her sister's behavior. How Bobbie longed to console him, to tell him it had not been his fault. How many times in the intervening years had she imagined making a home for him and Sam, the kind of home her sister had denied them?

She leaned forward, her hands on her knees, saying the only words she dared. "Perhaps now you can have a fresh beginning with Sam."

He said nothing at first, but when his gaze returned to hers, he took a deep breath. "That's one of the principal reasons I came back. I'd like to discuss Sammy's future with you." He cleared his throat. "Once you've gotten your bearings a bit, I mean."

"S-Sam's future?" She began to feel a sense of disquiet although she tried to hide it with a smile. "But he's only th-thirteen." Goodness, she was stuttering as badly as she had when she'd been Sam's age and first met Luke. Even at fourteen, she'd been drawn to him and had never met another man who was his equal.

"Yes, I know." The quiet words once again made her feel guilty, as if she'd been the one who'd robbed him of the chance to know his son. "It's a good time to look at his education now that your father is no longer here to have his say."

Her heart sank. He wouldn't propose to send Sam away to school again, the way he had when the boy was seven? Her eyes remained fixed on Luke, her fear growing. Before she could muster the courage to ask him what he meant, he continued. "But we needn't talk about it now. I came to pay my respects and tell you how sorry I am for your loss."

Her fingers knotted together. She must tell him how things stood as soon as possible. Maybe if Luke knew the contents of her father's will… "Yes, I think it's very important that we speak about Sam's future as well as… other matters, as soon as it is convenient." She hesitated. "I don't know how long you plan to be in London." She held her breath, awaiting his reply.

He gestured with a hand. "A few days…I suppose."

That was all? Her hopes plummeted. Perhaps, he'd change his mind when he heard… "If you come to the office tomorrow, we could discuss everything then."

He blinked. "The office?"

"Yes. I—I'm managing things there until we find someone…"

His eyebrows drew together. "There is no one to take your father's place?" Even before she could think how to answer, comprehension filled his green eyes. "Of course. He was used to controlling everything. But surely there is a chief engineer?"

She shook her head. "There is no one suitable," she whispered. *Only you.*

He let out a breath but said nothing more. Then he straightened, speaking briskly. "Very well. I shall come around tomorrow. What time would you like me?"

"As soon as you can. I shall be there by nine o'clock, in any case."

"Good enough. I shall come at ten." He stood. "Don't bother showing me out. I know the way," he added with a bittersweet look in his eyes.

Bobbie controlled the urge to get up and follow him to the door.

What would the morrow bring? The tension ebbed from her body as she turned her gaze from the empty doorway toward the fire. She'd pinned her hopes on Luke's return. Her dreams had taken flight. Reality left a cold pit of fear in her stomach.

Chapter Two

As soon as Luke left, Bobbie went in search of Sam. Not finding him in his room, she climbed to the top floor of the house and headed to the old nursery, the room that had always offered her solace as a girl from life's hurts.

Her nephew lay on the hearth rug, his head propped on an elbow, an open book beside him, one foot pushing his old rocking horse up and down. The same rocking horse she and Irene had ridden when they'd been young.

Despite the childish position, in his mourning suit the thirteen-year-old made a strikingly handsome boy on the threshold of becoming a young man.

Luke had noticed his resemblance to his mother. What if it hindered his efforts to get to know his son? After all, it could very well remind Luke of Irene's betrayal every time he beheld his son.

Bobbie suppressed a sigh, hoping it wouldn't be so. Father and son had been estranged far too long. Yet, fear filled her as she recalled Luke's words. *It's very important that we speak of Sammy's future.*

Entering the nursery, she forced a smile to her lips. "I thought I might find you up here."

Sam looked up from his book, his face solemn. "Has he gone?"

Bobbie closed the door softly behind her and joined her nephew on the rug. "If you mean your father, yes, he just left."

"Please don't call him that."

"What shall I call him?" How she longed to take away the boy's hurt. Had she made it worse for Sam over the years by making up stories about his father when Sam had been younger? Bobbie had no answer to that question, and only hoped Luke's return would help heal the breach and not damage the child any further.

Sam shrugged. "I don't care. Mr. Travis—Luke—whatever you are accustomed to calling him."

Bobbie smoothed the worn nap of the carpet. "It would be a bit strange to refer to him as Mr. Travis each time I speak of him, when you share the same name."

"I wish my name was Gardner like yours and Grandfather's. It should have been."

Bobbie reached forward and pushed back a stray lock of hair off Sam's forehead. "Oh, my dear, if it weren't for your father, you wouldn't have come to be—and I couldn't imagine that!"

Sam looked fixedly at the page before him. "Why did he have to come anyway?"

"You know we had to notify him of Grandfather's death."

"He certainly wouldn't have bothered coming for any other reason."

She racked her mind for a way to assure Sam to the contrary. Why hadn't Luke written to his son or visited him? "Perhaps your father needed a reason. Did you ever think he might be afraid to come back?"

Sam's blue eyes rose slowly to meet hers. In their reflection, Bobbie read a mixture of doubt, fear and longing. "Why should he be afraid?"

"Afraid that you won't care anything about him anymore." Bobbie took a deep breath, trying to formulate how to say what she wanted. "I believe your father thought he was doing the best thing by leaving you here with us after your mother passed away. He didn't think he could provide you with a proper home.

"And I refused to have you sent away to school," she added. "You wouldn't want to have gone through what poor David Copperfield did, would you?"

One corner of Sam's mouth lifted unwillingly in a gesture similar to Luke's. A second later, Sam's lips turned downward, his eyes filling with tears. "I wouldn't have asked for anything."

Bobbie put her fingers under the boy's chin, forcing him to look at her. "I know you wouldn't have. But children need things. They need a stable home and a mother and father…." She smiled. "And an auntie who is always after them to pick up their toys and brush their hair and clean their nails."

Once again, a smile tugged at the corner of Sam's lips. Bobbie caught her breath. For another instant, he looked just like Luke when he found something amusing but didn't want to let on. Her heart pounded erratically in her chest as the image of his handsome father filled her head.

Banishing those thoughts from her mind, Bobbie returned her attention to Sam. She bent down and put her arms around her nephew, the way she'd always done when he was younger and in need of comforting. He'd shot up so fast in the last year, that she missed the little boy who would run to her when he was hurt, dragging his stuffed bear behind him.

"I don't want to see him anymore." Sam sniffed. His voice cracked and he began to cry silently against her shoulder. He hadn't cried in a long time. Bobbie rocked him, smoothing his shaking back.

Would Luke stay long enough to get to know his son? He'd said only a few days. But how else would he get to bond with Sam? He didn't intend to take him away, did he? *Oh, dear God,* she prayed, *don't let him take Sam away.*

The next morning, Luke stepped out of the Tavistock Hotel, an old establishment in the north piazza of Covent Garden. He preferred it to the larger, more modern hotels springing up across London because it had the feel of an old club more than a hotel.

"Good day t'you, sir," the porter greeted, holding the door for him.

Luke nodded to him then headed down the arched portico and made his way the few blocks to the Strand.

He hadn't slept much and needed a brisk walk to clear the lingering fuzziness from his head. Unfortunately, after yesterday's rain, the day was foggy, the air dank and cool.

What had plagued Luke's sleep most was the impact of seeing Sammy—Sam, he reminded himself grimly. Memories he'd long shut away kept surfacing all night long, no matter how much he told himself it was futile to recall them now. Nothing would change the past.

It had also amazed him to see Bobbie so serious and womanlike. He'd always thought of her as Irene's baby sister. To find her in charge of the household—and her father's firm… He shook his head.

But he couldn't get over how grown his son was. Soon Sam would be a young man. Where was the little baby Luke had held in his arms, the little toddler balancing on his chubby legs? So much had been stolen from him, since the day Irene had left him. Luke clenched his hands, the bitterness that had no outlet threatening to choke out every other consideration. He'd lost a decade of the boy's life, and no one could make that up to him.

Yesterday had proved to Luke that he hadn't the least idea what to say to his thirteen-year-old boy. If it hadn't been for Bobbie's encouraging words, Luke would have been tempted to turn around and leave again.

With effort, Luke steadied his breathing, forcing himself to reason things through. There was a lot to be considered and he had only a few days to come to any decisions.

But Bobbie gave him hope that Sam would come around. Luke was so deep in thought he didn't see the portly gentleman in his path until he slammed into him on the crowded sidewalk.

"Pardon me—" Luke quickly backed away, ignoring the man's glare and mutterings of "watching where one was going."

The Strand was already jammed with pedestrian and coach traffic. Luke resumed his walk, this time mindful of the others on the sidewalk heading to work. But soon his thoughts returned to Sam. A sense of failure and of something precious missed had plagued him all night long.

He hadn't realized how much it would hurt to be viewed as a stranger by his own flesh and blood, a child he'd helped bring into the world. How did one make up for the years lost? Did he even want to try? A snatch of a Bible verse came to his mind, something he'd heard once in a sermon. *The years the locusts have eaten.* Wasn't there also something about a cankerworm?

He felt like a man whose treasure had been plundered by the locusts and cankerworm. Sammy's silent glare and set mouth accused him more than any words could. Bobbie's words came back to soothe the bitterness that threatened to erupt. She'd talked of a fresh beginning with his son. Did she mean it?

Besides Bobbie, who did Sam have now? The only father he'd known, Luke's father-in-law, was gone. There were no other males in the family.

Luke had a moral obligation to see to his son's upbringing. Yet he'd already sensed a withdrawal in Bobbie when he'd brought up Sam's future.

With nothing resolved, and only doubts bombarding him, Luke arrived at the nondescript office of the late Robert Gardner's engineering firm. It was located in the heart of London, in one of the old brick buildings dating back more than a century, sandwiched between two other similar buildings, one housing a tea importer, the other a coffee shop.

Gardner & Quimby, Civil Engineers. Once, he thought his name would grace the brass plaque. That illusion had left him soon enough after taking the job of junior engineer in his father-in-law's firm.

He shook aside the old aspiration and turned his attention to the coming interview. What else did Bobbie want to see him about? She'd mentioned "other matters." Well, he was here to talk about Sam's future. He braced himself for the expected battle. Would she oppose his plans for the boy's schooling? Is that why she'd preferred meeting at the firm instead of at the house, so Sam wouldn't be around to hear their conversation?

He was willing to concede Bobbie had been right six years ago. Sam had been too young to be sent away from home, but at thirteen, he would surely benefit from a good boarding school.

Would Bobbie agree this time?

The porter of the engineering firm held the door open for Luke.

"Thank you." He stepped inside the building he hadn't been in for over a decade. Like a typical office in the city, the front room had a busy, slightly untidy look to it.

A young clerk looked up from his high perch behind a desk.

"Gardner and Quimby," he stated.

"Third floor." He indicated the lift with a nod of his chin.

Luke knew the way. Hadn't he made his way there every day for two years? Until he'd quit and taken on a job with a British firm in India—as far from Robert Gardner's reach as he could get. He'd needed to sever ties not only professionally but also personally.

Once at the third floor, Luke strode down a narrow corridor to his late father-in-law's office, and knocked.

Instead of Robert Gardner's impatient bark, Bobbie's quiet "Come in" bade him enter.

He stepped into a room where he used to pore over blueprints with his father-in-law. It was crammed with books and rolls of drafting paper. Blueprints and drafting instruments were spread out over every work surface. Framed photographs of railroad tracks and bridges hung on the walls.

Luke stopped short on the threshold, not expecting to see a white-haired, bearded gentleman in a black frock coat and cravat seated in a chair before the desk.

He frowned. The man looked like a lawyer. Luke had little fondness for solicitors, since one had ensured the irrevocable separation from his son.

"Hello, Luke," Bobbie greeted him from behind her father's battered oak desk, looking somehow younger and more delicate by its wide, plain surface.

He nodded to the two, wondering at the presence of the dignified-looking gentleman. "Good morning."

Bobbie rose and came around the desk, her two hands clasped in front of her. The black gown made her appear pale and austere although she didn't look any older than she had six years ago. A wave of sympathy passed through him, as he realized how much her slim shoulders must be carrying at the present.

Her smile seemed uncertain as she looked at him from behind the oval, wire-rimmed spectacles. He wondered if she'd ever felt overshadowed by her beautiful sister. The two were so different in looks and personality. Her fair-haired, blue-eyed sister had taken after their mother; Bobbie looked more like her father with her dark brown hair and starker features.

Although not unattractive, her face had a squarer look than her sister's. Her mouth was wider, her jaw firmer—like her father's—her nose sharper, her dark eyebrows a trifle too straight and wide to be deemed feminine.

She had never seemed to care about her appearance, her nose usually to be found buried in a book. Any attempt of her mother's to get her to attend to the things a young lady should be concerned with had been greeted by a scoffing attitude.

But behind the spectacles, however, she had deep-set eyes of an arresting slate blue, fringed by dark lashes, which would command a second look from any man. He wondered why she'd never married.

"Thank you for coming by so early, Luke. Do you remember Mr. Hargreaves, my father's solicitor?"

Luke slowly turned to the man. Hargreaves. The name was forever engraved on his memory, from the various letters and legal documents he'd received with the lawyer's name printed across the top. Hargreaves, Colby and Smith. The legal firm that had taken away his rights to his only child. A metallic taste filled his mouth as Luke stared at the benign-looking older gentleman who had the face of Father Christmas but was as canny and unyielding as a fox.

"No, I don't believe we've never met in person," he said, laying a slight stress on the last words. He didn't offer his hand to the solicitor, who'd stood. "Although I believe we've met through correspondence."

The man inclined his snowy-white head, his dark eyes regarding him keenly below tufted, white eyebrows.

Luke took the seat Bobbie indicated in front of the desk.

"I appreciate your time in coming here, Mr. Travis," the old gentleman began once Bobbie had reseated herself. "There are some matters of importance in the late Robert Gardner's will that you need to be apprised of." As he spoke, he took up a thick document from the desk.

"Mrs. Gardner and her daughter are aware of its contents. Forgive us for not waiting for your arrival, but as we were not certain when, and if, you would be able to return to London, I took the liberty of already informing them of the contents of the will. As the more immediate members of the family, it seemed the right thing to do."

Luke rested an elbow on the chair arm, his chin on his fist, wondering what could be of possible interest to him in Mr. Gardner's will. Unless it had to do with Sam. In that case, Hargreaves would be greatly mistaken if he thought this time Luke would cave in to the late Gardner's wishes.

The solicitor cleared his throat and Luke realized the gentleman expected a response from him. "I don't really see why you needed me here. I'm sure my late father-in-law left everything in good order."

Mr. Hargreaves eyed him over his narrow octagonal spectacles, taking on the tone of an elder chiding a young man. "Your presence is needed here, sir, because you are named as a beneficiary in the late Mr. Gardner's last will and testament."

Luke stared at the man. No words could have been more unexpected than the ones the solicitor had just uttered.

Bobbie had been sitting on the edge of her seat since the moment Mr. Hargreaves began to speak. In fact, her hands were clasped so tightly together, her knuckles had turned white.

Luke sat up. "I don't understand." His glance went from Hargreaves to her as if for confirmation of the lawyer's statement.

She nodded, wishing she could read his expression. "It's true."

"That makes no sense—unless Mr. Gardner left me some drafting tools—as a parting gift." Luke gave a short, mirthless laugh.

Old Mr. Hargreaves did not acknowledge the sound

by so much as a bristle of his eyebrows. "In point of fact, sir, you are named among the principal beneficiaries, along with Mrs. Gardner, his daughter and grandson."

Luke frowned. "What do you mean, among the *principals?*"

"Exactly what I have stated," Mr. Hargreaves huffed, as if his professional integrity were being questioned. "I will read you the portion of the will pertaining to the bequest." Without waiting for a response from Luke, the solicitor adjusted his spectacles and perused the document.

Luke folded his arms across his chest and sat back. His lips were set in a firm line and his jaw jutted forth, conveying a belligerence she didn't understand. Shouldn't he be at least curious about her father's gift?

Despite her anxiety, Bobbie couldn't help but note how handsome Luke appeared in his black frock coat and charcoal trousers, his white shirt neatly pressed, a dark blue silk tie at his neck. He had lost all the awkwardness of the college student he'd been when she had first met him. Now he looked urbane, rugged, completely aloof.

The solicitor scanned the first page of the document, taking his time. Then he turned it over and laid it facedown on the desk, beginning with the second. "Ah, yes, here we are." He cleared his throat. "I quote, 'I bequeath the firm, Gardner and Quimby, hereafter referred to as "the firm", of whom I am the sole proprietor, equally to my youngest daughter, Roberta Jean Gardner, and to my son-in-law, Luke Langston Travis, in trust for my grandson, Samuel Luke Travis, on condition that he remain as chief engineer and manager of said firm. Moreover, this bequest is contingent upon Luke Travis's agreeing to groom his son to take over the firm in his place when he has come of age and finished his studies.'"

The solicitor looked up. "That is the pertinent portion, sir. Your son has also received the sum of £10,000, when he comes of age. That, of course, is from Mr. Gardner's personal assets and has nothing to do with the distribution of his firm."

Bobbie hardly dared breathe as she gauged Luke's reaction. Would he reject her father's olive branch out of hand? For surely that was what it was? Wasn't it her father's way of making amends from beyond the grave for all the sorrow and pain his oldest daughter had caused Luke?

By the end of Mr. Hargreaves's careful reading, the hard expression on Luke's face had given way to bewilderment. As soon as the lawyer came to a stop, Luke held out his hand. "May I…see that?"

"Certainly. But you will note that it is just as I have stated." Mr. Hargreaves handed him the sheaf of papers.

Luke stared down at the paragraph indicated by the gentleman. He seemed to be taking a long time to read it through, as if the document was in a foreign language and he had to go over it a few times for the meaning to penetrate. She could well understand, remembering her own disbelief when she'd first heard the terms of the will. Her father and Luke hadn't spoken to each other in years. In fact, her father had refused to speak of Luke after Irene's funeral.

When Luke finally finished reading the will, he handed it back without a word. Then he turned to Bobbie. "What do you make of this?"

Bobbie answered thoughtfully. "I didn't expect it

myself. But Mr. Hargreaves assures me it is all in order. You own half of Father's firm."

Luke looked down, rubbing his forehead. A moment later, he narrowed his eyes at the solicitor. "There must be another will."

Mr. Hargreaves gave him a disbelieving look. "I can assure you, sir, there is no other will."

"Gardner must have changed his will at some point after this one was written!" He gestured impatiently with his hand to the document in the solicitor's hands, as if it was an obscene object.

Mr. Hargreaves harrumphed. "I repeat, sir, this is Mr. Gardner's one and only last will and testament."

Luke stared coolly at the older man. "Would you have known?"

The solicitor drew himself up. "I have been the late Mr. Gardner's solicitor for the past thirty years."

Bobbie turned to Mr. Hargreaves, striving to alleviate the sudden tension in the room. "When was this will drawn up?"

"The date is here on the last page, signed by Mr. Gardner and witnessed by myself and a clerk from the firm." As he spoke, Mr. Hargreaves turned to it. "25 September 1875."

"I think that proves my point."

The lawyer raised his white eyebrows at the note of satisfaction in Luke's tone. "If you would care to elaborate?"

"He drew up that will right after my son was born."

Mr. Hargreaves nodded to indicate agreement.

"As I am sure you are aware, I resigned from my father-in-law's engineering firm a year later and accepted a post in India with a different firm. You are further aware that a year after that, my wife left me and returned to Europe." He didn't add "with another man," although Mr. Hargreaves knew all the family history, having been acquainted with the Gardners' private affairs for as long as Bobbie could remember.

Luke made a motion with his hands, undoubtedly bothered to have to recount the difficult summary of events. "Five years later, my wife was killed in a train accident in France, where she resided at the time. I had no further contact with my father-in-law. He and his wife, along with Miss Gardner, were given custody of our only child, Samuel."

Mr. Hargreaves inclined his head. "Your summation of the events concurs with my own acquaintance of the facts."

Luke leaned forward, a gleam in his eye. "Therefore, I am quite certain—and I am sure you will agree— that Mr. Gardner had effectively written me out of his family and business. He would have no earthly reason to bequeath me half the business he spent a lifetime building up."

Mr. Hargreaves adjusted his glasses on the bridge of his nose. "Be that as it may, this is Mr. Gardner's last will and testament to the best of my knowledge."

"He must have amended it at some point," Luke insisted stubbornly.

Bobbie spoke up, realizing it was going to be more difficult to convince Luke of her father's intention than she had thought. "I never heard of any other will. I'm sure Father would have consulted Mr. Hargreaves if he had wished to change his will. He trusted him implicitly." She turned to the older gentleman. "You handled all Father's personal and business affairs, isn't that right, sir?"

He bowed his head. "Since he founded this firm."

Luke fixed his gaze on Bobbie. "Surely you'll agree this bequest is highly unlikely?"

She tried not to falter under his steady look. "I think it made a lot of sense at the time Father wrote it. Think about it…you were his son-in-law, a fellow engineer, working in the firm." Would she be able to convince him that for whatever her father's reasons, this was for the best? That it was an answer to her prayers—to reunite him with his son…and save her father's firm?

"Precisely, but surely a few years later, it was the last thing he would have wanted."

Bobbie looked down at her knotted hands atop a blueprint, debating. She didn't want to press too hard, yet Luke was their only hope. "Father must have had his reasons for not changing it. I don't know… He never discussed it with Mother or me. Perhaps he'd always hoped you'd come back…."

"No."

Bobbie blinked at the sharpness of Luke's tone. "How can you be so sure?"

"Because your father made sure I wouldn't return." His glance went to Mr. Hargreaves. "Didn't he, Mr. Hargreaves?"

The solicitor pursed his lips. "Whatever he did at the time of his daughter's demise, he did for the interests of his only grandchild. It did not mean he would not favor your return in the case of his own demise."

Bobbie furrowed her brow in confusion. "What are you talking about?"

Neither replied to her question, staring at each other as if in a showdown.

Luke gave another cynical laugh. "When my son was grown and with such provisions that he would still control us from beyond the grave?"

Mr. Hargreaves cocked a bushy, white eyebrow upward. "I hardly consider being handed a successful engineering firm 'controlling you from the grave.'"

Luke turned to her, as if she would be more reasonable. "Even if by some stretch of the imagination, your father had once considered me a successor to his firm, do you honestly think he maintained that intention in the years since Irene's death?"

She made a helpless gesture. "You knew Father. Perhaps he never thought anything would happen to him… so he didn't bother to change his will."

The solicitor interrupted them. "Begging your pardon, Ms. Gardner, but I disagree that your father thought himself invincible. It is true, none of us likes to think of our end, but your father was a very responsible man where his family was concerned. He always had his affairs in order, his papers up to date." He folded his hands atop the document. "In light of this, it is my firm belief that he considered this his final will and testament."

The three of them sat silent a few seconds.

The lawyer shuffled his stack of papers together and began putting them back into his leather portfolio. "If that is all for the moment, I shall be on my way." He looked at Luke. "If you should have any questions, you may be in contact with me. In any case, Ms. Gardner has all the pertinent information."

Luke stood and nodded. "Very well."

When Mr. Hargreaves had departed, Luke sat back down and eyed Bobbie across the desk.

She ventured a small smile. "The terms of the will must have come as something of a shock."

He gave a slight grunt. "An understatement." After a moment, he asked, "And you or your mother had no idea of your father's intentions?"

She shook her head. "None whatsoever, not even when he first wrote it. I'm not surprised by his decision then, of course." She smiled sadly. "He was blessed only with daughters. He was so pleased when Irene married you. To have a fellow engineer in the family, you don't know what that meant to him." She eyed the ruler and compass on the desk, hesitating with what she was about to say. "Even if he had had a daughter who was interested in the field."

His eyes widened. "What, engineering?"

She lifted her chin. "Yes."

He emitted a sound of disbelief. "You?"

Bobbie tried to hide her disappointment at his reaction. "Is that so outlandish to you, too?"

His green eyes showed the first sign of amusement since he'd heard the will's contents. "You can't mean that you wanted to become an engineer?"

What had made her think he would be any different? "Don't you believe a woman is fully capable of the profession?"

He seemed at a loss for words. "I know there are a few—a *very* few. I don't believe it is a profession that comes naturally to…most women."

Her sense of disappointment in Luke deepened. Was he as narrow in his view of women as her father had been, as most men were? As a girl, she'd admired Luke because he did seem different—superior—to other men. For one thing, he'd looked beyond her spectacles and pigtails and seen the person behind them.

But then Luke had, after all, fallen for her sister, the epitome of all that was dainty and feminine. Didn't that prove how little Luke thought women capable of?

He rubbed his forehead, his puzzlement evident. "I suppose you were too young when I lived in England to notice what you were interested in. You certainly didn't seem to have a lot in common with Irene," he admitted ruefully.

"Very little." At least they agreed on that. "She loved parties and the social life that London had to offer, while I loved books and wanted more than anything to go to university."

The humor had left his eyes. They held a distant look as if he were seeing into the past. "When she didn't have her dark moments that no amount of socializing could snap her out of."

She remembered her sister's bouts of melancholia. "Oh, Luke, it must have been so difficult for you. I was too young then to realize how troubled she was. To me she was just a spoiled older sister."

He sat forward, rubbing his fingers over his temples. "Nothing I did seemed to make any difference."

How she longed to come around the desk and reach for him and offer what comfort and reassurance she could. "She'd been like that ever since she'd entered adolescence. I know Mother and Father tried everything to make her happy." She cast her eyes downward. "I know that's why they were so happy when she fell in love with you. They thought you were the answer to a prayer—an upstanding young gentleman who would make her happy and best of all, work alongside Father. Irene would bear your children and finally settle down." She sighed, unsure if her words would help him or stir up the past too painfully.

His lips twisted. "They never understood why it didn't work out that way. I suppose it was easier to believe I was the unfeeling one who dragged her off to India." He expelled a breath. "When all the while, I thought a change of scenery would help her."

She felt heartened that at last they seemed to be able to talk about it—as one adult to another.

Instead he changed the topic. "So you wanted to attend university?" He smiled with a shake of his head. "Somehow that doesn't surprise me."

She returned the smile with a half shrug. "Unfortunately, Father would have none of that."

Luke seemed to be listening to her. "Not many young ladies go to college, but it isn't unheard of. Doesn't the University of London accept women now? And, of course, Girton."

She nodded, encouraged by his serious tone. "Yes, University College began conferring degrees in '78, but Father insisted no young lady attended university, when I broached it." And that had been around the time Sam had come to live with them. She said nothing of that, not wanting Luke to think for a moment that she regretted taking care of her nephew in any way.

But he didn't seem to make the connection. His lips curled upward. "Irene used to despair of you, saying you were too tomboyish and bookish to ever have a proper suitor."

She grimaced. "Unfortunately, that didn't discourage Mother from foisting every bachelor of her acquaintance upon me in hopes of marrying me off."

"And was there no one who tempted you to give up your independent ways?" he asked with a lift of his eyebrow, a faint twinkle in his light green eyes.

She looked down at the desk, afraid of what he might read in hers. He'd never had an inkling of her girlish infatuation—and she must make sure he never did. She traced a line of the blueprint with her forefinger, hesitating. "I…was on the verge of accepting a proposal of marriage from a young gentleman…a nephew of a friend of Mother's…when you brought Sam."

"Don't tell me you gave up your prospects to care for my son?"

"Oh, no, no!" She hurried on, hearing the concern in his tone. "Quite the contrary, in fact. I was so relieved to have a good reason to refuse him—my suitor, that is," she said with a nervous laugh.

Instead of looking relieved or amused, his eyes narrowed. "So, you used the excuse of taking my child to save yourself from unwanted matrimony?"

Chapter Three

Bobbie's mouth fell open. "Of course not! It wasn't like that at all!"

He said nothing, but the look in his eyes remained skeptical. What had happened to the comradeship she thought they had enjoyed just moments ago? She folded her hands carefully atop the blueprint. "I did not use Sam to save myself from marriage," she said, quietly enunciating each word. Her eyelids fluttered downward at the next words. "I realized I…I wasn't in love with the gentleman…and I wanted to offer Sam a home."

When he said nothing she risked a look into his eyes. Even though she felt she'd confessed the secrets of her heart, she detected from his expression that he remained unconvinced. They seemed to be at the same impasse as when he'd heard the contents of the will.

Her spirits sank. Nothing was turning out right. Why did Luke resent her having taken care of Sam? Why was her father's bequest so unwelcome to him?

Before she could think what else to say, Luke sighed, sitting back again. "It's a pity you didn't achieve your dream of following in your father's footsteps. If I'd known, I would have put in a good word for you...not that your father would have listened to me."

"Father was quite opinionated," she acknowledged with a sad smile, relieved that Luke's anger at her seemed to have dissipated.

"Another understatement."

"But never more so than when he cared."

Luke looked away from her. "Cared about achieving his goals."

"He cared about you. His will confirms it."

His mouth hardened. "I repeat, I'm certain he changed his will after I left."

She shook her head. How could she make him see how ideal the situation was? "Is it so very bad?" she said in a small voice.

He looked at her as if she had said something extraordinary. "You can't mean that you and your mother accept this situation?"

"Why wouldn't we?"

He made a futile gesture with his hand and began to speak then stopped as if searching for words. Finally, he said, "I find it extraordinary that neither of you wish to contest the will."

"For what reason? You are an engineer in the same field as my father. We have no one to run the firm. Isn't it logical to think you might be the perfect candidate for the position?"

"I am the last man for the position!"

She blinked at the vehemence in his tone.

After a moment he said, "I can't accept the terms of your father's will." His tone was calm but the look in his light green eyes was as resolute as granite.

* * *

Bobbie looked at him through her spectacles in that thoughtful way she had, as if she were examining all sides to a question. "You can't...or you won't?"

Luke gestured impatiently, finding it absurd that he was obliged to have this conversation. "I have no desire to take anything offered me by your father."

"I know you and Father didn't see eye to eye on things when you worked for him, but that was so long ago—"

A sound issued from his throat. "You think taking my son away from me was nothing?"

She stared at him. "He didn't take Sam away from you! You left him with us! I know you had no choice but—"

"Leaving him in your care didn't mean I wanted no input into his life."

She opened her mouth to say something then stopped. Once again, she observed him. He remembered that pensive, bespectacled look when she was a young girl. "What did you mean earlier when you told Mr. Hargreaves that Father made sure you wouldn't return?"

"Exactly what I said." He could hardly believe she hadn't known, yet her puzzlement seemed genuine.

"I...don't understand."

"After you fought to take care of Sammy, your father made sure your family had sole custody of him."

"Wh...what do you mean?"

"Your father and your esteemed Mr. Hargreaves made me sign a document relinquishing all rights to my son until he came of age." He gave a sharp laugh. "I'm surprised they didn't make him take on the Gardner name."

She flushed, making him wonder if indeed that had

been considered. "B…but you said you'd never met Mr. Hargreaves."

"I didn't, but I certainly remember the name plastered all over the official documents I received."

She looked beyond him, her forehead scrunched up. "But why would Father do such a thing? Why wouldn't he want you to visit Sam and take an interest in his upbringing? I never meant for you to have no contact with him. In fact, I—" The color in her face deepened.

"You what?"

She shook her head and said quickly, "Nothing. I…I just didn't want Sam sent away to school at such a young age."

Could she be telling the truth? At the time it had seemed as if the whole Gardner clan had closed ranks to shut him out of his son's life. With no way to take care of his son, his hands had been effectively tied. "I have no inkling how your father's mind worked, though I got a fair amount of insight into his professional methods in the time I worked for him. He would stop at nothing when he wanted to achieve his aims."

She scanned his face, as if truly at a loss. "I don't know…I still can't believe he would do such a thing to you."

He shrugged. "I have the document to prove it."

She swallowed. "I…I'd like to see it. Not that I don't believe you—" she quickly added. "It's just that I want to understand…"

He realized Bobbie had probably been too young to remember. And yet, she'd made it easy for her father to have his way, conveniently giving up her own aspirations to take care of his son. He looked away, drumming his fingers on the chair arm. It was all moot now. But something about Bobbie's desire to understand drew him to articulate things he hadn't spoken of to anyone.

"Once I resigned from the firm and took your sister overseas, there was no forgiveness from your family. I 'stole Irene away,' as your father put it. You must know he blamed me when she left me—no matter that she chose someone else. Ultimately, both he and your mother held me responsible for her death, though I was nowhere near her at the time and hadn't seen her for a couple of years."

"I'm sure he didn't blame you!"

He debated saying more. What did it matter now? Except for that absurd will. Bobbie needed to see why it was impossible for him to accept even part ownership of her father's firm. "Your father told me so in no uncertain terms at Irene's funeral."

Bobbie drew in a sharp breath. "He must have spoken those words in grief. Oh, Luke, you weren't to blame that Irene was so unhappy in India."

He regretted bringing up the past. The last thing he wanted was to revisit it. Right now they needed to deal with the present. "How does your mother feel about the will? I can't believe she accepts it."

If she thought his question abrupt, she gave no sign. "You know Mother. She trusts Mr. Hargreaves to handle everything. I don't think she quite understands the reality of having Father gone. She assumes the firm will run itself."

He felt a sudden tug of compassion for the responsibilities that had suddenly fallen to Bobbie—her mother was a helpless, vain woman, then there was Sammy... and now a thriving engineering firm. He steeled himself against feeling sorry for Bobbie. Her problems were not his. His only concern was Sam.

At least Bobbie had had the privilege of seeing his son grow up.

"Perhaps…if you stayed in London now, it would give you a chance to get to know Sam. It's not too late."

He made a sound of disbelief. "You saw his reaction yesterday. I think I'm the last person he wants to be acquainted with."

"But he needs you so much right now. He has just lost the only father he has ever known—" She bit her lip, as if realizing how painful the words were for him to hear.

Luke sat forward, loosely clasping his hands. She'd given him the opening he needed. "As a matter of fact, I wanted to talk to you about Sam. I thought that was what you had wanted to see me about this morning." He shook his head, still amazed. "The last thing I expected was to be discussing your father's will—much less be a part of it."

"What…would you like to discuss?"

He cleared his throat, feeling the note of caution in her tone. "You could say I want to continue the conversation we had six years ago, when I deferred to your wisdom regarding Sam's education."

She moistened her lips, looking suddenly very young—the way he remembered her. "Wh…what exactly do you mean?"

"I mean, I think you should consider a good school for Sam now."

She blinked, her eyes wide behind her spectacles. "School? B…but he has a very qualified tutor—and I teach him myself."

He restrained his impatience. "That may be. But I'd like to discuss the idea of sending him to the school where I was educated. It's a fine old school and would help prepare him for university, either Oxford or Cambridge."

"Perhaps in a year or so…" she began. "When he's had time to get over Father's death."

He would not be so easily persuaded this time. "I realize I gave up my rights to Sam's upbringing when I left England. But your father is gone now, and I would like to have a part in my son's life."

Instead of disputing this, her face brightened and she smiled. "I think that's wonderful." Before he could take comfort from her encouraging words, she continued. "But you can do it best by assuming your place in Father's firm." Her voice hurried on, gaining momentum. She waved at the blueprints spread across the wide desk. "Doesn't it make perfect sense for you to take over this project right here in London? That way you'll be nearby for Sam." She gave a slight gasp, her eyes growing rounder. "Perhaps that was why Father never changed his will! He realized how wrong he'd been to take Sam away from you—and wanted to atone for that!"

He refused to consider such a notion. "You can imagine anything you'd like, but I know he would be turning over in his grave right now if he thought I'd be taking over Sam's upbringing!" He stood. "No, I'll get any other job before working for this firm again."

Bobbie's slate-blue eyes took on a stormy cast. "You heard Father's will. What of Sam's inheritance?"

"I care little for your father's stipulations."

"The firm will be Sam's one day. Do you have so little regard for that? You have a duty to see it continue as successfully as Father made it."

Any compassion he'd felt for her evaporated at her hard tone. His first supposition had been correct.

She was merely a younger, feminine version of Robert Gardner.

Perhaps interpreting his continued silence as hesitancy, she pressed on. "This is your son's legacy. My father has a good name and reputation throughout the British Isles. Few firms have the list of projects his company completed. Do you want it to go to nothing because my father died so suddenly? Is that fair to Sam?"

He shook his head, expelling a long breath. "Perhaps you're the stubborn one here, the one who takes the most after your father."

She jutted out her chin, resembling her sire all the more. "Perhaps that is why Father left things the way he did."

He raised an eyebrow. "So you could coerce me into submitting to his will?"

She seemed to recoil at his words, but a second later she rallied, standing. "To ensure the success of the firm for his grandson and future generations. He knew I couldn't oversee it by myself. And he knew that no paid manager would ever lead it the way someone with a vested interest in it would—the way he had." Before he had a chance to refute her logic, she held up a hand, her tone softening. "Please, think about it. And if you are serious about having a role in Sam's upbringing, spend whatever available time you have at the house. Actually, I'd meant to invite you to dinner tonight."

From forceful and unyielding, she had reverted to a gentle entreaty. Something in her eyes tugged at him against his will, reminding him of the young girl who'd peered down at him so long ago from the thick oak tree. And the woman who earlier had seemed so understanding and sympathetic about Irene.

He nodded. "Very well. But I don't think either Sam or your mother will be very pleased to see me."

Knowing his fight was not over—that it had only just begun—he was willing to call a truce for the day.

Bobbie sat at the long dinner table across from Sam and Luke. She'd deliberately seated Sam beside his father. Thankfully, she'd also thought to invite Mr. Southbridge. The retired rector tutored Sam in most subjects, while she oversaw his mathematics lessons. Luke would soon recognize that Sam's education had not been neglected.

It didn't help Bobbie's composure any that Luke looked so handsome in his dinner jacket and black cravat, his white shirt gleaming. She, in turn, felt like a dowdy spinster in her old black silk. She'd worn the same gown when her sister had died.

If not for the rector, the dinner conversation would have long ago floundered. Thankfully, Mr. Southbridge asked Luke all kinds of questions about his work and travels. Bobbie couldn't help notice how Sam listened to his father's replies, though it was clear Luke wasn't the kind of man to enjoy taking center stage.

Since Sam wasn't exactly forthcoming with information, Bobbie had to admire the way Luke had obtained a fairly broad view of his son's education by asking the rector a few well-directed questions.

But as the dishes of trifle were served for dessert, even Mr. Southbridge fell quiet, as if conceding the fight to the oppressive discord permeating the air.

Bobbie glanced to the foot of the table where her mother sat. As always, Mrs. Gardner presented an elegant picture, even in her heavy, black silk. Her fair hair was liberally laced with gray now under her white cap, but her face was still largely unlined. She had refused dessert after only picking at her meal.

Even though she had greeted Luke with all decorum, there had been no warmth in her manner, and she had scarcely glanced at him throughout the meal. She carried a lace handkerchief in her left hand, dabbing at the corner of her eyes every few minutes. Bobbie braced herself for one of her mother's crise de nerfs later in the evening.

Across the starched-linen tablecloth, Luke and Sam sat bent over their dessert flutes. Their hair shone under the light from the chandelier above them, one head a wavy, light brown, the other only a shade lighter, straight and golden as burnished wheat.

Bobbie looked toward the head of the table. The empty chair seemed to resonate the most loudly. Even from the grave, her father still dominated his family. What would he think of the dinner tonight? Wouldn't he be happy to have Luke back in their midst? She believed so. Truly, truly she believed her father had wanted him to return and that was why he had left his will unchanged over the years.

Mr. Southbridge patted his napkin to his mouth, setting down his empty flute. "Where are you staying, Mr. Travis?"

"I beg your pardon?" Luke looked up from his dessert.

The rector repeated his question.

"At the Tavistock in the City."

Bobbie gripped her napkin, an idea suddenly forming. She offered up a silent prayer before continuing. "Why don't you come and stay with us while you're in London?" Giving him no chance to refuse immediately, she turned to her mother. "Wouldn't it make much more sense to have him near?" Her mother had been apprehensive with no man in the house since Bobbie's father had died. Whether she liked the idea of having Luke or not, she was too well-bred to refuse.

"I don't think…" began Luke, as if understanding Mrs. Gardner's hesitation. But her mother's eyes were fixed on her, her expression brittle. Bobbie knew that look. It meant she would speak to her later.

Then Luke turned to Sam as if to gauge his reaction. The boy was looking at him, his eyes round with surprise, but as soon as Luke's gaze met his, Sam lowered his head and focused on his dessert once more.

Bobbie gestured toward Sam. "It would allow you to be closer to us—especially since you only plan to be in England a few days," she couldn't help adding with an edge to her tone.

The sarcasm wasn't lost on Luke. "Yes, that is true," he returned with a cool look.

Mrs. Gardner laid down her napkin with a resigned sigh. "You are certainly welcome here, Luke." The words sounded perfunctory, as if only to fulfill the requirements of a good hostess.

"Thank you, ma'am, but I wouldn't want to inconvenience you."

"Pray, do what you find most convenient for yourself," she replied, looking away from him.

"I think it's a grand idea!" the rector exclaimed. He beamed at Sam. "Wouldn't that be wonderful, Sam? To have your father with you?"

The boy only looked sullen as he stared at Bobbie.

She knew she was going about it all wrong. She should have waited and talked to her mother and nephew privately and then to Luke. But after this morning's confrontation, she realized how deep Luke's animosity toward her father—toward them all—ran. No matter how justified, it was time for healing to begin.

She pinned on a bright smile and faced Luke. "Good, it's settled then."

Luke made no reply.

Bobbie cleared her throat in the silence. "Why don't we go into the drawing room? Sam, perhaps you can play the piano a little for us." Her heart sped up once more at the anticipation of seeing Luke's reaction to his son's accomplishment in music. She ignored her own wish to prolong the evening.

"Hear, hear!" the rector said. "What say you, Sam?"

Sam made no reply, but stood when the others stood.

"I shall retire, dear," Mrs. Gardner told her before turning to Luke. "Pray excuse me. I am not feeling quite up to entertaining. I am sure you understand."

"Yes, of course. Please pardon my intrusion."

She waved aside his words with her handkerchief and left them.

The atmosphere lightened immediately.

Bobbie led them to the upstairs drawing room, indicating an armchair for Luke beside the rosewood grand piano. Reverend Southbridge took his accustomed chair nearby and sat back, prepared to enjoy himself. "The perfect digestive, a concert," he murmured.

Sam sat down at the piano and opened the instrument.

Bobbie remained standing, too nervous to sit.

Sam scanned the sheet music already on the stand then poised his fingers above the keys for several seconds.

As the silence grew, Bobbie thought Luke would be able to hear her hammering heartbeat as she waited to see his reaction. For reasons she couldn't quite comprehend, his approval meant the world to her.

Suddenly, Sam's fingers touched the keys and the opening notes reverberated in the room.

Good! Beethoven's *Sonata Pathétique*. Sam had been practicing it for weeks. Bobbie glanced at Luke.

His focus was entirely on his son.

Irene had been quite musical, to the extent that Bobbie had never tried to compete with her, giving up the violin after only a couple of years of lessons.

She held her breath, listening to the familiar notes she'd heard Sam practice over and over. Slowly, her breathing steadied as her nephew acquitted himself. It was not an easy piece, especially for a thirteen-year-old, but Sam had shown such amazing skill with the piano that Bobbie had encouraged him, hiring a special teacher a few years ago.

Sam's fingers—long and slim, so apt for piano playing—skipped along the keys, mastering the rapid movements without a stumble, then slowing to the haunting, drawn-out notes.

Luke turned to Bobbie, raising his eyebrows. Quietly, she brought a footstool and set it down beside his chair. "He's been playing since he was five," she whispered. "He practices quite diligently."

He nodded and said no more, but turned his attention back to his son.

Bobbie released a sigh as she allowed herself to sit back on the cushioned footstool. For the first time that evening, she allowed herself to relax. Perhaps music would break down the barriers nothing else could.

Luke recognized the piece at once. It took him back to an evening at the Sheldonian Theatre in Oxford. He'd been in his third year at the university and had recently met Irene at a friend's house.

She'd accompanied him to the concert that evening to hear a noted pianist play.

If he hadn't been in love with her before, he fell in love that evening. The music, passionate, intense, at times exquisitely heartbreaking, expressed what he couldn't yet put into words, for fear he'd scare this beautiful young lady away.

She had played the same piece for him some months later, having mastered it, she said, to play especially for him. The gift had touched him so deeply, he'd declared his love for her then. The next moment they were engaged.

Now, he was watching his son's profile and slim hands as he managed the familiar rapid notes. Could it be coincidence that he'd chosen the same piece? How could he or anyone know its significance for Luke?

And now, so many years later, his son was a stranger to him.

A stranger who played with the beauty and pathos of someone beyond his years. Of someone who'd known pain. The pain of abandonment? Did the hard stare he'd given Luke at the dinner table and the pointed disregard of him hide agonizing hurt? If that was the case, how would Luke ever make up for it?

The mournful notes of the sonata filled the silent drawing room, echoing in the lonely chambers of Luke's heart. Irene had not only wrecked his life the day she'd left him, but had destroyed her young child's home as well. What would things have been like if she hadn't left him that fateful day?

With an effort of will, Luke brought his thoughts back to the present. Glancing down at the crown of Bobbie's dark head, he noticed that she, too, seemed immersed in the music.

At twenty-eight most women would be married with children of their own by now. Did she, too, struggle with regrets from the past? She'd almost been betrothed. Despite her denials, had Bobbie given up all hopes of a home of her own and contented herself with raising his son and keeping house for her parents? One wrecked life was enough. He didn't want her ruined hopes on his conscience, too.

And now that her father was gone, would she feel obligated to continue on at home, looking after her widowed mother and Sam?

He remembered her shy confession of wanting to be an engineer. His lips turned upward at the defiant tilt of her chin when he'd expressed disbelief. He tapped his forefinger against his cheek now. Perhaps there was something he could do for her to make her dreams come true. After all, he owed her a large debt. The boy playing the piano so flawlessly was not a child he could take any credit for.

Luke thought of the terms of the will. Mr. Gardner expected Sam to take over his firm one day. He glanced at his son again. Is that what Sam wanted?

In four or five years, Sam would be ready for university. The thought brought him up short. It would be as if Luke had never had a child. At his age, he probably never would again.

Did he want to give up all chance of fatherhood? Even if Sam rejected him, wasn't it worth trying to get to know his only child?

When the last notes of the piano died away, they were all silent a moment until Luke began to clap. The rector immediately joined him, saying, "Bravo! Bravo, my boy!"

Bobbie clapped as well, standing from the stool she'd set at his feet.

Sam gave Luke a quick look as soon as he began clapping, but when Luke smiled at his son, he looked away, quietly closing the piano.

The boy stood, ignoring Luke, and walked to Bobbie. "May I be excused?"

Bobbie sighed but nodded. "Yes, dear. Say good-night to your father."

Without turning to him, he said, "Good night, sir."

Luke tried to ignore the pain the quiet, polite words caused him, telling himself he had no right to expect any differently. "Good night, Sam," he said gently, longing to do something to show how proud he was of him. "Thank you for playing for me. It was beautiful. You're very talented."

Sam said nothing, his lips a rigid line, reminding Luke suddenly of himself when he would be reprimanded as a boy and would struggle to show no feeling.

The boy made no acknowledgment of Luke's compliment but turned to the door after bidding his tutor good-night.

"I shall accompany you out, Sam, and say good-night to all of you," the rector announced, rising with a deep sigh and approaching Luke. "It was a pleasure meeting you, sir."

"Likewise," said Luke, shaking his hand, his attention still on Sam.

When the door clicked shut, leaving him alone with Bobbie, he sat back down and rested his head against the chair back, feeling very old and weary. Was he up to the struggle ahead?

"I've engaged a special piano teacher for Sam."

Luke opened his eyes, having almost forgotten that Bobbie was still there. "I'm glad. Sam shows amazing skill." He paused, meeting her eyes. "He takes after Irene."

She nodded. "I…think he surpasses my sister's abilities. He is very diligent as well."

He shook his head. "Hearing Sam play such a difficult piece makes me more amazed than ever that Irene and I could have produced such a fine child. It's thanks to you and all you've given him."

Her pale cheeks turned pink and she looked down, hiding her eyes but revealing to him how rich and dark her lashes were. He'd never really noticed before. She truly was a very attractive young woman, but it was hidden behind the spectacles and plain mourning clothes—and she'd always been overshadowed by a beautiful older sister.

She cleared her throat in a very businesslike way, her hands clasped primly in her lap. "I only did what any auntie would do. You have every right to be proud of him. Sam is doing very well with his studies. The rector thinks highly of him."

It was his chance to take up the topic of a good school, but he didn't want to destroy the mood. Bobbie's words were comforting, and that's what he needed at the moment. He'd always enjoyed her company but he'd never really known her as a woman. "What does he like besides music?"

"Most subjects." Bobbie smiled. "He has an aptitude for mathematics. I think that runs in the family."

He quirked an eyebrow. "Yours or mine?"

"Both."

"How competent is Mr. Southbridge?"

Bobbie bit her lip. "He came highly recommended. He no longer pastors a church, so he enjoys tutoring. He is teaching Sam Greek and Latin as well as a full curriculum comparable to whatever a boy would get in a grammar school."

"Don't you think he would benefit by the company of other boys his age?"

"Of course. But he has a few boys his age who live close by. He sees them occasionally…." Her voice dwindled off as if realizing how inadequate it sounded. "We've tried to give him every advantage. When he is not at his lessons, I take him to museums and galleries. He sees his piano teacher once a week. He keeps quite busy. He has had a few tennis lessons and swimming… We didn't want him to feel…" Her voice dwindled off.

"The lack of a father and mother," he filled in for her, his tone grim. "I understand. I'm very grateful for all of you have done for Sam."

Mere words could not possibly express how much he appreciated the personal sacrifices she'd made on his son's behalf.

Her bespectacled eyes gazed at him somberly. "It's not too late, Luke, to regain his affection."

He stood, coming to a decision. "I'll move my things in tomorrow, if your invitation is still open."

She smiled, as if in relief. "Of course it is. You won't regret it." Her smile faded. "Don't be discouraged at first, if Sam doesn't thaw to you right away."

He ran a hand through his hair, sighing. "I'm not expecting much, if anything. Part of me says it's too late already."

"Oh, no! It's *not* too late."

He felt warmed by her words, even if she was being optimistic. "I'd better be going."

She walked him to the front door and offered him use of the carriage but he declined. "It's a nice evening. I prefer to walk to the station."

She stood a moment on the stoop with him. "If…if it's nice weather on Saturday, would you like to go on an outing with Sam?"

He gazed at her face in the shadows. She was trying her best to make things easy for him, and it touched his heart. "Would he go somewhere with me?"

She bit her lip. "I could come along with the two of you. He likes to go to the Crystal Palace, which, you remember, they moved right here to Sydenham. There's so much to see and do there. If it rains, we can walk through the exhibits inside. If it's mild weather, we can walk on the grounds." She smiled. "Our favorite spot is the prehistoric island."

He returned her smile, feeling a glimmer of hope. "Very well. It sounds like a fine plan." He coughed, feeling suddenly magnanimous, as if her gesture had inspired it. "If you'd like, I can stop by the office and look over that project your father was working on when he passed away."

The relief in her eyes was so apparent, he felt stirred that he could offer her something in return for her generosity.

"Thank you," she said, her low tone fervent. "We're currently working on a tunnel under the Thames. I…I desperately need some expert help."

"Very well, I'll be there bright and early. Perhaps we can even go out to the site if there's time."

Is this what he wanted? With every word, he felt he was committing himself to staying in England for the foreseeable future.

Chapter Four

The following evening, Luke stepped out onto the darkened terrace at the back of the Gardner house.

He'd moved in late that afternoon and already wondered if it hadn't been a mistake.

The early April night was fresh but not uncomfortably cold. There was a sweet smell in the air and the night sky was clear, showing the first glimmer of stars, unlike the pall that habitually hung over London.

It felt good to be outside after another uncomfortable dinner in the household—this time without the relieving presence of Mr. Southbridge.

Luke had spent a good portion of the day with Bobbie at the engineering firm. First, they had looked at the plans for the new tunnel under the Thames, which would hold an underground rail to transport passengers from the heart of London to the southern bank of Southwark. They'd then gone to the site and he'd toured the work in progress with Bobbie and the junior engineer.

She clearly needed a project manager. The endeavor was challenging and innovative; he couldn't deny the fact that the work would be satisfying. It would be good to keep busy, doing work he knew and enjoyed while he was in London.

How long would he be in London? He sighed, running a hand across his face. Once again, dinner had not brought him any closer to his son. He glanced behind him at the house. Sam had excused himself immediately after dinner, turning down Bobbie's suggestion that he play them something on the piano.

Bobbie had put Luke on the top floor, to be on the same floor as Sam, she'd told him. Now he wondered how his son would feel about that.

He turned back to face the dark garden, leaning his arms on the balustrade. How he hated being back in this house. It brought the past back to him in a way he'd been trying for years to forget. Memories surrounded him, threatening to resurrect every feeling of guilt and stirring up unanswered questions, which had tortured him for years. Perhaps that was one reason he'd stayed in America so long. It was a land of new beginnings. People didn't care about one's family or history—all that mattered was a person's present-day accomplishments.

Here, he felt hemmed in by unseen forces: accusing voices, decisions made that had had forever consequences, and most of all a sense of failure from all that had resulted.

Was the Bible correct when it said one reaped what one sowed? What terrible things had he sowed in his youth to reap such a horrible marriage and aftermath? What had his son done to deserve losing his mother and father?

All he'd been guilty of in his youth was gullibility and naïveté, yet his choices had so changed the course of his life and that of his son and left Luke forever feeling a sense of incompetence in all his personal dealings.

The door to the terrace opened. For a second he thought maybe Sam had come out, but then he glimpsed Bobbie emerging and couldn't help a twinge of disappointment.

It would take time, Bobbie had told him. He had to be patient, he reminded himself with a suppressed sigh.

"Luke…"

"What?" he said curtly.

"A…are you all right?"

He took in a breath. "Yes, I just thought I'd get a breath of fresh air before turning in."

"I don't want to interrupt your solitude—" She took a step back as if to reenter the house.

But, he realized in that second that he didn't want to be alone. He extended his arm as if to hold her back. "No, don't go."

She joined him at the rail, wrapping her shawl more tightly around her shoulders.

"It's not too cold for you?" he murmured.

She shook her head.

They stood awhile without saying anything, but he felt it a companionable silence.

"I shall always be grateful how you rescued me from Mother's certain scolding that time you found me up in the tree." There was a smile in her voice.

He smiled in return, remembering. At least it was a pleasant memory. "You had swiped a cake from the platter and sneaked out back here."

"And hidden myself up in the tree there at the end of the garden." She motioned to the dark lawn. "Why *had* you come out back?"

His humor evaporated. "I was tired of fighting the pack of admirers around Irene. She had invited me to introduce me to her parents, and when I showed up here, it turned out to be quite a gathering with several young gentlemen vying for her attention."

"They were all her old suitors. I think she just wanted to show you off to everyone."

He shook his head. "She had a funny way of demonstrating that. I felt ignored most of the afternoon. I was trying to figure out why she seemed miffed with me—the first of many such times. I was just too young and new at it then to realize it would become a lifelong occurrence."

She sighed. "I sometimes think Irene was not truly well. I received a letter from her…shortly before the accident that ended her life. In it she sounded—I don't know—almost repentant for all the hurt she'd caused, but also helpless, as if she herself didn't understand why she behaved the way she did at times." Her voice filled with sadness. "I…don't think she was happy with the person she was with."

He stared at her in the dark, having a hard time imagining Irene repentant about any of her thoughtless actions. He should feel a sense of satisfaction that the man she'd left him for hadn't succeeded in making her happy, but all he felt was pity. "I'd like to see that letter some time if I may."

"Of course," she said softly.

He shook aside the negative memories. "Anyway, that afternoon of the party, I had just about decided to head back to the train station, when I decided to walk out here instead."

She giggled. "You didn't see me up in the tree…until I dropped my piece of cake on your head." Her laughter gurgled out.

It was a pleasant sound, causing his own mood to lighten, and he began to see the scene from her young eyes. "For an instant I thought it was a bird dropping on my head and I lifted my hand, terrified, thinking I'd have to go say my goodbyes to everyone with my head soiled, but then the cake bounced off my head and landed at my feet. I knew birds didn't eat cake—"

Her laughter grew. "No, only fourteen-year-old girls with a sweet tooth! You still had some crumbs on the crown of your head—and I was confounded. H-how was I to tell you?" she managed between her laughter.

"I shook my head like mad to ensure I didn't, as I looked up—quite indignant, I'll have you know, until I saw you between the branches. You looked more worried than I."

Her eyes sparkled. "You smiled at me and said, 'I don't believe I've ever met a cake-eating bird.'"

"I was all ready to blurt out a thousand apologies. Instead, you made me smile."

Her girlish joy was beginning to rub off on him. "All I could think about was whether I had icing sticking to my hair. I remember continuing to shake my head until you assured me quite a few times that there was not a trace of cake on me." He chuckled. "Such was not the case with you."

She frowned at him in mock indignation. "You didn't tell me I had chocolate icing around my mouth."

"You were quite a sight, with your hair ribbon askew, as I recall, a pretty-colored frock and your mouth smudged with chocolate."

"There I was conversing with you as if I was a young lady, and never once did you let on about my face."

"Until your mother came out, looking for you."

"I scampered down that tree so fast I tore the trim from my skirt and snagged a stocking. Just as Mother appeared, and I was busy smoothing down my skirt and hair, you handed me your handkerchief and said in the most matter-of-fact tone, 'Wipe the chocolate off your face,' then you greeted Mother as if nothing extraordinary were happening." Laughter erupted from her lips once more. "There I was, furiously scrubbing at my mouth and cheeks, while you were asking Mother about the hydrangea bush nearby. If I hadn't been so mortified, I would have found the situation amusing."

He chuckled. "Your mother forgot why she had come out there. I paid her a few more compliments, told her how parched I was and she led me away to the punch bowl."

They fell silent, then he added, "You know you never did give me back my handkerchief."

She looked away from him in what seemed embarrassment. "Oh—no, I suppose I didn't. I meant to—I was going to wash the chocolate stains from it and press it and give it back to you…." Her voice trailed off.

He shook his head in pretended disappointment. "And to think it was one of my favorites, one that my mother had monogrammed for me when I went off to Oxford."

"Oh, I'm terribly sorry—"

He shrugged. "Don't worry, I survived the loss."

Once again, a comfortable silence fell between them. Funny, he'd forgotten how companionable her presence was. Suddenly, in the still night air they heard a sneeze above them. They both looked up but could see nothing but the roof of the terrace.

"There must be an open window upstairs. I'll have to check when I go up," Bobbie said in a serious voice. "Do you think that was Sam?"

He craned his neck upward but could make nothing out. "I don't know…."

"I hope he hasn't caught a chill. I'll look in on him when I go up."

He gazed at her. She was more concerned than Irene had ever been over her own child. "I can, too, if you'd like."

"Oh—yes—only I don't know if he'll…"

His mouth turned downward. "Yes, quite. You'd better do it."

She reached out a hand and touched him lightly on the forearm then drew her hand away. "He'll come 'round. You'll see."

Her confidence comforted him, as had her brief touch. He realized his mood had lifted considerably since he'd first come out. The way it had that long ago day in this same garden, when then fourteen-year-old Bobbie had caused him to forget his own troubles for a few minutes. She had a remarkable ability to brighten his spirits even when he was feeling at his bleakest.

"You know you need a chief engineer for the tunnel," he said, looking at her in the semidarkness.

She sighed. "Yes, desperately. As you saw, we're already falling behind schedule and Father's only been gone a fortnight. There are two other firms working on the rails linking to the tunnel, so we can't afford to hold things up. The new line is scheduled to open in a year and a half."

Luke drummed his loose fists against the railing. He felt he was balancing on such a rail, unsure which way to fall. Stay in London, or concede defeat and leave? Finally, he took a deep breath, hoping he was choosing the right way. "I'll oversee the project—at least until I can find a suitable manager." He would use the time to reach out to his son, that was the only reason he was willing to knuckle under to the late Mr. Gardner's dictates.

Her eyes lit up. "Oh, Luke," she breathed, the relief palpable in the words, "would you do that?"

He nodded, feeling a warmth spread through his chest at the gratitude in her eyes.

She said nothing, and he was thankful she didn't press for more—or remind him of the terms of the will.

He took a step back from the railing. "Well, I think I'll take a short stroll before turning in."

She nodded. "You can leave through the garden if you'd like, but it might be a bit dark now. The street in front is lighted."

"I remember. Yes, I think I'll go out through the front." He turned to go inside. "Coming?"

"N-no. I'll stay outside a few minutes more. Thank you, Luke," she said in a fervent tone as he opened the door.

When Luke had left, Bobbie turned to the dark night. *Thank You, Lord,* she prayed, *for answering my prayer. Thank You for bringing Luke back home. Thank You that he decided to stay to help on the project. Thank You most of all for bringing Luke back to Sam.*

Please heal the breach between them. Show Luke what to say, what to do…how to be a father to his son.

When she reentered the house and climbed the stairs to her room, feeling bone-weary from the multiple stresses of the day, she remembered hearing that sneeze. She realized it could only have been Sam, though his room was two flights up. She entered the rooms on the first floor, but all the windows were shut tight in the bedrooms overlooking the back. She climbed the back staircase up to the nursery and servants' quarters. She glanced toward the front room she'd given Luke, but the door was closed and no light shown under it. He must still be outside. Then she passed the nursery and came to the door of the room they'd fixed for Sam once he'd outgrown the nursery. It, too, was closed. She hesitated, not wanting to wake him, but finally, tapped softly.

No answer. She waited a few more seconds after tapping again. Finally, she turned the handle as quietly as she could and stepped into the dark room. She immediately felt a cold draft.

"Goodness," she said under her breath, groping her way toward Sam's bed. She heard the boy's even breathing as she glanced at his shadowy form. Then she leaned over and pulled the dormer window closed and rearranged the curtains over it.

She looked at Sam once more when she had straightened. He continued sleeping. Her eyes had adjusted to the dark, and she could make out his features better. He looked peaceful and vulnerable in his sleep, his head slightly to one side, one arm curled under his pillow. The blanket rose and fell softly over his chest.

Finally, she turned and walked back toward the door.

Just when she reached it, Sam's voice stopped her. "Are you sweet on him?"

Her heart thudding in her chest, she turned slowly and walked back to the bed. "Whatever are you talking about?" she asked in amazement, refusing to acknowledge that she knew deep down whom he was referring to.

"I heard you talking and laughing with him. You sounded like sweethearts."

Her heart pounded even harder. Surely, it had not

sounded that way! She tried to inject a sound of humor to her voice. "And how, pray, do you know what sweethearts are supposed to sound like?"

"All giggly and talking in low tones, the way you two were."

Her cheeks flamed. "Oh, Sam, of course we're not sweethearts!" She sat down on the edge of the bed and reached out in the dark to touch his face, but he turned away from her, curling his body into a ball.

"Why'd you have to go and invite him here? He's not my father. Grandfather was my father. I don't need him!" His low voice became more vehement, and all Bobbie could do was rub his back, praying silently for God's peace to come upon him.

"I'm so sorry, Sam. I didn't mean to upset you. I just thought it would be easier to have him close by. You know how nervous Grandmother has been since Grandfather passed away. And...and we need someone to help us at the firm." Her voice grew eager. "Your father has agreed to oversee the tunnels. I know he wants to do it so he can be near you. He wants so much to get to know you." Her hand continued to rub the boy's warm back, though he didn't respond by so much as a motion or sound.

"Won't you give him a chance?" Finally, she sat back, letting the boy go. He'd need time.

By God's grace, surely Sam would see how much his father loved him.

When she left the room, she climbed downstairs to her room. In the darkness before turning up the gaslight, she remembered Luke's remark about his handkerchief. He'd caught her by surprise. Never did she think he'd remember it!

She hadn't been completely honest with him. She had

intended to wash and press it and give it back to him. But when it was clean and white again, neatly folded and still warm from the iron, she had stared at the monogrammed *LLT.* She'd brought it up to her nostrils, inhaling the clean, starchy smell. And then she'd put it away in her keepsake chest, where it still lay.

Chapter Five

Bobbie paused atop the hill at the end of Sydenham Park, Luke on one side of her and Sam on the other. They'd been at the Crystal Palace grounds for about an hour and already she felt the tension between her shoulder blades from having to make conversation and pretend all was well when it clearly wasn't. Luke hadn't made many overtures toward Sam, as if sensitive to the boy's hostility, but every friendly word he'd directed had been met with silence.

They had arrived shortly after noon, when the great park and exhibition hall opened. The day had turned into such a mild one, that they had kept their excursion to the Crystal Palace an outdoor one, bypassing all the fascinating indoor displays of faraway places from the Alhambra Court to the Temple of Karnac to walk instead around the terraces, gardens and fountains. The bulbs were beginning to open up, colorful crocus, bright narcissus and heady-scented hyacinth.

Now, they stood on a hill at the far end of the park and stopped to look at the lake below them.

It was surrounded by trees that hinted at the pale green and yellow of leaves just budding. Forsythia bushes gave a burst of color at different spots. A few villas were visible through the trees beyond the lake on the street bordering the park.

With a glance at Luke, Bobbie motioned to the small islands on the near side of the lake. "Have you viewed the statues of the prehistoric creatures?"

"Once, years ago with Irene," he answered briefly.

Sam's gaze flickered to his father but he quickly averted his face when he met Bobbie's eye.

"It's our favorite spot, isn't it, Sam?" She felt as if she had to prod every word out of her nephew. Thirteen-year-olds could certainly be stubborn!

Luke lifted an eyebrow. "I can understand that." He pointed below. "I think I spy some of the dinosaurs from here."

Bobbie smiled, following his direction. "Yes, I think you can see iguanodon on the middle island. And, look, Sam, which ones are those lying in the water?" She knew perfectly well, but wanted Sam to participate. Along the walk through the gardens and fountains, she'd felt like a schoolteacher, pointing out all the landscaping features, and wondered if Luke were feeling lectured. How she wished Sam would be more forthcoming, but he'd trudged along beside her, hardly saying a word, making sure she was always between him and his father.

"Ichthyosaurus and plesiosaurus," he mumbled. "And those two over there are teleosaurus," he added, pointing to a pair.

If Luke was surprised at this sudden volunteering of the information, he didn't show it.

"They look almost like modern-day crocodiles— from what I've seen in picture books, of course," Bobbie said with a laugh, relieved Sam had been forthcoming on his own. Perhaps he would continue to open up with the dinosaurs, since he knew so much about them. "But these are much bigger, or so I've read."

"Yes, the actual crocodiles I've seen are only three or four feet long."

They both turned to look at Luke in amazement. "You've seen croco—" Sam stopped midword, blushed, then finished "—d-diles?"

Luke nodded, his eyes on his son. "In India."

Bobbie turned to him. "Oh, yes, of course, during your years there. You must have seen many exotic things."

"Yes, it's a very exotic land," he confirmed.

"Did you ever see a snake charmer?"

Luke blinked at Sam's sudden question, but immediately gave the boy his full attention. "Yes, several times. They travel from town to town with their covered baskets. They'll sit cross-legged on the ground and a crowd gathers. They play their flute and out rises the cobra. If you're lucky, it spreads its hood."

"You mean the wide part of its neck?"

Luke nodded to his son. "That's right. It looks a little like a hood, hence the name."

"How does the charmer keep from getting bitten? Is it magic?"

"They say the music serves to hypnotize the snake. The snakes are slow to move anyway. And, handled correctly, I suppose it isn't so hard to get them to go where you want."

"I read about snake charmers in a book on India."

Luke nodded at his son. "Some charmers have more than one snake in their basket. Sometimes the snake is stubborn, or lazy, and doesn't want to come out of his basket. The charmer will be playing for all he's worth, his cheeks bulging out, and still the snake doesn't emerge."

Sam's lips turned upward, his blue gaze fastened on his father's face. "What does he do then?"

"He'll flick his fingers in front of the snake, like this—" Luke reached out quickly and almost touched Sam under his chin then drew his fingers back as Sam flinched. "See what I mean? The snake feels attacked and immediately lifts up his body out of the basket. That's the peculiar thing about cobras, how they can lift a good third of their length straight up."

Sam continued to be a captive audience so Luke kept the momentum going. "The charmer will continue teasing the snake in this way, all the while playing his flute with one hand, the other fluttering his fingers in front of the snake fast enough to prevent getting its fangs sunk into them."

Sam nodded as if digesting this information. Thankfully Luke had touched on a topic that fascinated the boy. When silence threatened to take over again, Bobbie motioned forward. "Shall we descend and step back thousands of years in time?"

Luke gave a slight smile; she'd always found that smile extremely attractive, a half lift of one side of his lips, which revealed a quiet sort of amusement. "Lead the way." He stood back, allowing her and Sam to precede him.

As they descended the hill, she turned to Luke, pointing to the interesting rock face. "You as an engineer will appreciate the geological cliffs. They have recreated the different rock formations common here on the British Isles. Tell us about the rock, Sam."

Sam thrust his hands in his pockets as they all paused in front of a cliff made up of layers of different-colored rock. "They're called *strata*." As he spoke, he didn't take his eyes off his father. Luke nodded as his glance went from his son to the cliff face as if absorbed in what he was hearing. "Th-they show the geological makeup of the earth under the top crust."

Sam cleared his throat and continued, taking a hand out of his pocket and pointing. "The topmost after the soil is the 'tertiary,' it's made up of a lot of chalk, like that found in the cliffs of Dover. It's full of flint."

"Yes, I see. What about those fellows up there?" Luke gestured to the majestic group of deerlike statues poised above the cliff.

"They're prehistoric elk—they're bigger than today's elk," his son explained.

Bobbie nodded. "Yes, the one standing looks at least twelve feet high from the tip of its antlers."

"They're based on skeletons found in Ireland. They lived during that period." Sam turned away from the rock cliff and pointed downward to the island nearest them. "Just like the dinosaurs found on this island."

They continued walking down the narrow pathway between the cliff on one side and the island on the other.

They finally came to a stop before a group of the animal statues they had seen from above, some half-submerged in the water, others standing on rocks beside the island.

"They certainly are massive seen from here," Luke said.

"Yes, I'm always astonished each time I come here." Bobbie pointed to one in the water near the island's edge. "Doesn't that one with the smooth gray skin look like a funny sort of dolphin, and the other like a long, skinny lizard with a snakelike neck?"

"Mmm. The teeth on that large one certainly look sharp," Luke agreed.

"This is the Secondary Epoch."

They turned when Sam once again volunteered the information.

"Can you tell me anything more about it?" Luke asked quietly, giving his son a keen look.

Sam cleared his throat then indicated the rock strata behind them on the path. "It's called the Wealden Formation. It's where the largest fossils have been found and the most vegetation. It's where they first found the bones of iguanodon."

Luke gave the boy an admiring glance. "How do you remember all these names?"

Sam only shrugged.

Bobbie laughed. "It only shows you how many times we've been here! Of course, we studied them all at home and viewed the fossils at the British Museum of Natural History," she added more seriously. "We looked up each one in natural history books as well. Show your father the famous iguanodon, Sam."

Her nephew led them a little farther and pointed. "Those green ones."

"Amazing." Luke showed the proper awe at the two massive creatures. One was lying on the scrubby earth, looking upward, its teeth bared, its long tail outstretched. The other stood slightly above it on an outcropping of rock, on all four of its thick legs, its sharp teeth also bared.

Bobbie shuddered. "Look at those clawlike toes! I wouldn't want to have been within its reach at dinnertime."

After studying the creatures for a few more moments, they continued walking along the bank. A sculpted dinosaur standing on four thick legs stared down at them from the island across the narrow channel of water. It had a hump on its upper back and a long tail that lay on the grass.

Luke pointed to it. "Which is this, Sam?"

"Megalosaurus."

Another giant reptile resembled a huge iguana with a row of sharp spikes down its back. "That one's hylaeosaurus," Sam said before Luke could ask him.

They arrived at the last island and saw no giant statues, although the island was as luxuriant in vegetation as the previous one. "Which period is this?" Luke queried.

"This is the oldest." Sam turned back to the rock strata and showed them the black layer at the bottom. "This is coal. There's only plant life. If we go a little farther, we come to the limestone." They followed him and heard the tinkle of a waterfall. A narrow channel of water fell between the cliffs above them to the tidal lake below. "This is where all the microscopic animal forms are found," he told them.

They studied the plant life of the island then Bobbie turned to Sam. "We must show your father the lead mine. That's just up ahead here. We can enter into the mine and see stalactites and stalagmites."

"That should be interesting," said Luke, who was studying the layers of grit and stone in the cliff.

"You must have worked in a lot of similar material," Bobbie said in an effort to encourage Sam's interest in his father's work.

"Yes, I've been involved in several projects blasting and tunneling through rock and silt. Limestone, ironstone, sandstone…" He identified the various layers on the rock face before them.

Sam listened but didn't ask any questions. Well, at least a start had been made this afternoon, thought Bobbie, following her nephew into the mine shaft opening.

She slowed her steps so Sam would be forced to walk next to his father. Luke began to tell him of working on a railroad tunnel and point out the similarities to the mine shaft, where a replica of a train transporting coal stood on the tracks.

Listening to him, Bobbie began to plan more such outings. Time, that's all the two needed together.

Sam's accusations about being sweet on Luke returned to her. She'd have to be extra careful how she behaved around Luke, even if it meant reining in the natural affinity she felt toward her former brother-in-law. She was no longer the younger sister, but a full-grown woman of twenty-eight.

The feelings Luke inspired in her now that she was an adult woman were much deeper and more powerful than the girlhood infatuation, she realized. Between working alongside of him at the firm and accompanying him on outings with Sam, she would be spending a good part of her days with him.

Would her heart be able to withstand the torture of loving him without giving her feelings away?

Chapter Six

Luke descended the stairs from his room. After spending the whole afternoon on the grounds of the Crystal Palace, they had returned to rest a little before tea.

He felt encouraged that Sam had begun to open up a little. Perhaps Bobbie had been right—spending time with the boy—and giving him attention—would allow Luke another chance at fatherhood.

He heard the lad's playing from the drawing room and made his way there. Once again, Sam was playing Beethoven's *Pathétique*.

Rather than disturb his son, Luke sat on one of the lower steps of the staircase outside the room and contented himself with listening to the haunting sonata. The stirringly familiar piece had the ability to transport him to another time and place. This time, instead of the early days of his courtship with Irene, he was back in India, a few years after their marriage.

He'd been away for a week on a railroad project in the north and had just arrived back at their bungalow in Delhi tired and dusty.

He entered the cool hallway and set down his portmanteau when the envelope caught his eye. It was propped against the Chinese porcelain bowl used to hold the day's mail, there for all to see. He recognized Irene's small, neat schoolgirl script right away.

A mixture of relief and irritation filled him as he concluded it was a note telling him she was off for a few days with friends, an increasingly frequent occurrence. He felt ashamed of feeling relief. It meant peace and quiet at home. Lately, Irene had begun to rail at him for bringing her to this outpost of the Empire, full of provincial British officials and their narrow-minded wives. She wanted to go back to England and tour the Continent.

But it irritated him that Irene's absence also meant she'd left young Sammy in the care of the infant's ayah again. A very nice, competent nanny, but not the child's mother.

While he'd been taking out his frustrations by working longer hours away from home, Irene had filled her days socializing with the British community, at the club or going off on weekend house parties so that he'd gotten used to coming home and finding her absent.

He sighed now, breaking open the envelope's seal.

Dear Luke,
By the time you read this, I'll be on my way to
Bombay to catch the steamship to Marseilles with
Anthony. Please don't try to stop us. Take care of
Sammy...

Anthony? Who in the world was Anthony? His mind searched all their British acquaintances. Not Sir Anthony Forbes-McKinney, the handsome young ne'er-do-well who purported to paint but was rumored to be nothing but a remittance man, sent abroad by his family for committing one too many indiscretions back in England?

He sat down on the lower step, just as he was doing now, hardly grasping the reality of Irene's hastily penned words.

Since when had the artistic dilettante she'd played a game or two of tennis with at the club become so close to her, she was willing to go off on a jaunt with him?

It took until the end of the note for Luke to realize that his wife hadn't gone off on a jaunt—but that she'd left him for another man.

Only then, in the empty silence of the house, did he come to realize Irene was *gone*. Gone for good. And that the marriage he'd fooled himself into believing still existed was only a sham to present to their small, snobby social circle in India.

He dropped his head in his hands, acknowledging to himself at long last how truly finished his marriage was, no matter how much he'd tried in recent years to pretend otherwise. The thin veneer of polite conversation, which had passed for communication between him and Irene the few times they met over the dining table, had only masked an uneasy truce, ready to break apart at the least pressure.

How foolish he'd been.

But he'd never believed her vivacious manner—the same charms she'd used on him—would ever lead her astray. She was a married lady with a child, a leader in society, no matter how much she flirted with the dashing officers in Her Majesty's army, the wealthy British planters or the handsome gentlemen's sons adventuring far from home. Luke had never questioned her fidelity. He'd trusted her.

He crushed the letter in his hand, too numb with

disbelief to feel anything—except to wonder who was going to take care of Sammy when he heard the boy's crying from far off in the nursery.

He rose like a sleepwalker and ascended the stairs and went down the corridor, his steps silent on the reed mats.

Farida was jiggling the toddler in her arms, murmuring a Hindi lullaby to him. She turned startled eyes to Luke when she perceived his presence in the room.

"Travis-Saahib—you have returned." She held the child out to him. He approached her, taking Sammy in his arms. The boy's chubby cheeks were rosy, his arms and neck damp.

"Papa," he murmured contentedly. "Papa back." He snuggled against his father. Luke turned toward the window, curtained with a filmy muslin and held the boy gently. "Yes, Sammy, Papa's back." He stared at the boy, rocking him gently until he fell asleep again. His dark blond lashes curled against his plump cheeks.

The pain stabbed him then. How could Irene leave their child?

Oh, dear God, he prayed, *what am I going to do?* Suddenly, he felt helpless. How was he to take care of a child? Where had Irene gone? Should he go after her?

He couldn't think yet.

In the days and weeks that followed, he operated like an automaton, going through the motions of his work, making discreet inquiries, discovering his wife had indeed taken a ship back to France. He cabled her parents, but Irene did not return there. Instead, she finally wrote to them that she had settled for good in France—a country that didn't inquire too closely into a person's liaisons or marital status.

The pain of rejection and humiliation, followed by the

crushing sense of failure, would come in the months and years ahead. He wondered if this had been the first time Irene had deceived him. Even when he'd first known her back in London, had she been true to him? The thoughts had tortured him as he remembered her winning manner.

Finally had come the hardening of his heart, until all Luke knew was his work.

He survived the humiliation of Irene's desertion by plunging himself more deeply than ever into the railroad projects. It was the only way to escape his own thoughts as well as the scandal and stunned disbelief of the small British community around him, the shocked whispers about that "ideal young couple" he and Irene had presented to the world. So Luke took off into the vast interior of India to oversee the laying of track and the building of bridges and tunnels, leaving Sammy more and more in the care of his ayah—ignoring his earlier accusations of Irene's doing the same thing.

His final rupture with Irene had occurred only a few months later when he'd undertaken the long journey to bring Sam back to England. India was no life for a young European child. Unrest was growing and the climate was brutal.

Had he committed the greatest mistake of his life by relinquishing his only child through his own selfish pain and self-pity? Was it too late to regain ground?

The sounds of the music penetrated Luke's mind, pushing aside the events of so long ago and forcing him back to the present.

Slowly, he rose, feeling uncertainty assail him once again, as he approached the doorway of the drawing room.

Sam was hunched over the piano. He clearly was

unaware of anything around him but the music—plaintive, soulful, coming almost to a standstill then recommencing at a lightning pace.

Luke stepped silently into the room, watching the boy's long fingers move rapidly over the ivory keys. There seemed anger in his playing this time, which Luke had not detected the first evening. The music ended abruptly. Sam, as if finally realizing someone stood in the room, started and looked up at Luke.

"That was the first piece your mother ever played for me." Luke hadn't expected to say that.

The boy's mouth worked, his blue eyes staring up at him. But he said nothing and turned his gaze back to the keys, his back still hunched, one foot kicking the carpet beneath the piano bench. From the gifted virtuoso, he looked once more like a normal adolescent boy forced to sit at the piano. Luke wanted to smile, if his heart weren't aching so.

He cleared his throat. "W-would you like to play something else?"

The clock ticked a few seconds then Sam got up from the bench so fast he almost knocked it backward. "No, thank you." With quick strides, he walked past his father and left the room.

Luke gazed at him in amazement, wondering what he'd done to bring about the change in his son from this afternoon at the park.

A second later, Bobbie peered into the drawing room. She must have been standing there when Sam rushed out. Luke stifled a sense of humiliation at his son's rejection.

Bobbie entered the room and approached him, her dark eyebrows drawn together. "What happened?"

He shrugged impatiently and turned away. "You

know him better than I do. I merely told him…that it was the first piece I ever heard his mother play—and then asked him if he cared to play another. He said no and left."

"I'm sorry." Her soft words calmed him. "He seemed to be warming to you today, but it will probably take more than one outing."

Luke raked a hand through this hair. "I realize that. I never presumed that spending a few hours in his company and asking him a few questions about his hobby would erase years of neglect."

There was so much sympathy in her eyes that Luke felt ashamed of his anger. He continued looking at her, noticing the delicate bloom in her cheeks and the soft fullness of her lips.

Abruptly, she broke contact with his gaze. "Why don't you sit down? I've rung for the tea."

Unwilling to spend the next few hours before dinner brooding about the past and the futility of having returned to England, he did as she bade and sat down across from her on the settee.

They said nothing for a few minutes. Luke closed his eyes, rubbing the bridge of his nose with his thumb and forefinger.

"When you first left Sam with us, I used to tell him about both you and Irene."

Luke stopped the motion of his fingers and slowly opened his eyes. She was not looking at him but at the coal fire burning in the grate. "I beg your pardon?" he asked.

"I told him that his mummy and daddy had had to leave him with us because they were in a dangerous place. I told him about the lions and tigers in India." Her slim, tapered fingers made a motion, although he couldn't see the expression in her eyes. "I don't know what other nonsense I spoke, since all I knew of India was what I had read in books. I just spun all kinds of fantasies about this wild, exotic place. I told him how you were busy bringing civilization to this vast continent of people—building bridges and laying railroads."

She smiled, continuing in her faraway tone. "When Sammy came to us, Father promptly bought him a train set even though he was much too young to be able to play with it. But I used it to show him the kind of work you were doing." She clasped her hands tightly together on her lap and finally looked across at him. "Then I did something I know I had no right to do."

Luke stared at her, wondering what she was going to say.

"I began writing letters." The color in her cheeks deepened, and her large, slate-blue eyes seemed to entreat him behind her spectacles. "I know I had no right, especially without consulting you. But I didn't know then how to get in touch with you. I didn't want to write to your solicitor and I hadn't heard a word from you when you first left."

"What kind of letters?" he asked carefully.

"Letters from you and Irene—to Sammy."

Luke drew his brows together, still finding it difficult to understand. "Letters from us?"

"I pretended to be one of you in turn and wrote to Sam. Then I would show him the letters and tell him they came all the way from India."

When he said nothing, she cleared her throat. "I would take him on my lap and read them to him. Later, when he was older, he'd sit right up close to me, sucking his thumb." She smiled, reminiscing. "I'd put all kinds of expression into my tone, the way I did when I read from his picture books. You had some impressive adventures, let me tell you."

She sighed, sitting back, as if coming out of the past. "I doubt he remembers much of them now. I stopped 'writing' when Irene died."

Luke sat silent, both shocked and alarmed at her revelations. How dared she toy with a young boy's feelings? What had been the effect upon Sam?

Bobbie swallowed, trying to read Luke's expression. But he looked stunned.

She leaned forward a little, trying to explain further. "I pretended that you...and Irene were still together. I said nothing to him about his mother being only across the Channel in Paris." She felt nervous at the steely way he was regarding her. "My parents and I decided it was best that way. I kept writing my sister, urging her to come and see Sam. I heard nothing from either of you—until you sent Sam a Christmas gift."

He rubbed his jaw and looked away. "I should have written," he finally said in a gruff tone. "What does one say to a two-year-old when one is as lost as he is?"

Her heart ached for him. She gave a self-conscious laugh. "I would tell Sammy all about the lions and tigers, trains and soldiers—and snake charmers, of course— and scribble little pictures in the margins, which I knew would make more sense to a young child than a lot of words."

Luke was looking at her now, almost as if she were a stranger—or as if he had a hard time understanding what she was saying. "Why didn't you tell me this at the time?"

She bit her lower lip, giving an embarrassed shrug. Was he going to be upset with her? It was so many years ago now. "I don't know," she whispered. "At first, I didn't know how to get in touch with you. Then when I did have a return address with the first Christmas gift you sent Sam, I didn't quite know how."

She faltered but he bored his eyes into hers, urging her to continue. "I was unsure how you'd feel, especially as I made it sound as if Sam's mummy and daddy were still together in India. I didn't think Sam would understand why his mother had gone away. He was too young to carry that burden. And I was…probably a little afraid you'd tell me to stop." She shrugged again, looking down, kneading her fingers together. "I'm sorry. I know I overstepped the bounds."

When she didn't hear anything from him, she dared to peek up at him. He only shook his head, as if not knowing what to say. But he didn't look happy about her confession.

She continued on. "It got harder and harder as time went on. A child of four and five can be very astute, I discovered," she said with another abrupt laugh. "I ran out of things to write, for one thing, and his curiosity grew. He wanted to know when you two were coming to visit him…to take him back with you."

Luke dropped his head in his hands.

She hated causing him more pain, but felt he had to know the extent of Sam's hurt if he was ever to build a bridge to his son's heart now. "He so looked forward to your yearly birthday and Christmas gifts, but there was never any note from you but one scribbled line wishing him a happy day," she whispered. "I—I felt I had to supplement that. And then even your gifts stopped."

"I realized at the time that my gifts would only cause him more confusion. A clean break was best."

They stared at each other a long moment. Finally, he asked, "What happened when Irene died?"

She took a deep breath, reluctant to remember those awful times. "I spoke with Mother and Father about how we should break the news of Irene's death to Sam. We gave him as much of the truth as possible. He was only seven then, so he was still too young to take in much of what had happened. We had agreed that it was better to keep up the fiction that she and you had been together. We told him that she had been killed in a train accident, but left him to assume that it had been in India.

"When you showed up for her funeral, Sam, as you can imagine, was too stunned by it all to say much of anything to you. By then you had become a stranger to him, no matter how many letters he had had from you." She looked up at him. "Especially since you had little to say to him at the time, either."

His eyes strayed toward the fireplace. Was he thinking of that visit?

"I hardly remember that time now. It was as if I was in a dense fog. When I got your cable, I could scarcely believe what it said...that Irene was really gone." His words were halting and low. "She was only twenty-seven. How could she be gone?" He shoved a hand through his hair. "Sammy had seemed so scared then, clinging to you. I hardly dared approach him."

"I know he needed you so much then. I think he dreamed of his father from the letters he received, but when you appeared in person—so large and solemn— you must have seemed forbidding to him. From his childish perspective, I don't think he could make the jump from the jolly-sounding, brave man who fought tigers, to the silent man dressed in black who stood by the graveside."

Luke sat back, a look of defeat in his green eyes. "And now?"

She tried to infuse a tone of encouragement in her words. "It will take time. But please don't give up. You saw him today. He wants so much to know you."

He drew in a deep breath, looking unconvinced.

She cast about in her mind for something to say. Suddenly her eyes widened, and she smiled a little. "Why don't you take him on a tour of the tunnel?"

He blinked. "You mean the project your father was working on?"

She nodded eagerly, hurrying on. "You can show him a bit of your world—what you really do," she said with an abashed smile, remembering her made-up letters.

He was already shaking his head. "That's your father's work."

She spread her hands wide. "It doesn't matter. It's still the kind of work you do."

He continued shaking his head. "I'm sure your father has taken him a number of times to view a project."

"Very seldom. A few times after a project was completed, but lately Father had been so busy and Sam equally so with his studies. Many times the projects were farther afield in Britain so it wasn't practical. With this one so close to us, it's perfect." She smiled again, praying silently that she would be able to convince him. "You could take him down to the tunnel and show him the hydraulic pump in action. What boy wouldn't like that? You saw how interested he was when you talked of tunnels in the mine shaft this afternoon."

Suddenly one side of his mouth turned upward in that endearing way he had. "And some young ladies as well, I take it?"

Her insides flip-flopped and she could feel the color

rise in her cheeks. "I don't think many. I'm as odd as I was in my likes and dislikes as when you first saw me up in that tree." Did *he* think she was odd?

"In a likeable sort of way," he said softly.

Her smile felt wobbly. How could a man—a man who'd been married to her sister—still affect her the same way he had when she'd been fourteen? She cleared her throat and smoothed down her skirt, searching for any topic of conversation to mask how giddy she felt inside. "Tomorrow is…Sunday. W-would you like to accompany us to church?"

His eyes widened slightly as if her question had surprised him. "I—I haven't been to church much in recent years."

"Oh." Did that mean he no longer attended church, or just that he hadn't been able to? "We go right nearby here…to St. Bartholomew's. It's a very nice old church." She felt she was moving too quickly.

A closed look came over his face, and too late she understood. "Yes, I remember it."

He and Irene had been married there. Oh, how could she be so clumsy?

"I'm sure it's as nice as…it was then." He rubbed the back of his neck, clearly uncomfortable with her invitation.

She hurried to fill the awkward moment. "Mother, Sam and I go every Sunday morning. And the servants, too, of course. The vicar is very good, truly dedicated to his flock." She should change the subject or apologize, but something inside her felt the need to press on. Perhaps it was what Luke needed the most—to be in the Lord's house.

"I…don't know."

She left it at that. She would pray for him tonight. The Lord was the only one who could draw him and bring healing to his heart.

Luke stood at the dormer window in his bedroom, looking down on the moonlit garden in back. His heart was troubled. Too much of the past had been stirred up today. For so many years, he'd run from it, and thought that by burying it, it would cease to exist. But now, he saw the results of the past…a boy on the verge of manhood, the fruit of his brief, unhappy marriage… his heritage. Luke had a responsibility to see that Sam developed into a worthy young man.

He sighed, thinking of the next day. Would he stay home in the morning or accompany the family to church? It would mean a lot of looks and questions from the parishioners, he was sure. Had Bobbie thought of that? He'd forgotten to ask her how she planned to reply to her neighbors and acquaintances about his sudden reappearance among them. If she had lied to his young son about Irene, what had she and her family told their friends and acquaintances about Irene and him? And Mrs. Gardner, would she suffer his accompanying them to church?

But if he stayed home, it would mean precious hours away from Sam. By Monday, Luke would be busy at the site, and have little time to see his son.

He thought again of Bobbie's suggestion that he invite Sam to the tunnel. Perhaps it wasn't such a bad idea. It would probably only attract the boy on account of his grandfather's role in the project, but who knew? Maybe it would help him understand Luke's work as well.

He thought again of Bobbie's astonishing revelation

earlier in the evening. She'd written letters on his and Irene's behalf to young Sammy. Luke leaned against the cold panes of glass, not knowing if that had done more harm than good, knowing only that Bobbie had done everything to make the young boy's life better, at a time when he'd been abandoned by both parents. He owed her a debt of gratitude he feared he could never repay.

Luke sighed. He didn't deserve a second chance with his son.

Only by God's grace could he hope to obtain favor and forgiveness from his boy again.

He fisted his hand against the sash. He'd go to church tomorrow. His lips quirked upward, imagining Bobbie's eyes lightening with pleasure. It would cost him very little to give her this joy.

He sighed. For too long, he'd run from God as much as he'd run from his past. Maybe it was time to run toward Him. He'd certainly need God's mercy to make any inroads with his boy.

Chapter Seven

By midmorning the next day, Luke had to steel himself to enter St. Bartholomew's Church. Besides his wedding, the only other time he'd been there had been for Sam's christening—another bittersweet memory.

Now, as he sat on the pew, listening to the hymns, memories of those two events in his life filled him.

Sam sat on one side of him, Bobbie on the other. Mrs. Gardner sat on her other side, and it was almost as if Bobbie had deliberately put herself between Luke and her mother. Another sign of Bobbie's thoughtfulness. Every day in the Gardner household, he was discovering what a kind, sensitive soul she was. He felt he'd never really known her, or seen behind her awkward, adolescent exterior.

Mrs. Gardner had only glanced at him with a slight lift of her eyebrows and murmured, "You are accompanying us this morning?" when he'd come down to join them.

Despite her mourning, Bobbie looked very pretty, dark tendrils of hair arranged around her face beneath the short black veil of her small hat. Her cheeks were flushed a delicate pink against her pale skin.

Reprimanding himself for noticing his former sister-in-law in that way, Luke settled back and looked around him. It had been a long time since he'd been inside an English church. They were very different from the white clapboard buildings with their tall, single steeples he'd seen so often in the smaller towns across America.

St. Bart's, though only several decades old, instead of centuries as so many in Britain, reflected the growth of this once small village since the railroad had come to it. Bobbie had told him on the way over that it had already been enlarged.

Three tall, stained-glass windows graced the altar end of the church. The morning sun pierced them, bringing out the brilliant blues and reds of the glass. He remembered facing Irene as she'd walked down the aisle on her father's arm.

She was a beautiful woman, but that day she'd been breathtakingly lovely in her white satin gown with its long train and lacy veil.

She'd come to stand before him, her face just visible behind the filmy veil. She'd worn pearls in her earlobes, he remembered.

As the hymns ended and the daily collect was read, Luke remembered repeating the vows of his marriage. The vicar had been different from the one presiding today, thankfully. Luke didn't want to face a man who had blessed a union that had ended so disastrously. It was bad enough that he would have to greet people after the service, who had been witnesses to it.

He glanced around but didn't recognize anyone on cursory inspection.

He tried to focus when the vicar took his place in the pulpit to begin his sermon. He was a middle-aged man, still handsome, and mild mannered in address.

"'Looking diligently lest any man fail of the grace of God; lest any root of bitterness springing up trouble you…'"

The words caught his attention. For a few seconds, they resonated with him. *Root of bitterness.* It described so aptly what he felt he was carrying around inside him since he had come back to Sydenham.

The vicar described the futile anger and acrimony that had been so familiar to Luke, feelings that were further frustrated because they had no outlet. Those whom he could have lambasted were dead. Only he remained to castigate. And he was doing that in full measure.

He listened intently to the sermon for a while until deducing that they held no answers for him. *Nail it to the cross, root out that bitterness, prayer and supplication, God's grace, the redemptive power of Jesus Christ…* All words that had little reality or meaning for Luke, who was used to dealing in hard facts. He started with a blueprint and watched it become a structure of iron, brick or steel.

Prayer…he'd prayed years ago. Prayed that Irene would come back. Prayed that he'd be the right kind of husband.

But she hadn't come back.

And he'd never had the opportunity to ask her why he hadn't been enough.

He'd stopped attending church after Irene had left him. There hadn't been much point in the small British community in India. He didn't want to be looked at in pity or as a curiosity…or worse, be accosted by single women offering their sympathy.

Never again would he give his heart to a woman.

When the service was over, they shuffled out of the crowded church. The parishioners all seemed well-to-do, Luke concluded, eyeing the ladies' small beribboned hats and fashionable attire and gentlemen's well-cut dark suits and silk top hats. He listened to the rustling of the women's high bustle skirts and the murmur of conversation as everyone made their way through the nave to the exit.

Several women greeted both Bobbie and Mrs. Gardner. Curious looks, as he'd anticipated, were cast in his direction, but no introductions were made as they moved forward. But once they stood under the tall elms and maples in the churchyard, Mrs. Gardner stopped to talk to friends. Most were still offering their sympathies on her bereavement. She sighed and thanked them, bringing her handkerchief to her face. When they turned to him, Bobbie made the introductions.

"Mrs. Lynds, do you remember my brother-in-law, Mr. Luke Travis?"

The elderly lady peered at him through her ivory-handled lorgnette. "No…indeed, I do not." She turned her focus on Bobbie. "Brother-in-law?" She pursed her lips, deepening the wrinkles around her mouth. "Ah, you undoubtedly refer to your late sister's husband."

"Yes, that is correct," Bobbie answered quietly, holding the lady's gaze.

Mrs. Lynds turned back to him and gave him a thorough going-over from top to bottom. "Where have you been these many years, sir?"

"In America."

She pursed her lips again. "What would you want in that place?"

"He is an engineer, like Father," Bobbie said quickly.

The lady barely heard her as suddenly her gaze fell

on Sam then slowly returned to Luke. "You are the father?"

"That's right." He saw Sam's glance go quickly to him and he held the boy's gaze, the way Bobbie had done to him, as if to give him courage. Sam swallowed and looked away.

"Well, it's about time you returned home," Mrs. Lynds admonished.

Another lady, middle-aged, with a pleasant face, who had been standing beside Mrs. Lynds, smiled and dipped into a curtsey. "So pleased to make your acquaintance, Mr. Travis. How thoughtful of you to return in the Gardners' time of need."

"May I present Mrs. Allston?" Bobbie said.

There followed several more introductions to various ladies and gentlemen who came to pay their respects to Mrs. Gardner. One of the gentlemen asked him straight out, "Are you taking over Gardner's firm?"

Before Luke could formulate a reply, the steely-haired man, doubtless a banker from the city, continued. "You're a godsend. The firm will go under without someone at the helm to replace the founder." He shook his head, as if seeing the profits already ebbing. "It'll be difficult to replace old Gardner. You say you've been in the States? What type of projects have you worked on?"

"The same sorts—railroads, bridges, tunnels…"

The man nodded. "Well, I wish you success. If anyone can take the reins here, it'll be you. Always good to keep things in the family when possible." He smiled amiably. "A pleasure making your acquaintance. If you need any advice, don't hesitate to call on me." He handed him his card, and sure enough, he was a banker.

"Thank you, sir," Luke murmured, as the man tipped his top hat to him and turned away, taking his wife by the arm.

"Mother, are you ready to go?"

"Yes, dear, I am feeling quite done in." Mrs. Gardner looked at Luke. "This is my first outing since the funeral."

"Let me accompany you to the carriage, ma'am."

"Thank you." He gave her his arm and made a way for them through the dispersing parishioners.

When he had helped both her and Bobbie up, he decided on the spur of the moment he would prefer to walk back and enjoy the beautiful spring day. Not allowing himself to get his hopes up, he turned to Sam. "Would you like to walk back with me?"

He thought the boy would shake his head. Instead, he glanced into the interior of the brougham, as if seeking Bobbie's approval. She began to speak, but her mother cut off her words. "Oh, dear, no, it's too windy out there. Come along inside, Sam."

Perhaps it was only a boy's natural desire to be outside rather than cooped up, but Sam suddenly took a step back and said to his grandmother, "I'd like to walk, if I may, ma'am."

Bobbie had to clutch her hand to keep it from reaching out to Sam. Why did she suddenly feel abandoned because Sam chose to walk home with his father? It's what she wanted, wasn't it?

"All…right," she said, forcing herself to smile at her nephew.

Her mother gave a resigned sigh and sat back on the seat. Bobbie looked at Luke. "It's not too chilly?"

"No, it's quite nice."

"Yes, of course." Actually, she wouldn't have minded a brisk walk in the sunshine, but Luke hadn't invited her. She tried to brush aside the disappointment. She nodded then thought of something else. "You know the way back?"

He smiled and glanced at his son. "Yes, I'm sure between the two of us, we'll manage."

How foolish her worries were. "W-we shall see you at the house then."

"Yes, we won't be long." He secured the carriage door and stepped back from it.

Bobbie tried not to think how final the thud sounded. Luke waved the coachman forward then turned to Sam. "Well, let's be off, so we don't feel cold."

She slid the window down. "You'll be back in time for dinner?"

He nodded and lifted a hand in farewell. Chiding herself for her needless cautions, she forced herself to sit back as the carriage rumbled off.

Before she could examine her feelings any further, her mother frowned at her, smoothing her gloves. "Why has he come back now?"

Bobbie moistened her lips, deciding how to answer. "Because of Father. I had to cable him about his will." She wouldn't say anything about Luke's interest in Sam yet.

"I don't like it. We've been fine without him until now. Why suddenly appear and rake up the past?" Her mother's pale blue eyes stared at her, worry clear in them. "What if he should want to take Sam away?"

Bobbie's deepest fear, so hidden she had hardly been aware of it herself, suddenly gaped wide open. She laughed, which sounded unnatural even to her own ears. "Oh, dear, no. He wouldn't do that." She tucked a strand of hair into her hat. "Besides, we need him here. Don't forget, Father trusted Luke enough to leave him half the firm."

Her mother lips puckered into a frown. "That's another thing! What could your father have been thinking?"

Here, she could reassure her mother more fully. "Because Father knew Luke was the best person to take over the firm if anything should ever happen to him." She reached out and patted her hand. "We need Luke right now. You'll see, he'll stay and be a good father to Sam."

Her mother nodded slowly and finally looked away at the passing scenery. Bobbie allowed herself to lean back, thankful she had been able to set her mother's worries at rest, even if her mother had succeeded in arousing hers.

"Irene should never have married him."

Bobbie's eyes widened at the decisive statement. She sighed, knowing it was futile to argue with her mother. She had never seen a fault in her oldest daughter. "You forget how much in love they were…" Bobbie remembered all too well that Luke was so infatuated he had eyes for no one else….

"But he never understood Irene's sensitive nature. She needed someone more attuned to her, someone she could lean on…."

Bobbie said nothing. She remembered her sister's moods, one moment up, the other so down, no one could say or do anything to help her. A husband would have had to be superhuman to have been everything Irene needed.

Bobbie wondered why Luke had never remarried. Had his experience with Irene soured him to marriage for all time? How sad, if that were the case. Bobbie stared out at the trees, their branches arched over the road, thinking of the type of woman who would make Luke a good helpmate and companion.

Someone who was steady, shared his interests, helped him in his career. Someone who loved his son unconditionally and who could help him to laugh again…

Someone like she herself.

Luke turned to Sam. "Shall we?"

"Yes, sir."

The two began walking briskly down the wide, tree-lined avenue toward home. Birds chirped all around them.

He thought of how to begin a conversation with his son. "Do you like going to church?"

Sam shrugged. "It's all right."

"The vicar delivers a good sermon."

"Yes. I like listening to him."

"How do you like your lessons?" Luke queried.

"Well enough."

"You've never wanted to go to school with other boys?"

Sam looked at him, his blue eyes wide and guileless. "I—I don't know. I've never thought about it."

Luke paused at the corner. "We have to turn down here, don't we?"

"Yes, sir."

Kirkdale. He glanced down the street. The deep green of the hawthorn and yew hedges behind low fences hid the large houses set closely together down the long, broad street.

The village of Sydenham had continued growing since he'd been here last, with several more brick villas lining its streets, evidence of its continued attraction to the prosperous middle class commuting to London.

Six years ago, he'd gone down this street. It had been a spring day just like this one. Irene's favorite time of the year—probably because it coincided with the height of the London Season.

And he'd come back to attend her funeral. All he could think of then was the irony of the soft blue sky and puffy white clouds, the daffodils bobbing in the breeze, their yellow trumpets sprinkled by the brief showers, signs of new life against the tragedy of Irene's short, chaotic one. Had she finally found peace?

Luke shook aside the memories. He was here to get to know his son. He took a deep breath, seeking another topic of conversation. "You must enjoy your music lessons quite a bit."

The boy nodded. His hands were stuffed into his jacket pockets, his shoulders hunched forward, his stride almost as long as Luke's. What would it be like when he surpassed Luke's height? He could hardly conceive of having a grown son. "When did you first discover you loved music so much?"

Sam shrugged. "I…don't know. Always, I guess."

Before Luke could formulate another question, Sam surprised him with one of his own. "Wh-when did you know you wanted to be an engineer?"

"Hmm. That's a good question. Not as young as your age, that's for certain." He chuckled.

The boy looked sidelong at him, a puzzled look in his eyes. "You didn't?"

"Oh, no. All I cared about then was playing rugby and cricket and beating the teams we played against in school."

Sam listened intently. "Where did you go to school?"

Luke smiled in recollection. "Oundle. It's quite an old grammar school near the village where I was born."

"Did…did you like it?"

"Very much. Maybe not at the very beginning. I was younger than you when I first arrived. Even though my family was not that far away, I still missed home. My father had attended the school when he was a boy, therefore I was expected to go as well."

He kicked at a small stone in his path. "Once I got over being homesick, I loved it. I made lots of new friends. When you live together, eat together, go to class together, it creates the kinds of friendships hard to find elsewhere."

Sam seemed to be listening with rapt attention.

Hope began to grow in Luke that perhaps he'd be able to convince Sam of the benefits of school, and in that case, Bobbie's opinion would be irrelevant. He didn't want to do anything to offend Bobbie, but neither would he let the boy's education suffer because of her ill-founded fears.

Women tended to be overprotective of children. She had been raised with only a sister. She didn't understand perhaps how boys were—rougher, more eager for adventure.

She'd looked so worried when he'd suggested walking home. He had to smile. As if the two of them would get lost and not be home in time for dinner. Despite her blatant overreaction, he couldn't help but be charmed by her tender concern.

Sam's voice interrupted his thoughts. "Tell me what it was like."

"What—oh, yes." Luke began to recount some of his best memories of his boyhood school days.

Gradually Sam began asking more questions. Once, he smiled.

"What is it?"

"Aunt Bobbie made boarding school sound horrible, as in David Copperfield."

"I see." He rubbed his chin, wondering how he could lessen the negative image Bobbie had painted. "Well, times have changed since Mr. Dickens wrote. Schools vary quite a bit, and, of course, each boy's experience is different."

Sam nodded as if considering.

Luke was surprised at how quickly they reached the house. As they opened the gate and turned into the walkway, he asked his son, "Would you like to go to a piano concert in the city?"

"A-all right."

His acceptance—no matter how hesitant—brought such a sense of relief to Luke that he almost came to a stop. He managed to keep his tone casual. "We can invite your aunt, too."

The boy gave him a sharp look, which he wasn't sure how to interpret. "Very well, sir." His tone sounded a little stiff, and Luke wondered what he'd said.

"I saw posters for a Chopin concert at Covent Garden. I'll discuss it with your aunt and get tickets."

Sam said nothing more, but opened the door and led the way inside.

Luke's heart lifted. Maybe he was making progress.

He remembered the scripture reading. *Looking dili-*

gently lest any man fail of the grace of God; lest any root of bitterness springing up trouble you...

Mustn't he get rid of the bitterness in his heart if he hoped to begin again with his son?

Chapter Eight

Bobbie breathed a tired sigh as she left her mother's room. Ever since her father's death, she'd had to help her mother settle down almost every night, sitting by her bedside and sometimes reading to her until the laudanum drops had their effect and her mother drifted off to sleep.

She heard the muted sounds of Sam's piano playing through the drawing room door and smiled, glad that Sam was playing for his father. As she approached the door, the music ended, and Bobbie had to swallow her disappointment that she'd just missed it. Her mother had been particularly fretful since Luke had moved into the house.

Bobbie opened the drawing room door quietly and stepped inside. Sam was still on the piano bench, turned toward his father. They broke off their conversation and looked at her, making her feel almost like an intruder.

But then Luke smiled at her. "There you are. Is your mother all tucked in?"

Bobbie returned his smile, sensing his understanding. "Yes, indeed, thank you." She glanced around to see where she would sit. The stool beside Luke's chair wouldn't do. Neither did she want to sit too close to him, mindful of Sam's eyes on them. She paused halfway to the piano and addressed Sam. "That was lovely. Would you like to play another one?"

He shook his head. "No. I'm a bit tired."

"Very well. You had better get up to your room. You have a big day tomorrow." She turned to Luke. "I've asked Alfred, the man who takes care of the horses and grounds for us, to accompany Sam to the city tomorrow after he finishes his lessons with the rector."

Luke nodded. "I look forward to seeing you there, Sam. We'll go down into the tunnel and see the progress the men are making in the shaft."

"All right. I'll try to finish up my lessons quickly."

Bobbie chuckled. "No need, Sam. There will be plenty of time if you come in the afternoon."

Sam rose and bid his father good-night, a warmer good-night than previously. "Good night, Aunt Bobbie," he added to her as she finally chose the settee.

"Good night, dear. Don't forget to brush your teeth and don't stay up too late reading."

"I won't," he promised.

She watched him leave the room, suddenly conscious of being alone with Luke. She cleared her throat, turning to him. "Shall I ring for tea?"

"If you'd like."

"Very well." She did so, and when she returned to her seat, he said, "Your father would be proud of you."

At the sudden words, she could feel tears prick her eyes. She blinked them away and when she could speak, asked, "Why is that?"

"You are a devoted daughter and a dedicated aunt."

She picked up her embroidery hoop. "Oh…I just do what anyone in my place would do." Why did the compliment—sincere though it was—fill her with an odd sense of disappointment? Is that all he saw in her?

"I'm not so sure about that. Your mother seems to depend on you quite a bit."

Bobbie's hands fell still. "Father's death has hit her quite hard. It was so unexpected. And, of course, mother is of the old school. Father ran everything. His word was law, and mother admired and acceded to him in everything."

His eyes twinkled. "Of the 'old school'? You sound like one of the Langham Ladies."

She bristled. "The Langham Ladies only seek re-form for women in the areas of education, marriage and employment. It is in great part thanks to them that the Married Women's Property Act finally came to be passed."

He held up his hands as if fending her off. "I didn't mean to imply anything to the contrary. I beg your pardon. I am in full agreement with their laudatory aims."

Her color returned. "Forgive me if I sound a little defensive, but I am a great believer in the rights of women. I-it might not seem so from what you see of my life here…." She made a helpless motion.

"No, I would draw the contrary conclusion." At her surprised look at him, he continued. "It is perhaps because of your life that you take a greater interest in the plight of women. You had dreams of going to uni-versity and becoming an engineer. Instead, you have been saddled with my son, and you have been a dutiful daughter." He sighed heavily. "Now, you are obliged to see to your mother's needs when you should be enjoying a home and family of your own."

She could feel her face flush with shame. Did he pity her? She stared at the half-finished circle of embroidery. "If I—I don't have a home and family of my own, it's out of my own choosing."

"What was your fiancé like?"

She glanced up, taken aback by the question. "I beg your pardon?"

He smiled that half smile, a twinkle in his eye. "I'm trying to imagine what kind of young gentleman attracted your admiration. Enough to consider marrying him." He waved aside the beginnings of her protest. "Don't tell me you were forced into an engagement by your parents. Not an independent young lady such as you. There must have been something to admire in the young man for you to contemplate an engagement."

She looked down at the rich colors of her cross-stitch, remembering Graham for a moment. She rarely ever thought of him anymore, and when she did, it was with a sense of guilt. "He was a…a very nice young gentleman."

"What was his name?"

"Graham Harrison."

"It sounds like a fine name…for a fine man."

She touched a hand to her throat, uncomfortable with the questions coming from him. "Y-yes, he was a fine man."

"How did you meet?" he asked softly.

Wondering at his interest—was Luke just being kind?—she replied, "At one of Mother's soiree's. I told you that she was forever having her friends and acquaintances bring their eligible sons and nephews to introduce me to."

"And this young man must have been quite special to catch your attention."

She was hardly conscious of dropping her hands to her lap, her hold on the needlework loosening. "He was special in a way that didn't stand out—perhaps that is what attracted me to him."

"In what way was that?"

"He seemed quite shy and reticent. He did nothing to try to get my attention." She smiled, remembering Graham's diffident manner as he sat in the corner of the settee and never once said a word to her, yet every time her look chanced to cross his, she caught his gaze on hers—one he quickly averted.

"It sounds as if you wanted someone who was the direct opposite of your father."

She gasped, the thought never having occurred to her in all the time she'd known Graham. "I—I don't think so. I mean, I never thought of him in that way." Once again, she picked up her needlework and fixed her attention on it, unable to look into Luke's discerning eyes. "He was just a very nice person, kind and considerate… and steady."

She laughed, a nervous sound to her ears. "I suppose I thought I could ward off Mother's barrage of young gentlemen if I agreed to marry Graham. It would please Father as well. Graham wasn't an engineer like you, but he had a good job at a bank. My parents had known his parents for years." She paused. "But I had not yet accepted his proposal of marriage."

She chanced a glance at Luke when he said nothing. But he was looking at her as if he expected her to continue. She swallowed, her mouth dry. "Then Irene passed away, and Sam came to live here. And…and Graham enlisted in the army and later was killed in the Boer War," she ended in a whisper.

"I'm sorry, Bobbie," he said softly.

She wiped the corner of her eye. "Don't be. I always felt badly that maybe if I'd married him he wouldn't have gone off…" She hesitated. "But I realized I wasn't in love with him."

After a moment he said, "You were fortunate to recognize it was not love before making a grave mistake."

She looked at him and realized he was speaking of his own experience.

He sighed. "I was afraid you hadn't married because you had to take care of Sam."

She shook her head vigorously. "No, Luke. I never gave up anything important. Please believe that. And, even if I had married, I never would have taken your son away from you."

He drew in a long breath, his eyes leaving hers. "It wasn't your fault. It was my own. I know you would have done the best you could have for Sam. And…and—" He seemed to have difficulty speaking. "I would have preferred your taking him to live with you and giving him a normal family life than leaving him here."

She said nothing, realizing all that he meant without saying it. "Father was a good grandfather to Sam," she said quietly. "I think the years and the heartaches mellowed him. You wouldn't have recognized his behavior around Sam. The proof is the love Sam had for him."

Luke nodded, and she read the painful acknowledgment in his green eyes.

Just then the door opened and the maid wheeled in the tea cart. Bobbie rose immediately to help her bring it in. "Thank you, Mary," she told the young woman. "I can take it from here." With a hand that shook slightly, she poured a cup for Luke and placed one cube of sugar in his cup with the silver tongs, remembering how he took his tea. She had memorized every detail of his likes and dislikes in the short time he had been in their midst when she was younger.

"Thank you," he murmured, taking the cup from her. He had the most attractive hands of any man she'd ever known, slim yet square and manly.

"About tomorrow, what should we show Sam?" he asked after Bobbie had taken her seat once more.

"I was thinking, perhaps take him down to the work near Swan's Pier?" she replied, grateful that he'd steered the conversation away from Graham. "There's no need to go into the compressed air chamber since now we're boring through mud, not water. I wouldn't want to risk anything going wrong since Sam is still a boy."

He nodded. "Yes. Has everything gone all right so far with your workers?"

"Yes. In the tunnel being dug under the Thames, the men only spend shifts of four hours down there and then sit in the decompression chamber. There have been no reports of Caisson's sickness in any of them."

"That's good. I saw a number of cases on the work on the Brooklyn Bridge. It was a terrible thing."

She shuddered. "Very well then. We'll take Sam to the tunnel we've just begun that will lead to the King William Street station. The plans call for the tunnels to be right under the existing roads as much as possible."

He pursed his lips, nodding thoughtfully. "Yes, that does avoid a lot of complications with existing structures below ground."

"There was so much concern when the railroad first applied for permission to attempt an underground railway beneath London—people were fearful it would destroy sewer and gas lines, as well as building structures. They didn't realize how far down a rail tunnel was to go." She shrugged. "So, in the end it was simpler to align the tunnels with the thoroughfares above them."

He rubbed his hands together. "It's settled then. We'll go down at the Swan Pier site tomorrow afternoon."

Bobbie smiled at him, basking in the companionable feeling between the two of them. If only it would last… even if he never saw her as anything other than Sam's maiden aunt.

The next afternoon, after spending a part of the morning with Bobbie at her father's office, going over the tunnel project in detail, they took an omnibus to the north bank of the Thames, alighting near London Bridge.

Luke paused a moment, looking toward the river. It was a mild, sunny day with only a slight, cool breeze off the water, bringing its briny smell to his nostrils. He enjoyed the hustle and bustle of the river traffic, from small steamships ferrying passengers up and down the length of the city to the large hulks of sailing ships docked farther downstream along its quays.

He looked to see where their current tunnel project was.

As if reading his thoughts, Bobbie pointed west. "We've just about completed the first phase, the two tunnels spanning the Thames. They run atop each other, as you saw in the plans, just this side of the bridge." Her finger moved direction, pointing to a spot nearby on the quay. "There's the old Swan Pier shaft. We're using it as the place to lower the boring shield to proceed tunneling under the city now."

She continued directing his focus. "The two tunnels will now run side by side up from the riverbank under Arthur Street, which curves northeastward as you saw on the map, until it reaches King William Street. The terminus will be right by the Monument."

From where they were standing on the busy thoroughfare beside the bridge, they could make out directly northward the top half of the tall, fluted column that commemorated the Great Fire of 1666. The wide road leading to it was choked with vehicles from carts and coaches to omnibuses and drays.

Bobbie's voice rose. "Oh, there's Sam with Alfred."

Luke waved to his son across the street before taking Bobbie's arm to cross. She gave him a quick look but said nothing, turning her attention to the busy traffic.

"You're right on time," she said as soon as they had reached Sam and the man who had brought him. Luke nodded to Alfred, a tall and slightly stoop-shouldered man wearing a plaid suit and top hat. "Thank you. We'll bring Sam home with us."

After bidding him farewell, they turned toward the shaft. "We'll take the lift they've set up there to go down to the tunnel."

Luke tried to determine whether or not Sam was excited by the prospect of going underground into a tunnel, but the boy's expression didn't give much away. As they neared the area where a number of laborers were busy with a variety of tasks, all he asked was, "Did Grandfather go down often?"

"Yes, he would frequently visit the site to make sure everything was being done according to the plans—and of course, if the plans weren't working, he was down here to decide how to improve them." She turned to Luke. "Isn't that what you've found to be true as an engineer—that many times things don't work exactly as calculated on paper and you must improvise something at the worksite?"

He directed his reply to Sam as they approached the opening of the shaft. "Yes, unfortunately, such is sometimes the case. The more experienced the engineer, and the more familiar the project, the less often such miscalculations occur. But even the most experienced engineer like your grandfather would tackle new kinds of projects that would present unforeseen challenges."

"Yes, indeed, Sam." Bobbie led them into the interior, greeting workers as she passed them. "This project is something entirely new. We've never had this kind of an underground rail system beneath a city. We didn't even know at first what kind of a train to use, since a steam engine wouldn't be practical in such a confined space."

"What kind of engine are you going to use?" Sam asked, as they waited for the lift to come up.

"The City and South London Railway Company decided to use a cable to pull the engine and its cars back and forth from one end of the line to the other."

Luke added, "The same kind of cables are used in the American city of San Francisco."

Sam's eyes widened. "Have you been to San Francisco?"

"Yes. It's a beautiful city, though still rough around the edges. Nowhere near as big as London."

The large lift arrived with a loud grinding sound. Workmen emerged pulling wagons of dirt.

Sam's eyes widened even farther. "Is this what's coming out of the tunnel?"

Bobbie nodded. "Yes, and they bring it up this shaft to haul away by barges down the river. This way the city streets aren't tied up with all the rubble."

The lift operator touched his cap to Bobbie and Luke as they entered the platform of the lift. "Afternoon, Miss

Gardner, Mr. Travis. Going to inspect the work?" The
man spoke with a heavy Scottish brogue.

She smiled at the man, whose face and work clothes
were grubby, and gestured to Sam. "As a matter of fact,
we are taking my nephew, Sam, to see the works." She
had already introduced Luke on an earlier inspection
of the site.

"Well, young man, you're going to see a real feat.
Such a noise as you've never heard. That new tunnel
boring machine eats up the clay like a monster chewin'
through his dinner."

With a slight thud, the lift reached the bottom of
the shaft and they stepped into the dark tunnel, which
was about fifteen feet in diameter. A provisional set of
rails had been set down on the muddy bottom to pull
the wagonloads of dirt out of the tunnel. A half a dozen
men were in the small space and they could hear voices
farther up the dark tunnel. A few hanging lanterns lit
the way.

"Would you like me to take you up to the borin'
machine?" the man asked Bobbie.

"That would be kind of you. Thank you."

It was clear the workmen respected Bobbie. Luke
wondered if in time they would accept her as their boss.
They followed him through the sticky, clay mud. They'd
all been forewarned to wear heavy boots. The sides
of the tunnel wall were lined with iron sections. As
they approached the end, the noise of both voices and
machinery grew louder. Sam's face betrayed a curiosity
to see what was ahead.

The workman waved with a flourish. "There she is,
eatin' away at the dirt."

A couple of men were loading buckets of dirt into an
awaiting cart. A bulkhead faced them at the end of the

tunnel. Through it, a small opening, about five or six feet across and ten feet high, separated the completed tunnel from that being bored. Three men stood beyond the bulkhead, operating the machine, which could be heard but not seen. A wooden platform stood in front of it, and another wooden wall. The platform was heaped with the emerging clay and dirt, which the workmen were constantly shoveling into the tunnel, to be cleared away by the remaining men.

The Scotsman indicated the metal walls of the tunnel. "Just as fast as she bores out the earth, we line the walls with these iron pieces and frames so they don't cave in on us.

"Come along, and we'll see how it's done." With a wave, the Scotsman led the way toward the bulkhead and into the shadowy section beyond it.

The sound was deafening and they could just make out the turning motion of the giant blades beyond the final partition. Clay poured into the enclosure.

One of the workmen nodded at them briefly as he emptied a shovelful of wet clay into an awaiting wagon. "We got her goin' at ten feet an hour now!"

Sam stared at the activity around him. As soon as an area was cleared, the men erected the curved iron walls to prop up the tunnel walls. Every man seemed to know exactly what to do, all working in concert. In a little while, they managed to move the front-most partition forward another few feet and the procedure began all over again.

"Excuse us—" a workman said, walking past them carrying iron shields with another man.

Just as Bobbie and Luke moved out of the way, they heard shouts from the head of the tunnel.

A geyser of water poured out of the small opening, threatening to pull down the entire partition.

Luke didn't think but grabbed his son by the shoulders, shouting to Bobbie as he moved away from the flood of water. "Take him back up!"

His command seemed to bring her to life. Quickly, she stepped through the bulkhead back out into the completed portion of tunnel. Luke shoved Sam at her and gave them both a push toward the end of the tunnel from where they'd come.

As soon as he saw them begin to run, Bobbie clutching Sam by the arm, Luke turned back into the small opening, grabbing a man who'd been knocked down by the gushing water. The space was already knee high with cold water and continuing to fill.

He helped the man through the bulkhead. "Get some boards!" he shouted to the awaiting men. "We've got to shore this up and build another wall."

Chapter Nine

Bobbie paced the pavement, wringing her hands together, wondering what was happening below. If it hadn't been for Sam's safety, she would have stayed below to help.

Was Luke all right? She gazed toward the shaft. The lift had gone back down but not come up again.

"Will anything happen to…Papa?"

Sam's face was pale, his eyes stricken.

She stepped forward and took his two hands in both of hers. They felt cold. "I'm certain he will be fine. H-he's a very experienced engineer. I'm sure he has been in countless such situations before." Had he? Oh, dear, what was she thinking? It wouldn't mean he was any safer now than before. She squeezed her nephew's hands. "We need to pray for your father, and for all the men still down there."

He nodded and bowed his head, closing his eyes. Bobbie did the same and began to pray in a soft voice. "Dear Lord, keep Sam's father safe. Bring all the men out safely. Give Luke wisdom to direct the men. In Your name, dear Jesus, we pray, Amen."

As soon as she lifted her head, they heard the lift

returning. Both rushed over. A few of the men emerged, muddy and wet.

"What happened? Where are the others?" Bobbie asked immediately.

"Oh, Miss Gardner," said one, shaking his head, "it's flooded. We must have hit an artery of the Thames. Mr. Travis told us to bring down some materials. We need to block the water, build another bulkhead, he said."

"He—they're still down there?" She couldn't mask her dismay.

He nodded. "If you'll excuse me, miss, I'd better do as Mr. Travis asked. Don't know how long things'll hold otherwise."

Her hand flew to her mouth to stop her gasp. *How long things would hold?* She must remain calm for Sam's sake. Quickly, she moved out of the workman's way. "Yes, of course. Do hurry."

She watched the men load boards and sheets of iron and other material onto the lift.

Praying silently all the while, she watched it descend again, even as she thought of all the tunnel and mine cave-ins she'd read of in the past.

It seemed hours that they waited aboveground. Once or twice she tried to convince Sam to go home, but he shook his head, his mouth set in a firm line. "Please let me stay, Aunt Bobbie."

She nodded, not having the heart to deny the boy knowledge of his father's well-being. What if he came back up hurt—or worse? She shook her head, renewing her prayers and thanksgiving. *Dear God, thank You for keeping them safe, for bringing them all up safe and sound. Thank You for Your mercy and grace. You wouldn't have brought Luke all the way back to Sam*

*after all these years just to snatch him away again.
I thank You for your mercy and loving kindness toward Sam.*

Once more the lift came and went with more supplies.
All the men could tell her was that the whole tunnel was
filled with water, but that everyone was safe, working
like madmen to stop the onrush of water.

Finally, the lift returned with several men. One of
them came up to her. "We blocked it up, miss, and all
the workers are coming up for now."

She looked behind him. "Where are the rest?"

"They'll be on the next load. Mr. Travis is just making
certain everything's in order. He'll tell you all about it,
I'm sure. He's an amazing gentleman, miss." The man's
gaze and tone were filled with admiration. "He knew
just what to do. Just like Mr. Gardner would've done."
He nodded. "Yessir, he directed us in building the bulkhead and is already figurin' out how to proceed. Says
we'll need to use the compression chamber again."

Bobbie and Sam hurried to the entrance of the shaft
to await the lift's final return. When it did, the half
dozen remaining workmen alighted, talking and laughing with the others who'd already returned. They were
covered with wet mud but didn't seem to mind at all.

Bobbie scanned their faces, searching for Luke's. He
came last, behind all the others. Bobbie had to stifle her
sob of relief. He was all in one piece, apparently unhurt
as he walked toward them.

Like the others, he was soaked to the skin, his face,
hair and clothes smeared with mud.

"You're all right?" he asked them both, as soon as
he approached them.

She gave a burst of laughter. "We're all right! You're

the one we're concerned about. Are—are you un-hurt?"

He nodded impatiently, his gaze on his son. "You're sure you're all right?"

Sam nodded vigorously. "That water, it just burst out. Where did it come from?"

Luke glanced back toward the shaft. "It must have been some stream that flows into the Thames. We're only a few yards away from the river still."

"How did you know what to do?"

Luke ran a hand through his hair, and feeling the mud on his fingers, gave a self-conscious laugh, looking at his hand. "I guess I mustn't come into the house like this."

How she wished she could give him something—a towel, anything to dry off. All she had was her handker-chief, which she quickly took out of her pocket. Thank-fully, it was clean. "Here, I know it's not much but at least you can wipe off your face."

He smiled at her, and her stomach did a familiar flip-flop at the look in his light green eyes, crinkled at the corners in the sunlight. "That's right. You owe me a hankie. Thanks." His cold, wet hand touched hers as he took it from her. She had to resist the urge to reach out and clasp his hand in both of hers.

He took off the worst of the mud from around his face with her handkerchief. His attention turned back to Sam. "To answer your question, since the boring has mostly been under the Thames up to now, the men are familiar with working with water. They just need to go back to those conditions until we hit dry ground again. In the meantime, we'll set up the compression chamber once more, which is an airtight area behind the boring shield, and keep drilling as before. I'm sure this is only a pocket of water."

He turned back to Bobbie. "Thank you for getting Sam out so quickly."

"I—I just acted on instinct," she stammered, feeling flustered by the intense emotion in his eyes.

"I wish I could have stayed down to see what was going on," Sam interjected.

Luke smiled, turning back to the boy. "Not until you're a full-fledged engineer, son. We weren't sure what would happen, and I wouldn't want anything to happen to you. You have a whole life ahead of you."

"We'd better get you somewhere where you can get some dry clothes. You'll catch a chill if you stay out here," Bobbie said, feeling the breeze off the river.

"Yes, ma'am," he replied with a grin. "Let me just see about the men, and we'll figure out where everyone should go."

She watched him direct the remaining workers. Some had already returned with blankets and a wagon. "We'll head to the building at the King William Street terminus. They've brought some dry clothes there. Why don't we meet you there?" He frowned at her garments. "You are none too dry yourselves."

"We're dry enough to make it home. We shall meet you at the King William Street site and take a hackney to the train station from there."

"Very well."

She watched him walk away to rejoin the men. Her heart swelled with pride, thanking the Lord for everyone's safe return and filled with wonder at how Luke had probably risen in the laborers' estimation in the space of a few hours.

By the time he finished the project, everyone would

look up to him as the new owner of her father's firm. She knew in her soul her father would have wanted it that way.

When Luke emerged from his room after bathing and changing his clothes, he was surprised to find Sam in the corridor, almost as if he had been waiting for him.

He smiled at the boy. "Hello, there. How are you feeling now after your adventure?"

"A-all right." He cleared his throat. "How are you?"

Luke's smile widened. Did he sense a thawing in Sam's manner? He'd been quiet on the train ride back, but Luke had caught him looking at him whenever he turned to his son. "Nothing a hot bath and a clean change of clothes couldn't fix."

Sam returned his smile and Luke felt a warmth spread through his chest. Then his son's smile faded.

"What is it?"

Sam looked down and stubbed his toe against the carpet. Luke waited a few seconds, giving the boy time. His patience was rewarded when Sam looked back up at him, his blue eyes earnest. "Weren't you scared?"

Luke thought back to that moment in the tunnel then cracked a smile. "You know, I think it happened so fast that I didn't have time to be scared. All I could think of was the men who might be trapped in there."

Sam nodded, his eyes riveted to Luke's. "You've probably been in a lot of situations like that, where you might be killed, so now you're used to them."

Luke considered before answering, not wanting to appear more than he was to his son. "I've had my share of near misses, so in a way, I'm not as easily scared as I was when I first started out in this line of work. But it's not to say I don't get scared." He rubbed his chin. "I think the fear comes later, as a reaction." He grinned. "Probably tonight, when I wake up and it comes back to me. I'll especially be terrified when I think of the danger you might have been in."

Sam's lips gradually curled upward. "You pushed me at Aunt Bobbie, and then she almost dragged me to the lift, as if I was still a little boy."

"We probably both still think of you as a little boy." He cleared his throat, realizing his mistake in reminding them of all the lost years between them. "I guess what scares me more than a tunnel caving in, is the past."

Sam cocked his head. "What do you mean?"

Not sure how his words would be received, he ventured with honesty. "I mean, I can't change the past, the mistakes I made and the time I lost. I can't bring back that time."

Sam said nothing but he looked thoughtful.

Luke gestured toward the top of the stairs. "Shall we go down? I believe your aunt Bobbie said something about hot tea when we arrived home. Shall we see if she's had a chance to change?"

Sam nodded and walked beside him to the stairs. "It *was* scary for a moment though," his son repeated as they walked down the steps. "All this water just burst out of nowhere, it seemed."

Luke chuckled. "Yes, like a gusher except horizontal instead of vertical."

Sam glanced at him, his eyebrows drawn together. "A gusher?"

"Yes, you know, an oil gusher."

He shook his head.

"When they drill for oil, sometimes they hit a pocket of oil that's been lying there for millennia, building up pressure, and as soon as the drill hits it—" he opened his hands "—kaboom! The thick, black oil comes shooting out hundreds of feet into the sky."

Sam's lips parted in fascination. "Jiminy! Have you ever seen one?"

Luke shook his head as they reached the next floor and they glanced into the drawing room in search of Bobbie but she wasn't there. Hopefully, she was already in the parlor below. He wanted to make sure she was well recovered, too. Maybe she, like Sam, was suffering the aftereffects. He wondered if she had often visited her father's engineering sites. "But they can be very dangerous. Petroleum is highly combustible. Sometimes the gusher catches fire and then everything goes up like an inferno."

"What do they do then?"

He shrugged as they made their way to the front parlor. "There isn't much they can do...let it burn out, move everything out of its way that hasn't already gone up in smoke. The best thing is to prevent a fire, and even then, they lose so much oil, since it all spills over the ground."

He opened the door and allowed his son to precede him. "Oh, there you are," he said with a relieved smile at Bobbie who was already seated before the tea table.

She returned his smile and he thought how pretty she looked, her cheeks rosy, her dark hair brushed back. "I'm glad to see you in one piece."

"The feeling is mutual." He took a seat on the settee opposite hers and to his surprise and pleasure, Sam came to sit beside him. He compared it to his first day there, when Sam had remained at the opposite side of the room.

Bobbie poured a cup of tea. "Here you go, Sam, would you give this to your father?"

Sam jumped up to do her bidding and handed him the cup.

"Thank you." He took a sip. "Ah, that tastes good, nice and hot."

Sam approached his aunt's table for his own cup. "Aunt Bobbie, do you know what a *gusher* is?"

She pursed her lips, tilting her head. "I believe I've heard the word but…no—" she shook her head "—I don't know the meaning of it."

"It's when a tower of oil comes gushing out of the earth, like a volcano, isn't that right, P—" Sam looked at him for confirmation, stopping abruptly as if he had been on the point of saying something else. The boy's cheeks deepened in color, and he quickly looked at his cup and took a swallow.

Luke wondered if he had been going to call him Papa. He remembered the way Sam used to say "papa" when he was a little tyke. He quickly replied to Sam's question, to cover the boy's confusion. "Yes, you could call it a tall, narrow volcano. Or a geyser."

"Isn't that a—a—" Sam's brow furrowed as he struggled to come up with a description.

"It's a hot spring that sometimes shoots up in the same way—not as high or as dangerous as a gusher, but impressive nonetheless. There are some famous ones in Iceland, and they've discovered one out in the American West. We'll have to bone up your knowledge of geology and geography," he quipped, taking another sip of tea.

"Sam has—I mean, the rector has taught him geography," Bobbie put in. "He hasn't had the advantage you have had of traveling all over the world and seeing firsthand some of these geological phenomena—"

Luke held up his hand at her increasingly defensive tone. He hadn't meant to point out a lack in his son's education, although he had noted the gap and wondered briefly how much his son was missing out on by not attending a good school. "I realize that." He smiled at Sam, a thought occurring to him. "Although, now that you're older, maybe you can travel with me sometime and see them for yourself."

The boy's eyes grew round and he turned to Bobbie. "Aunt Bobbie, do you think I could do that?" He swallowed, turning back to Luke. "Maybe even go to America…with you some day?"

Luke hadn't thought that far afield, but…why not? The boy was almost a young man. Slowly, he nodded, feeling a profound sense of relief flood him. Perhaps it wasn't too late to regain his son's regard. He kept his tone deliberately light. "Why not?" He glanced at Bobbie, who was biting her bottom lip and staring at them both, as if she'd just heard one of them had been stricken by cholera. His momentary excitement diminished. "What do you think, Bobbie?" he asked deliberately, curious how she would answer.

She seemed to make an effort to smile. "I'm sure that would be exciting for Sam…for any boy…*someday*. But right now, he is busy with his studies and his music."

Sam's smile disappeared. Luke, not wishing to create ill feeling when they had all just been through a harrowing experience, decided changing the subject was the best recourse for the moment. But now that the idea had been formed, he would definitely take it up with her at a later date. "Speaking of music, do you ever go to concerts or musicals in the city?" His look included both of them.

When Sam shook his head, Bobbie explained. "We've gone to an occasional concert. We also try to take in the annual Handel festival here at the Crystal Palace every summer."

"I know I mentioned a Chopin concert but what about something lighthearted, since we've all just had enough of a dramatic experience this afternoon?"

Sam was already nodding vigorously so Bobbie said, "That sounds nice. What did you have in mind?"

"I was thinking of a matinee in London." He considered, then snapped his fingers, remembering a show bill he had seen near Convent Garden when he was at the hotel. "What about a Gilbert and Sullivan? I think I saw something about a revival."

Bobbie nodded slowly. "Yes, I believe I heard that *Pirates of Penzance* is going on right now."

He set down his cup and saucer. "I'll see about the tickets tomorrow."

The next morning Luke told Bobbie of his intention of going back to the site of the flooding.

"I'll go with you," she announced promptly.

He paused in the act of putting on his coat. "Don't you need to spend the day at the office?"

"It's all right—I can go there afterward. I'd like to see what all of you managed to rig up so quickly."

"I can describe it to you in detail."

Her dark eyebrows drew together over her spectacles. "What is it? Don't you wish me to go along?"

He let out a disbelieving laugh. "After the collapse yesterday? I should hardly think so."

She blinked. "Why should that prevent me?" Her fine chin jutted upward. "You're going down, aren't you?"

"You did put me in charge of this project, didn't you?" he reminded her.

Bobbie regarded him steadily. "And as part owner,

I feel it my duty to determine the extent of damage yesterday."

Luke gestured impatiently. "Bobbie, be reasonable, you're a woman—"

Her mouth fell open. "What does that have to do with it?"

He tried to curb his irritation at her stubbornness. "Please, Bobbie, let me go down first. We have no idea how structurally sound it is down there. You can go down as soon as I determine it's safe."

She waved aside his attempts at a compromise. "We'll be in the compressed air chamber. Surely, you don't think anything drastic will happen inside it?"

"Yes, but there is the decompression time afterward."

"Oh, but we wouldn't be down for long. And it's not as deep as all that."

"I'd feel more secure knowing you were not down in the tunnel with me." As he'd told Sam, his reaction to yesterday's accident had come later. He'd woken in the night reliving his fear that something might have happened to Bobbie or Sam.

"Nonsense. There's no danger now." She reached for her own coat and hat. "Now, we'd better be on our way."

He said no more, unable to refute her argument that as co-owner, she needed to be as involved as he in the oversight of the firm's projects. Would working at Gardner and Quimby—with Bobbie Gardner as co-owner—be similar to how it had been working with Robert Gardner? Would Bobbie always use her ownership as her trump card to get her way when they were at odds?

Chapter Ten

Bobbie sat in the darkened Savoy Theatre, feeling the magic she always experienced the moment the house-lights were dimmed and the curtain raised. In this theater, the moment was particularly dramatic, as it was the only theater with all electric lights, keeping the air comfortable, unlike gaslights, which overheated the interior. The theater was quite new, the decor Italian Renaissance, the curtain a shimmery gold satin.

Luke had secured very good seats for them, only a few rows from the orchestra pit. She glanced around her at the balconies and stalls behind and above her. Every seat was reputed to have an unobstructed view of the stage. There was a good crowd this afternoon.

A hush descended as the stage was unveiled.

The orchestra began to play. The small lights in the pit reflected off the shiny horns, trumpets and cymbals. The bows moved in rhythm across the violin strings. Bobbie settled back against her blue, velvet-upholstered seat with a sigh, prepared to be captivated by the fantasy of the stage for an hour or two.

What a good idea Luke had had of bringing them to a comic opera after their terrifying experience. She'd talked to Sam that first night as he lay in bed, but the boy hadn't seemed traumatized by the flooding tunnel. Instead, all he'd talked about was his father's bravery.

"He wasn't even scared. His only thought was for the men. Isn't that what a real hero would do?"

"Yes, indeed." She smoothed down Sam's coverlet, thinking to herself how Luke had always embodied all the attributes of a hero to her. Larger than life, admirable, beyond reach....

Was he still beyond reach? Would he always be beyond reach? She glanced at him in the theater, sitting on the other side of Sam. His head was bowed toward his son as he whispered something to him. Sam grinned and nodded, before the two sat back.

Bobbie found herself experiencing a twinge of something unpleasant, and it took her a few seconds to identify it as jealousy. The thought shocked her so much, she quickly averted her head and sat back, fixing her gaze straight ahead of her even though she noticed nothing of the characters on the set.

She forced her mind to the musical. The actors hadn't moved on the stage. They were all male, dressed in pirate uniforms, some seated on rocks along a make-believe seashore, some holding goblets in their hands, toasting and drinking. Others were playing cards. In the background was a backdrop depicting the sea, with a ship in the distance.

All at once, the men burst into song.

Bobbie had been to see the original opening of *The Pirates of Penzance*. She struggled to remember how old she'd been then. Twenty. Irene had left Luke a couple of years before. Bobbie had come to see the production with Graham, she remembered now. She'd been able to laugh that night at the sheer absurdity of the words and situations on stage. It had seemed such a long time since she'd laughed with pure abandon.

When she returned home, she'd had another note from Luke with a birthday gift to Sam. It was then she'd decided to decline Graham's offer of marriage. For how could she marry one man, when she still had feelings for another?

The lighthearted singing that began on the stage now helped dispel the sad thoughts of the past. Bobbie laid her program on her lap and settled down to enjoy the show. Of course she wasn't jealous of her own nephew! How absurd. She was delighted that he was beginning to look on his father as someone admirable.

Sam burst into laughter and she glanced over in time to see Luke's answering grin at his son. Luke's eyes lifted to meet hers and she felt her lips lift, even as her heart began to melt.

How could she be so susceptible? She was a grown woman—a spinster—so why was she acting like a young, impressionable schoolgirl who felt giddy at her former brother-in-law's smile.

Once again, she forced herself to concentrate on the music. Soon she found herself smiling and at times even laughing at the songs and situations. Most of all, she was gratified that Sam was having such a good time, hopefully dispelling any lingering horror from the day in the tunnel.

During the intermission, Luke bought them refreshments in the lobby.

As they stood among the milling crowd, sipping their lemonade, Sam said to his father, "That song the major general sang was funny."

Luke agreed. "Did you understand what he was saying?"

The boy thought for a moment. "Well, he sang about how much he knew about so many things. There were mathematical words like *equation*."

Luke smiled. "'Simple and quadradical.'"

Sam returned his smile. "'The square of the hypotenuse.'"

"'I am the very model of a modern major general!'" they both ended, laughing. Then Luke sobered. "Have you had any of those concepts in your mathematics lessons yet?"

Bobbie immediately bristled. Was this a way of quizzing Sam again about his schooling?

"Yes, sir."

Bobbie lifted her chin. "I have not yet introduced him to the binomial theorem, however. Were you introduced to them in your public school at thirteen?"

One side of Luke's lips tilted upward in a way that made her forget her irritation. Made her forget everything. "No, I can't recall that I was until perhaps the latter end of algebra." He lifted an eyebrow at her, a twinkle in his eyes. "I'm relieved to hear that Sam hasn't yet been exposed to it at his tender age."

She could feel herself flush, as if he knew what thoughts were crossing her mind.

His glance reverted to his son. "Nor to differential calculus."

Sam shook his head. "No, sir."

Bobbie was quick to point out, "I don't think any thirteen-year-old has had differential calculus."

"I shouldn't think so," Luke said in a mild tone, and Bobbie flushed even more, realizing he was only teasing.

"'In short, in matters vegetable, animal and mineral—'" Sam mimicked from the score.

Bobbie and Luke joined him as they ended the refrain, "'I am the very model of a modern major general,'" and they all laughed, though Bobbie felt hers was a bit strained.

Luke became serious again. "Do you know why else the song is funny?"

Sam's dark blond eyebrows drew together. "No, sir. Why?"

"Because it's a satire. Know what that is?"

He scrunched up his nose. "I'm not sure."

Bobbie explained. "It's a way of ridiculing or poking fun at something in society. It's often used in literature. Here, Mr. Gilbert has used it in the words to the songs."

Sam nodded as if digesting this. "Is that why so many people laugh at different times during the singing?"

"That's right," Luke said. "A lot of people saw this opera when it first opened almost ten years ago, so they know what it's about. Good satire only gets funnier each time you hear it."

Sam tilted his head to one side, his eyes on his father. "So, what makes the major general's song so funny?"

Luke looked at her as if giving her a chance to explain, but she made a slight motion, deferring to him. It was good for the two to have the kind of talks she'd grown accustomed to with Sam.

"If you notice, most of the first half of the song is the major general bragging about all the things he knows about. It sounds rather impressive, don't you agree?"

Sam nodded.

"Then it's only in the last stanza that he begins to sing about modern military warfare, and if you listen carefully, you'll notice he is admitting his ignorance of these things. In one of the last lines he states that his military knowledge only goes to the beginnings of this century."

Sam scrunched together his eyebrows and thought for a few seconds. Then recognition dawned in his blue eyes. "You mean, he only knows about how wars were fought in the early 1800s?"

"That's right, about the time Napoleon was fighting our soldiers."

Sam laughed. "But that's ridiculous when he's a major general! How's he supposed to know how to fight today?"

"Of course it is. The songwriter is saying that today's officers spend so much time learning all kinds of information but not enough studying about modern warfare."

Luke's gaze met Bobbie's and she saw in that moment the pleasure she'd enjoyed for years, that of imparting the tools of knowledge to a young mind and witnessing the pupil's use of reason to come to the answer himself.

She smiled at Luke, thanking the Lord once again for reuniting Sam with his father.

The smile Luke gave back to her made her feel the long journey leading to this moment had been worth every single step.

A few days later over breakfast Luke told Bobbie he wanted to visit other portions of the underground rail tunnel, those where the excavation was already complete. This time, before she had a chance to volunteer to come along with him, he suggested it himself.

She blinked and he almost laughed at the look of surprise behind her spectacles. "Are you sure it won't be too dangerous?" she asked in an exaggerated tone.

He chuckled. "You've proven you're just as intrepid

as any man. I think you, Miss Gardner, have all the makings of a fine engineer." She'd impressed him the other day with her levelheadedness and quick ability to grasp the situation and offer solutions. By morning's end, his irritation over her stubborn determination to accompany him had evaporated and he'd been gratified by her presence.

She looked down at her plate and her cheeks took on a pretty tint. "You needn't just say that."

"I'm not." He felt a sensation of pleasure that he was able to encourage her in something she obviously loved. Perhaps it wasn't so farfetched a notion that she pursue an education in her father's field. "So, what do you say about coming along and showing me some of the completed sites?"

She set down her toast and clasped her hands, her slate-blue eyes meeting his. "Very well."

"Where do you suggest we begin?"

She considered a moment, pursing her lips. "What about the Elephant and Castle site across the Thames? Yes," she said with a nod before he had a chance to reply. "Another firm is overseeing the tunnels in Southwark and it will give me the chance to introduce you to the various workmen and foremen. They need to know you as head of Father's project."

The reference to her father's work gave him pause, until he realized it didn't really bother him. When had this change in him occurred?

"Very well, I defer to your judgment."

Bobbie narrowed her eyes as if to detect any irony in his tone. But he was serious; he trusted her judgment. And, he found he was looking forward to a morning out on the project site with her.

Now, as they descended from a hansom and walked

toward the site of the tunnel, Bobbie said, "This location was originally to be the terminus of the southern end of the line, but work has already commenced beyond it to extend the line as far as Kennington." Her eyes shone. "The railway owners are already seeking permission from the government to take the line all the way to Clapham. Can you imagine?"

He looked around the area. It was a busy part of Southern London, crowded with buildings, the roads teeming with traffic. "It will certainly ease the congestion above ground."

"Indeed."

"It will also bring in more people from the suburbs."

"Oh, yes. This is designed so people who get off the trains from, say, Sydenham, can then take the underground tube into the city."

They reached the site of the future station and rode down in a lift. It came to a thud at the bottom and they exited into the tunnel, whose iron walls were being bricked over. "I noticed on the plans there is quite an incline in the tunnel up from the Thames on the other side, toward the King William Street terminus," he remarked, looking around him. "The foreman and I were analyzing the burst of water. We probably hit a pocket of water as the tunnel was going upward."

"Yes, an unfortunate result of having to go up toward the city station. It is the one negative of the plan. The engines will have a steep grade to climb to and from that station."

They walked around the future underground tube station. A few electric lights were already strung along sections of its length.

"This one is quite a bit wider than the other tunnel," he noted, impressed with the progress so far.

"Yes, here it was possible to have the two tunnels side by side, instead of one atop the other, with the platform in the middle. Come, have a look."

She led him to the large, flat area where the two tunnels met. "Can you imagine—" she turned to him, making a sweeping arc with her arm "—some day, trains will be stopping here. Who knows…perhaps as often as every quarter of an hour?"

He nodded, picturing it, catching her excitement. "The initial train will only have a few cars, won't it?"

"Yes, three at most, in addition to the engine. They'll have to see what the demand of passengers is. Everyone expects some initial resistance as people overcome their fears of going so deeply underground."

They walked around some more and spoke to the workmen, one of whom took them farther down into the shadowy chamber.

When they emerged some hours later, the sun was shining bright and high in the sky. Luke blinked a few times to adjust to it, taking a better look at the area around them. It, too, had grown rapidly from his earlier years in London. But the Elephant and Castle pub still stood where it had for centuries.

He glanced at his pocket watch. It was a little past noon. He glanced over at Bobbie, who was talking with the workman who had ridden up with them on the lift. When she nodded her dismissal and turned back to Luke, he asked on the spur of the moment, "May I offer you some lunch at the Elephant and Castle?"

She looked across the street at the pub, with its timbered facade. "I didn't realize it was so late. We must have been underground quite some time."

"I don't know about you, but I could use a bite to eat and something to drink."

She smiled with a quick glance at him then away. "Yes, I suppose I could as well, thank you."

He took her by the arm and guided her across the wide thoroughfare to the corner where it met a narrower street. A traditional wooden sign showing an elephant with a red castle painted above its back, swung gently over the door. "This has been here forever, hasn't it?"

"Oh, yes, to medieval times, though this isn't the original tavern. I believe it burned down in the last century."

He led her to a table by the mullioned windows in the shadowy interior of the pub. Quite a few people patronized the place at that hour.

"It was formerly a coaching inn," Bobbie said over the buzz of voices around them as they sat down, "bringing everyone from southern parts of England here to the city."

"And now it's the trains, which will soon connect them with the underground."

She smiled at him across the small table. He smiled back at her, enjoying just being in her company.

Before he could analyze this feeling, a waitress came by. After ordering a bowl of a hearty barley soup for Bobbie and a plate of shepherd's pie for himself, Luke sat back with a sigh, satisfied with their morning's work. He realized how good it was to have a full partner in a project, someone who had an equal stake in the success of a venture. The question for him was, what *was* his stake?

Turning away from this disquieting thought, he looked across at Bobbie, who was staring out the window. "Did you enjoy the Gilbert and Sullivan the other afternoon?"

She looked back at him with a quick smile, and once again he was taken with how pretty she was. "Oh, yes, very much."

He cleared his throat. "Do you think Sam did?"

"I'm certain he did. Children that age haven't learned to feign an enthusiasm they don't feel."

He nodded slowly, realizing she was right. "I hope that doesn't mean you were only feigning an enthusiasm."

"Oh, no!" Her cheeks deepened in colour. "It was a very good production. I haven't laughed so much in—" her inky-black lashes fluttered downward "—well, at least since Father died." Her eyelashes drew upward and her eyes looked fully into his behind her spectacles, "And for that, I thank you. It was nice to forget everything for a brief moment."

He inclined his head slightly. "Then I am happy I could oblige." He found as he spoke the words how true they were. It gave him a good feeling to have pleased her and lightened her load if only for an interlude.

He picked up the linen napkin at his place, fiddling with it. "Do you think Sam would enjoy something a little more serious, maybe a piano concerto?"

"I'm sure he would." She moistened her lips, making them appear a deeper shade of crimson against her skin. "But you know you don't have to earn his affection with spectacular outings."

He raised his eyebrows a fraction, not having thought of it in that way. "Do you think that's what I'm doing?"

"I'm sure you want to take him places that he'll both enjoy and that will benefit him. I applaud you for that.

All I'm saying is that he will equally enjoy just being with you."

"I'm trying to do that as well."

Her lips curled upward in a warm smile. "He was so impressed with your quick actions in the tunnel. I think you are the first real-live hero he has ever known."

Before he could stop himself he asked, "Not your father?" He regretted the question immediately. "I mean, I would imagine Sam would have looked up to him quite a bit."

If Bobbie noticed his discomfort, she made no sign, but seemed to consider his question seriously. "Oh, yes, he admired Father. But it's not the same to see someone on a daily basis and never witness anything spectacular—than to suddenly watch someone save a person's life."

"I wouldn't go that far," he said modestly.

"Well, Sam saw what he saw and has drawn his conclusions."

He rubbed his jaw, seeing the perils in being someone's hero. "I don't want Sam to put me on a pedestal. I'll be bound to fall off."

Her eyes filled with sympathy. "I'm sure if you just be yourself around him, that won't happen. He'll come to respect and admire you in a healthy way—the way he always did as a child."

The waitress came by and set down their food and drinks. When she moved away, Bobbie bowed her head, and Luke quickly followed suit. He didn't remember her being so pious before.

"Dear Lord, For what we are about to take, please make us truly thankful, Amen."

They unfolded their napkins and began to eat. "Good, hearty, English fare," he said with a smile, when she looked toward him after she'd taken her first spoonful of soup.

"You haven't had much of that in recent years, I imagine."

"No, I can't say that I have. Eaten a lot of unusual things, though."

She looked immediately interested. "What was the most unusual?"

"Probably rattlesnake."

"Oh!"

After a few more bites, he wiped his mouth and set down his fork. "I really want to thank you for all you've done for Sam."

Her cheeks colored once more and her eyelids lowered. "I—I haven't done anything extraordinary." She gave a nervous-sounding laugh. "Please don't put me on any sort of pedestal yourself."

He considered her a few seconds, realizing his gratitude had only made her uncomfortable and sought a way to distract her. She clutched her napkin in one hand. Her black gown accentuated the paleness of her skin. "You know, the only times I've seen you as an adult, you've been in mourning."

Her dark eyebrows drew together a moment. "I—I hadn't thought of that, but, yes, I suppose you're right."

"You're still a young woman. You should be in bright, fashionable colors—" He gestured with his hand, awkward with the words he was trying to express. "I don't know…going about in society. I hate to think of you cooped up at home now with only your mother and Sam for company." He chuckled. "Or grubbing around in muddy tunnels."

She smiled, an impish look in her eyes. "What if I'm happiest down below there?"

He grinned back at her. "Well, if that's the case, I certainly won't try to stop you in future. Seriously," he continued, his tone sobering, "I'm very grateful for all you've given to Sam. Who knows what kind of life he'd have led—or what he'd be like today if you hadn't given him—" he cleared his throat, finding it suddenly hard to go on "—the love of a mother."

"Oh, Luke, I'm his aunt. I loved him like a…son from the moment I laid eyes on him."

They stared at each other for a few seconds. Her lovely blue eyes seemed wide and round all of a sudden. He looked away, almost as if there were things there he shouldn't see—or didn't want to see.

He cleared his throat, turning his thoughts to a safer subject. "Have you ever thought…now that your father has left you his company to run, that perhaps you could follow your dream?"

"What do you mean?" She sounded genuinely puzzled.

"Become an engineer."

She made a sound in her throat, between laughter and disbelief. "You—who sounded so skeptical when I first mentioned my childhood dream of following in my father's footsteps?"

"Well, I know I was surprised at first, but you wouldn't be the first. There are a few women who have gone into the profession—and some who've made quite valuable contributions. Hertha Ayrton, for example, or Helena Blanchard in America." He shrugged. "The more I've thought about it—and seen of you this last week— the more I realize it isn't such a farfetched notion. After all, you are owner of your father's firm. And you're right, it is a premier firm and you wouldn't want to see it go downhill just because your father is gone. Who better to ensure this but his own daughter, an engineer in her own right?"

She shook her head. "I still find it hard to believe you would support me in this. Besides, I'm too old. It's too late. I'm twenty-eight. And, there's Sam—" She stopped, as if aware of what she'd said.

But he didn't let her backtrack. "Sam will soon be a young man, and as much as you might not like to think about it, will need to go away to school someday."

Her lips firmed into a straight line and she focused intently on her clasped hands. He couldn't help but notice the knuckles were turning white.

Despite her resistance, he decided to continue with the idea Sam had brought up. "I was thinking…that perhaps I could take Sam with me to America."

Her eyelids snapped up. "Y-you mean for a visit?"

"Yes…" he replied slowly, bracing for an outburst. "There's a lot I could show him."

Instead, she moistened her lips and looked around her as if searching for an appropriate reply. "It's just that…he's never lived with you before." Her slim hand made a helpless motion. "This is his home, all he's ever known, really. He was too young to remember India. Oh, I realize that he always wished to be with you, and ideally, that would have been best, but you yourself made the decision that your life was not one that a child could adapt to." Her eyes held a pleading look in them he found hard to resist. She truly cared about the welfare of his son.

"But now he's older." He pushed aside his own dish and clasped his hands on the tabletop, leaning forward. "Don't you see, Bobbie, this might be my only chance to ever have a son? To really get to know him before he becomes an adult," he added.

How he wanted Bobbie to understand. For some reason, she was the only person he'd ever felt a real kinship with in the Gardner family. And now he sought her approval and her blessing.

"But why can't you travel here in England? There are so many places the two of you could go, which are closer to…home." She cleared her throat. "Father has given you a chance to follow your profession here. Have you thought any more about that now that you've begun to work at the firm?"

He looked away from her, sensing a profound sense of disappointment. She didn't understand; she was, after all, a Gardner. "You know this arrangement is only temporary. I made it clear I can't accept your father's will."

"*Won't* accept it, you mean?"

He met her gaze with a slight shake of his head. "It doesn't matter. It's all the same."

An uneasy silence settled between them. Luke looked toward the bar and signaled the bartender. A moment later, the waitress came by with the bill, and Luke reached for his wallet to settle it.

"Thank you for lunch," Bobbie said in a polite voice as she stood.

"Don't mention it," he replied in any equally polite and distant tone as he opened the door to the street, the food in his stomach feeling heavy. No wonder he'd rarely missed his country's cuisine.

Chapter Eleven

Bobbie peered out the rain-splattered window of the front parlor into the dark night.

Luke had taken Sam to the Chopin concerto as he had promised him. Bobbie had planned to go along with them, but her mother had complained of feeling faint after dinner, so she had felt obliged to stay home.

If Luke or Sam had been disappointed, she had seen no sign of it. Sam had been too excited by a night on the town with his father.

Bobbie had been on her way down to prepare some tea for her and her mother, when she'd thought she'd heard the sound of coach wheels. Her heart leaped, thinking Sam and Luke were already home.

Telling herself it was much too early for the concert to have ended, she nevertheless strained to see out the window. A lone streetlamp cast a yellow halo around itself, illuminating the steady rain that fell and reflected off the drops that slid down the windowpane. The wind howled outside, causing the newly budded trees to bend.

Bobbie made out the roof of a coach above the high hawthorn hedge. Who else could be out on a night like this? No one with any sense…except for Luke and Sam. But Luke had treated the weather as nothing at all, insisting he'd keep Sam dry with their mackintoshes and umbrellas, promising they'd take a cab to the station and from there to the concert in St. James's Hall.

If things had worked out, she, too, would probably not have balked at a little inclement weather.

She let the drape fall back and made her way into the entry hall to open the front door as soon as the passenger had alighted from the coach.

She opened the door before hearing a knock, curious to see who would be paying a call. She gasped at the sight of the rector shaking out his umbrella. "Oh, my goodness, Mr. Southbridge, what are you doing out on this awful night?"

He smiled. "A little rain doesn't bother me." He closed the umbrella and doffed his top hat. "I thought your mother might like some company." He peered at her as she stepped aside and urged him inside. "I thought she'd be alone, you see. Was it too nasty a night for you to attempt the concert after all?"

She flushed. "No…it wasn't that." As she helped him off with his topcoat, she explained. "Mother wasn't feeling quite well, so I decided to stay with her."

"I see."

She wasn't sure how much he did indeed see, from the kindly look in his gray eyes.

He tut-tutted. "That's a shame. Well, I don't want to disturb her if she's not feeling quite the thing."

"Oh, I'm sure she'd enjoy your company. I was on my way to fetch us both a cup of tea. Might I prepare you one as well?"

"That sounds lovely, my dear." He walked beside her toward the staircase.

"Why don't you go on up to the drawing room? I'm sure Mother would love to see you. I'll be up shortly with the tea."

"Very good, my dear, if you're sure I won't disturb her."

"No, you'll help take her mind off things."

He nodded in understanding. "It must very difficult for her right now with the loss of your father."

She nodded before turning away and proceeding to the kitchen.

When she returned, she found her mother and the rector in conversation and was relieved to see her mother had perked up as they discussed parish news.

"I do hope to see you once again in the Ladies' Guild, Mrs. Gardner. We do so miss your presence. And your help was invaluable."

Her mother looked down demurely. "I shall try, but it has been difficult these past weeks."

"Of course, dear lady. Take all the time you need. I just don't want you to shut yourself away. You are too—" he cleared his throat, and Bobbie noticed his hesitancy for the first time "—young a woman and much too vital to pine away."

Some color rose into Mrs. Gardner's pale cheeks, making Bobbie envision her mother as a young woman. It reminded her of the way Irene used to look when Bobbie was still in childish pinafores. Her sister would hold court over her admirers and they would appear enraptured, just as old Mr. Southbridge looked at the moment.

"Thank you, my dear," Mr. Southbridge said as she handed him his cup of tea. "You are so thoughtful."

They talked awhile longer. Bobbie complimented him

on his sermon the past Sunday, and he brought them up to date on some of the parishioners who had been ill.

The rector set down his empty cup and saucer. "You must be so happy to have your long lost son-in-law back in your midst," he said to Bobbie's mother.

Mrs. Gardner's mouth opened and shut, and Bobbie felt a twinge of pity as her mother hunted for the right words, knowing she could not express her real opinion to the kindly rector. "I—I—"

Bobbie finished the sentence to give her mother a chance to collect her thoughts. "I think Mother was too surprised to really know how to take it. With the shock of Father's passing, this was an additional shock."

"Of course." The rector looked immediately contrite. "It had been so many years. How is young Sam adjusting to having his father again?"

Bobbie circled the rim of her saucer with a forefinger. "At first it was difficult. But gradually, he has accepted his father's presence. Something happened the other day to hasten things along."

The rector raised a gray eyebrow.

Bobbie filled him in on the mishap in the tunnel, keeping things as benign as possible for her mother's benefit. Mrs. Gardner had only been given a very scant summary of the event when they'd come home that day.

"Oh, dear…" Mr. Southbridge murmured, shaking his head. "How unbelievable. And to think how quickly it helped to soften Sam's heart toward his father. The Lord works in amazing ways."

Her mother drew her lips together. "Do you really think it was the Lord? After all, my son-in-law had practically abandoned his son for more than a decade.

What gives him the right to march back in here as if no time has passed at all?"

Mr. Southbridge considered, sitting back against the armchair and crossing his legs. "A fair question, my dear, and one to which there is no easy answer. God's grace is unfathomable at times. All we can do is trust that He works all things out to our eventual good."

Her mother's lips drew into a thin line but she said nothing more, having too much respect for the rector.

After a few more moments of conversation, Bobbie's mother rose to her feet. "I'm afraid I must retire." She motioned to the rector who began to stand. "Please, don't get up for my sake. Stay with Bobbie. She is used to my retiring early. I seem to be developing a bit of a migraine." She made a vague gesture. "The weather, you know, and the strain of everything still…"

Mr. Southbridge stood in spite of her plea, and bowed over her hand. "Courage, my dear lady. Know that I am praying for you and will continue to do so."

She nodded, touching her lacy handkerchief to the corner of her eye.

When she had left, Mr. Southbridge took his chair once more. "You're sure you don't mind my company? You'd probably prefer a good book, eh?"

Bobbie smiled. "I always enjoy your company and you know it. You are so good to Mother, too."

"I hope I didn't offend her with my last remark about Mr. Travis."

Bobbie smoothed down her skirt over her knees, choosing her words carefully. "If you did, it won't be for long. I know Mother values your counsel. I can't deny that Luke's being here has been difficult for her." She sighed. "You must understand that she has only had Father's opinion of Luke all these years. She hasn't really ever given herself a chance to get to know Luke himself, but always seen him through Father's eyes."

"Ah, yes, I see. A dangerous thing, that."

They sat silent a few moments. Bobbie didn't mind the quiet. She was used to the rector's company and had always found him a good, comforting soul.

She was staring into the coal fire, thinking of the various times in her life when he'd proved a good listener—more sympathetic and patient than her father. She'd gone to Mr. Southbridge with things she'd never have gone to her father with, no matter how much she admired him. When deliberating about whether to accept Graham's offer of marriage, for one, and when facing the challenge of taking care of Sam, beset with doubts about her capabilities to raise him.

So deep in thought was she that Mr. Southbridge's words startled her, bringing her abruptly back to the present. "How do *you* feel about having Luke back in your life?"

Her teacup clattered in its saucer as she looked up in surprise. Were her feelings that transparent? "I beg your pardon?"

The rector seemed unaware of the turmoil he'd created in her. "After all, you were just a young thing when Luke lived in London. You must scarcely remember him."

If only that were the case. "Er, yes…yes, that is so. Of course, I saw him again briefly when—" she cleared her throat "—when Irene died. That's the only time Luke came back…and, well, Sam was still very young then."

"Oh, yes, I'd forgotten about that time. It was a difficult period for all of you then."

"Yes." In more ways than one…

"Despite the sad occasion that has brought Luke back this time, I hope you are finding some solace in his presence."

"Uh, yes…"

"What a wondrous thing, just when Sam has lost the only father figure he has ever known, to have his real father come and take an interest in him."

She nodded. "Yes."

Mr. Southbridge regarded her a moment. "Are you having second thoughts about having him come home?"

She flushed under his discerning gaze. He'd known how much she'd wanted Luke to return, to be a father to Sam. She picked at a nub of thread on the arm of her chair. "No, of course not." She sighed. "It's just that—" Why was it so difficult to articulate?

"You've really been Sam's mother and father for many years," Mr. Southbridge said gently. "Of course, your parents were always here to support you, but they thrust on you the raising of Sam. Suddenly, in comes a stranger, the person Sam has dreamed about since he was a little boy, right after he lost his beloved grandfather."

She nodded, feeling a sheen of tears blur her sight. "It's an answer to prayer…and yet, it's happened so fast." She wiped at the corner of her eye, aghast at how she was losing control. What was wrong with her?

"Indeed it has. But isn't it good that Sam has a man to look up to? Your father is gone—what a hole was left in Sam's life. And what a worthy man to fill that place. No better man could have been chosen but the boy's own father."

She could only continue to nod, her eyes swimming with tears. All that he was saying were things she'd told herself more than once. Indeed, she didn't understand why she was feeling what she was feeling. It didn't make sense; it wasn't logical. "B-but what if he…he should take Sam away?" There, she'd said it, voicing her greatest fear.

He blinked in surprise. "Take Sam away? What nonsense is this?"

She removed her handkerchief from her pocket, feeling a bit like her mother—a thought that didn't please her at all. She had never been a watering pot!

"There, there, my dear, I didn't mean to upset you so. Now, why don't you dry those tears and tell me what all this is about?"

When she felt sufficiently composed, she sniffed a final time and said more calmly, "When Luke first returned, he mentioned his idea of sending Sam away to school."

Mr. Southbridge nodded, his lips pursed in consideration.

"But lately, I've heard Sam mention his desire to go to America with Luke. His father's been telling him of the places he's lived in, of course, and Sam being an impressionable young boy, finds it all so exciting."

"Yes, that is understandable."

"Luke is actually considering taking him to America for a visit when he leaves. A trip that far, who knows how long it would take."

The rector looked puzzled. "But I thought Luke was here to stay. Isn't he helping you run the firm? Didn't your father leave it jointly to the both of you?"

"Yes, but Luke has made it clear since he arrived that he is only here temporarily, to help me out until I find a suitable manager."

"Oh, dear, what a pity. He seemed the ideal candidate.

I thought it such a blessing…such an answer to prayer…" He shook his head.

Bobbie crumpled up the handkerchief in her hand. "So did I." She drew in another breath. "Father and Luke never really got along. When Irene left Luke, it made the rift more permanent. I…I so wanted to believe that Father's will was his way of reaching out and making amends to Luke, but…Luke doesn't see it that way."

The rector had been nodding throughout her explanation. "Well, my dear, perhaps all that is needed is time. Let the Lord have His perfect work. I will pray that the Lord guides Luke according to His perfect will."

Bobbie sighed. "Thank you." It was all any of them could do. But what if there wasn't enough time for the Lord to do His work?

After the reverend departed, Bobbie felt too restless to retire to her room until she knew that Sam and Luke had returned safe and sound. She stood in the darkened parlor, the fire still glowing at the far end. Finally, she took the window seat and continued to watch the rain fall in the dark night. The case clock sounded the hour— midnight—before she heard the hackney drive up and let the two off. Breathing a silent prayer of thanks, Bobbie saw them dash to the front door, being lost from sight for a few seconds before hearing the sound of the heavy front door opening and closing, and then the bolt being drawn.

She had deliberately left the door ajar, but now she sat frozen, mortified to have them see that she had waited up so long. Would Luke think she didn't trust him with his own son? But neither one peered into the room. Her tense posture relaxed when their soft footfalls sounded on the stairs.

Now she felt foolish all by herself in the still house. What was she to do? She didn't want Luke to see her come up now. She would wait until they were both in bed before making her way quietly up to her room.

But only a short time had elapsed, perhaps five or ten minutes, when she heard footsteps descend the stairs. Her heart began to pound and once again, she tensed. Perhaps Luke—for they were unmistakably his footsteps—was going to the kitchen for a cup of tea or late-night snack.

The footsteps reached the corridor and a couple of seconds passed before they approached the parlor door. She turned to stare at the sliver of dim light from the corridor. The door opened wider and she swallowed, seeing the outline of Luke's tall figure illumined by the light behind him.

He entered the room. Before he could turn up a light, she cleared her throat to let him know she was there.

He immediately stopped, directing his gaze toward the window. "Bobbie?"

Luke peered at the silhouette against the bay window. "Bobbie?" he repeated when he received no answer to his first query.

She gave an abrupt laugh, as if embarrassed to be caught there. "Yes, it's I." She began to rise.

He waved her down as he advanced toward her. "No, don't get up. I didn't mean to disturb you." He gave his own deprecating laugh. "I believe I was going to do the same thing as you."

She resumed her seat. "Oh, what was that?"

He reached the window seat and stood a few feet from her. "Sit in the dark and look out at the rain," he said with a smile. "It's a good way to think."

"Yes…yes, it is." Her voice mirrored his own humor

as she turned back to look out at the dim view of rain-drops on the glass. "How was the concert?"

"Very nice." He'd been sorry she couldn't attend. Annoyed as well, finding Mrs. Gardner's need for her daughter selfish and inconsiderate. He'd realized almost from the moment he and Sam had left the house how much he missed Bobbie's company. How he was grow-ing accustomed to having her with him. He cleared his throat. "I'm sorry you couldn't attend. How is your mother, by the way?" He was skeptical of Mrs. Gard-ner's ailment, although he sympathized with her recent loss.

"Better." Bobbie glanced up at him quickly, a smile in her voice. "Mr. Southbridge dropped by and seemed to cheer her up a bit."

He raised an eyebrow. "In this weather? I commend the fellow. You must be very special to him."

"We've known each other for ages. He understands what my mother has been going through better than the rest of us, for he lost his dear wife some years ago." She sighed. "He hasn't remarried, so I know he hasn't gotten over the loss."

Luke shoved his hands in his pockets and nodded.

"Is Sam all to bed?" Bobbie asked softly.

"Yes, he was tired. Not used to keeping such late hours."

"No, although sometimes, he stays up in bed reading till quite late. I usually stop in on my way to bed if I see a light under his door, because he knows I want him to get to bed early."

"I remember reading in bed past my bedtime when I was a boy." He felt badly that she'd had to sit home with her mother while the two of them had had a good time doing something they both enjoyed, but didn't know how to express himself.

He cleared his throat, not sure how she would receive his advice again. "You know, you should really think about going to university."

She sighed. "It's not as simple as you make it sound."

"I realize your mother needs you right now, but gradually she will resume her life."

She was shaking her head at his words. "She was so dependent on Father. We all were, I realize that now. He…he was such a strong personality—well, you know that. I'm not sure that Mother will ever adjust fully to having him gone."

He felt irritation growing in him. "That doesn't mean you should give up your life. You're still a young woman."

She made a sound of disbelief in her throat.

"From my perspective of thirty-six, twenty-eight is a mere babe."

"But for a man, thirty-six is still young!" she protested. "You're in your prime, both professionally, and… and as a…man."

She fell silent and he felt an awkwardness between them. The curve of her cheek was illuminated by the scant streetlight. It glinted off her eyeglasses. He could make out her delicate lips and pert chin.

Suddenly, he was very aware of her as a woman, a young, attractive woman. He wanted to laugh off the realization. She'd always been a child to him, Irene's little sister. But now, as he heard her soft breathing and noticed the rise and fall of her chest, he realized how easily he could lean forward and take her in his arms.

He stepped back, astounded by his own thoughts.

What was he thinking? It must be the result of listening to the romantic music this evening…the shadowy confines of the parlor…the fact that they were the only ones still up in the household.

He cleared his throat. "Well, you must be tired. I think I'll retire."

"Yes…of course."

He took another step back and another, finding it difficult to make his legs move, even when his mind was telling him to get out quickly.

But he wouldn't give in to some moment of loneliness. He'd made it alone this long. It was better this way. He wouldn't risk another failure.

He'd be mad to take on another Gardner woman.

The next afternoon, Bobbie took her garden tools out to the flowerbeds. She wanted to trim away dead branches from the perennials and begin weeding.

Working in the garden always relaxed her and she had gradually taken over most of its work from Alfred, leaving him the heavier chores of pruning the fruit trees and tilling up the vegetable garden.

She lifted her face to the warm sunshine and breathed deeply of the sweet scent from an apple tree in bloom nearby. Then, she donned her gardening gloves and began to spade up the soil, pulling up young dandelion plants before their roots got too big.

She still felt fatigued from having retired so late the previous evening. Even when she'd finally gone up to her room, a few minutes after having heard the last echoes of Luke's footsteps on the stairs, it had taken her a long time to fall asleep.

She kept hearing his tone of voice and pondering the look in his eyes those last few minutes that he had stood beside her—so close she was afraid he'd hear the beating of her heart.

Despite the shadowy light, she had sensed something between them. His expression—his tone of voice—was different. For a brief second in time, it was as if he had been aware of her as a woman.

But that was impossible, she told herself over and over, beating her pillow as drowsiness refused to come. Instead, her heart sped up each time she went over the words they'd exchanged.

It had all started when he'd brought up her age. He still thought of her as a young woman. If only she hadn't said such a silly thing about his age. *You're in your prime, both professionally, and…and as a…man.* Her cheeks burned each time she heard herself say those words. *As a man.* What had she been thinking?

As soon as the comment left her mouth, it was as if there had been an electric current in the room, igniting the very air between them.

He'd stared at her in the dark, not saying anything.

And then the next second, he sounded so strange and left so abruptly, almost as if running away from her.

Did he think she had…designs on him? She hardly dared articulate the thought, it was so abhorrent to her. What kind of woman did he think she was?

She stopped and took off a glove, retrieving a handkerchief from her pocket and wiping her damp cheeks and neck. It had turned quite warm in the shelter of the walled garden.

In the distance she heard a boy's shout, and she recognized it immediately as Sam's. Luke had taken him to a neighboring field at the back of the villas to toss a ball.

Quickly, Bobbie put away her handkerchief. The

wooden door at the far end of the garden opened and both of them returned. She gazed at the pair of them, both so handsome. Soon, Sam would reach his father's height.

Luke was hatless, his light brown hair gleaming in the sun. He wore a tweed Norfolk jacket and knickerbocker trousers. His son wore almost an identical suit.

She attempted a smile, as if nothing had happened the previous night—which was the truth, she reminded herself. "Hello. Back already?"

They strolled toward her, Sam with a wide smile, swinging a cricket bat in one hand, Luke with something not quite a smile—a more guarded look, she would say, before scolding herself for reading too much into it. She focused her attention on Sam.

"Aunt Bobbie, Papa can bowl the ball so fast. He taught me how to spin it. Did you know he played cricket at his school?"

She adjusted the brim of her hat to shade her eyes better as she glanced in Luke's direction. "No…" Why was he the only man capable of making her feel so aware? A few stray locks of hair had fallen over his forehead and his cheeks looked ruddy from the game; one hand casually gripped the ball. She swallowed, meeting his gaze briefly before addressing Sam. "So, he'll teach you to be a champion bowler?"

"Or batsman," he said with a proud lift of his chin.

"Sounds challenging. Why don't you two get a cold drink? Cook left a pitcher of lemonade for the athletes."

Sam ran off toward the house. Luke remained standing, and Bobbie felt more awkward and self-conscious than she had since he'd returned to England. As long as she thought he didn't really see *her,* just Irene's baby sister and Sam's maiden aunt, she had been able to hold her own in his company. But now, the memory of last night made her alert to every nuance, real or imagined, between them.

"You like to garden?"

"Oh—what? Yes, yes, I do." She looked toward the bed, which didn't look like much at the moment. Only a gardener would see its potential.

"Funny, I don't remember that about you."

She glanced up to find him looking at her, not at the bed. "I didn't realize I enjoyed gardening until a few years ago." She pulled off her gloves, giving a jerky laugh. "I guess that's a sign of advancing age…love of gardening."

"Possibly, but I wouldn't call it that in your case."

Her mouth felt so dry she didn't think she could get any words past her tongue. "No?" she whispered.

"No." He kicked at a dandelion she had pulled out. "Perhaps it's another outlet for a person who has too many talents and too much energy to spend her days sitting at home doing needlepoint and receiving visitors." Before she could think how to reply, he continued. "I was serious about your continuing your studies. If you'd like, we can go to the University College next time we're in the city and inquire about the degree-conferring program."

He was moving too quickly for her. "I don't know." The thought of studying what she loved most of all was so thrilling. It hardly seemed possible. And not if it meant losing Sam.

"Don't be so concerned about how others might react. You can deal with your mother after the fact. And as for Sam—" he shrugged "—I imagine he'll think it a lark, to have an engineer for an aunt."

She couldn't help a smile. Perhaps Luke was right. Slowly, she began to nod, though she didn't commit herself yet with words.

"Apropos of Sam, I was thinking of perhaps taking him for a little trip, if you could have him excused from lessons for a few days."

Her smile died. "A trip? Where were you thinking of going?"

He looked down at his shoes. "I thought perhaps up to Northamptonshire to show him where my family hales from."

"Oh." Suddenly, she felt a deep welling of sympathy and understanding. All Sam had ever known was her family. It was natural that Luke would want his son to know something of his heritage. "Yes, that would be nice. Do you have any family left?"

"A few cousins, I believe." He shrugged. "It'll probably be more a matter of visiting the cemetery plot and showing him old headstones and looking up church records. I can also show him the house where I was born. It was sold after my mother passed away." He squared his shoulders, reminding her of a gesture of Sam's. "And we can look at Oundle School, the place I attended."

"I see." They stared at each other as if in a contest of wills. Finally, she nodded. "Well, I shall glance at his lessons and see when a good weekend would be." She moistened her lips. "What about the tunnel?"

"Since the flooding, things have moved apace. I've been quite impressed with Melville. I think I can leave him in charge for a couple of days."

He seemed to have it all planned out. "All right."

"I appreciate it." His pale green eyes looked into hers a second longer before drifting toward the house.

He stepped back. "Well, I shall join Sam in that cold refreshment. Can I bring you something?"

"No, thank you. I'll come in in a bit."

"I shall leave you to your gardening then." With a quick bow of his head, he dismissed himself and walked off. She couldn't help but watch his purposeful stride, one hand in the pocket of his trousers.

What would Sam think after a few days alone in his father's company? Would he come back thinking he no longer needed his old aunt Bobbie for anything? She wiped her eyes with her sleeve.

She should feel a measure of relief that Luke had given no sign that yesterday evening had meant anything. Nothing but a spinster's overactive imagination.

The thought left her hollow.

Chapter Twelve

By the end of the week, Luke trudged beside his son on the paved sidewalk of the town of Oundle. They had taken the train up from London that morning to Northampton and switched to the small branch line to this market town.

He turned to his son. "What do you think?"

Sam looked around at the old yellow limestone buildings crowded along the street. "It's very nice."

Luke was surprised that it was still as picturesque as he remembered it. "It's quite ancient." He gestured to the building facades. "You know the stone is quarried locally. Jurassic limestone and Collyweston slate, if I remember correctly."

Sam narrowed his eyes as if calculating. "From the Mesozoic period."

He grinned. "That's right." They stopped to examine the stone of one building more closely. "When limestone was first being formed in the earth."

His fingers rubbed the rough surface. "Many of these structures date back to medieval times." He looked down the long street. "I'm surprised things are still so well preserved. It's got quite a bit more industrialized since my boyhood."

"What was it like growing up here?"

"Well, when I was only a little younger than you, I began boarding at Oundle School, one of the oldest public schools in Britain. We can tour the grounds if you'd like."

Sam nodded. "Yes, sir, I should like to."

"But first, since it's market day, let's head to the square and look at the stalls."

"All right."

The sights and sounds in the large square were typical of an English market, from the bleating of sheep and squawking of hens to the smells of baked goods and grilling sausages. It was too early in the season for farm produce except for those out of greenhouses but pots of spring bulbs abounded. Luke thought of Bobbie's gardens and how much she would have enjoyed the outing with them.

He immediately put a brake on his thoughts in that direction, something that was becoming more and more difficult. He thought a weekend away from her would help put things in their proper perspective. Instead, everything he saw reminded him of Bobbie in some way, from a young woman walking ahead of them on the station platform to a notice about a piano concerto being held in a few nights at a local hall.

What had been hardest had been keeping from thinking of that evening alone with her and how easy it would have been to kiss her—

He turned to Sam with a ruthless jerk of his head. His son was the sole reason he was here. "Hungry?"

The boy nodded eagerly.

They stopped at a stand and bought some freshly

baked currant buns and munched them as they strolled along the crowded stone square. "We'll continue down this street and reach the main church in town." He pointed above the slate rooftops. "See that spire? It's St. Peter's. I'll show you where some of your ancestors are buried."

When they arrived at the large stone church, they walked inside and admired the stained-glass windows and ancient carvings. The interior of the church was cool, the stone floor worn down in places.

Once back in the sunshine again, Luke pointed to the fenced-in churchyard at the side. "You probably know little of your forebears on my side."

"No, sir."

He opened the squeaky, black, wrought-iron gate and motioned for Sam to precede him.

The grass was already green but not yet mowed. A few dandelions already blossomed in the pathways. Old, worn gravestones stuck out of the earth, some leaning forward or back, some blackened with age.

Luke stopped before one. "When I was a boy, my grandmother would bring me here and show me the headstones. This was my favorite. 'Here lies Theophilus Andrew Stephens, son, brother, father and jolly companion to all.'" He chuckled. "I liked to think of him as this rotund, old man with white hair and beard, surrounded by his children and grandchildren."

Instead of smiling, Sam gave him a funny look. Was he thinking of the word *father* and all it implied? Luke cleared his throat. "Come, let's look at your family, the Travises." He led his son toward the rear of the cemetery. "You see, there are quite a few of us buried here." He stood before the lichen-covered stones of his great-grandparents. "Your great-great grandparents. They're getting a bit more difficult to read. 'Ebenezer Travis 1770 to 1851.' He lived to a ripe old age. 'His beloved wife, Eliza Hawthorne Travis 1778 to 1822.' She died in childbirth, I was told. They had quite a few offspring, as you can see. But old Ebenezer never married again."

They strolled around the graves, reading the various names off the headstones. Luke led Sam to the more ancient stones at the rear. "Your great-great-great-grandparents, Todd Anthony Travis and Elizabeth Ann Creighton Travis from the 1700s."

They read the inscriptions silently. Last of all, he led them to the newest stones. "Your grandfather and grand-mother, my parents. Although they lived in a nearby village when I was growing up, their family plot was here in Oundle, where the family originated."

Sam read the names. "'Luke Langston Travis 1820 to 1870. Died as he had lived, honorably and in full vigor.'" He turned questioning eyes to Luke. "He had the same name as you."

"Yes."

After a moment he asked, "How did…did he die?"

Luke squatted down and pulled away some of the grass growing high around the gravestone. "He was saving a family from a burning house."

Sam's eyes widened. "Was he a firefighter?"

"No, he was a curate at a small church in a neighbor-ing village. He also taught Greek and Latin at the village school. We can go there later. Anyway," he resumed the story, "the house next door caught fire one night and my father was the first one on the scene. He used to stay up late reading. He must have seen the flames. He was in there, waking the occupants before the fire wagons arrived. He survived but the smoke damaged his lungs. He died a short while later of bronchitis.

"I was only eighteen at the time, but I was away at Oxford by then studying for my degree." He gazed at the flat gravestone, standing amidst the green grass. No close family lived nearby anymore to take care of his parents' two plots. "It turned my world upside down. I expected my father to be around for a good long time." He sighed deeply, glancing upward at his son, whose gaze remained on the gravestone. "It was only a year before I met your mother."

Sam's eyes shot to his. "It was?"

Luke nodded, not having intended to talk to Sam about Irene, but the words had come out of him. Perhaps it was time. Luke stood slowly, brushing off his hands, as he tried to figure out where to start. He hadn't talked about these things to anyone in so long. "Yes. I was nineteen."

"How did you meet her?"

He smiled, recollecting. "At a party. A few fellow students and I were invited to a professor's house one weekend spring day—a day much like today, except it was in May, so more flowers and greenery were out.

"She was there. Your grandfather and grandmother were friends of this distinguished professor in the engineering school."

"Did you like Mama right away?"

He glanced at his son. It was the first time he'd heard him say the word *mama,* and it affected him in a strange way. Sam had lost a mother as much as he, Luke, had lost a wife and lover. "Yes, I did." He shook his head, again smiling. "I took one look at her at the end of the garden and was smitten."

Sam's blue eyes, so much like Irene's, stared into his, as if striving to absorb his very words. "She was beautiful. And so lively. She was surrounded by a bunch of

Oxford fellows. I didn't think I stood a chance, young, awkward, gangly engineering student that I was. I didn't even know how to talk to young ladies back then."

Sam's lips had curled upward as if he understood. "What happened?" he asked.

"I was finally introduced to her." Luke paused, remembering that breathtaking moment of looking into Irene's powder-blue eyes and being lost. "It was like magic. It was as if we were the only two people at that party."

Sam looked fascinated. "And then what happened?"

Luke shrugged. "Oh, I don't know. I stammered a few silly things, I'm sure, and remained in a fog for the next few months every time I was in her company. Which wasn't often, since she lived down in London." He paused. "But I began to go there every weekend and she'd arrange to come into town. We'd do things together, go to plays and concerts and visit friends of hers."

He sighed, reliving those heady times. "She knew a lot of people. Your grandfather was already a well-respected man in his field, so your grandmother and mother were invited to a lot of gatherings. I don't think I've ever attended as many parties as I did that year of courting your mother."

"What about Aunt Bobbie?"

He smiled, thinking back. "Aunt Bobbie was just a young thing then. She didn't attend any of the parties. Although I did meet her at a garden party shortly after first meeting your mother. This time your mother had invited me to her house—your same home in Syden-ham," he added. "She had planned this party to intro-duce me to her close circle of family and friends. I remember how pretty the flowers were in your back garden. I'd gone there to escape all the crowd of people for a bit." He didn't add how uncomfortable and out of his element he'd felt that afternoon.

"I spied this young girl, about your age. She was sitting up in that sycamore tree out at the end of your backyard. I saw a leg dangling through the dark leaves." He shook his head. "A scuffed black shoe and white stocking, all wrinkled around the ankle."

Sam grinned. "She's always getting after me if my shoes aren't polished or my hair not brushed."

"It seems we both had the same thing in mind—to escape the crowd."

He raised a brow. "What was wrong with it?"

Luke looked down at the gravesite, his hands in his pockets, remembering how he'd felt that day. "I didn't feel part of it. They were all strangers, except for your mother and a couple of others. As for your aunt Bobbie, she hated those parties. She didn't like having to dress up, but your grandmother wanted her to learn to be as ladylike as your mother."

"Aunt Bobbie still doesn't like parties. She prefers going with me to museums or places like the Crystal Palace."

He gazed at his son. "You're very fortunate to have your aunt Bobbie."

The boy chewed on a corner of his lip, also staring down at the grave. Then he looked at him, and he swallowed, as if finding it hard to say what he wanted to say.

"What is it, son?" The word just slipped out, and for a moment Luke was afraid that Sam would repudiate him, but the boy didn't seem to notice.

"Wh—" His voice cracked, and Luke reached out his hand. "Why did you stop writing to me?"

For a moment Luke drew a blank, then he remembered what Bobbie had told him about writing Sam letters in his name. He let his hand fall to his side without touching Sam. "I'm sorry. I mean—" He drew a deep breath. How to explain something that had no explanation because he'd never thought enough to write his young son in the first place? He looked around the churchyard as if seeking an answer. Seeing a bench outside the cemetery, he gestured. "Why don't we sit down a little while?"

Following his gaze, Sam nodded slowly.

They left the graveyard and Luke closed the gate behind them. When they sat on the bench, the sun shining through the leafless tree above them, Luke sat forward, loosely clasping his hands between his knees. "I'm sorry that I didn't continue writing to you." He didn't know whether to confess that the original letters weren't from him, but he didn't want to disappoint the boy any further. Enough damage had already been done. Perhaps someday he could tell Sam the full truth. "I—I was so stricken by grief…about your mother…that I couldn't think of anyone else."

He looked sidelong at his son. "Sometimes we get so hurt that we only think about ourselves for a while. I suppose that's what happened to me."

"Did Mama hurt you?"

Before Luke could decide how much to tell him, Sam said, "I've heard people talk…once in a while when they didn't know I was there. Grandmother and Grandfather, and sometimes Grandmother with her friend, Mrs. Allston, or with Bobbie. Mama left you." He regarded Luke somberly. "Is that true?"

How much of the truth could his son bear to hear? After a moment, he said, "Yes."

"Why?"

Luke looked down at his clasped hands. "I don't know. I truly don't."

"But…didn't she love you?"

What a difficult question. One he'd asked himself for years. He took a deep breath before meeting his son's gaze once more. "Not enough, I guess."

Sam looked troubled. How Luke wished he could help him understand. "How can someone not love someone enough? Aunt Bobbie loves me and I love her. Grandfather lo—" there was a hitch in his voice before he continued "—loved me. And so does Grandmother."

How Luke longed to put his arm around his son's shoulders, but he didn't dare. He'd lost the right to. "Yes, of course they do. They're your family." He bowed his head again, rubbing his forehead. "They say blood is thicker than water, and I guess it was true in this case."

"What do you mean? That because Mama wasn't your family, she didn't love you enough? But if she married you, didn't she become your family?"

Wise words. "Yes, that's what is supposed to happen when two people get married. But sometimes it doesn't."

"Did you love her?"

Luke nodded. "Very much. Maybe too much."

"How can you love someone too much?"

"I'm not sure. But sometimes you try too hard to do everything they want, and it's still not enough. Then you get tired and maybe you don't try hard enough." He paused, uncertain how much more to say. But his son deserved some answers. "She didn't want to move to India, for one thing. Maybe I shouldn't have made her go."

Sam seemed to ponder this. "Why did you want to go?"

Luke rested his back against the slats of the bench. This time he stretched his arm across the back, behind Sam but not touching him. "Well, first of all, I was offered an engineering job there. It seemed a wonderful opportunity. They were laying all kinds of railroad tracks over a very large, primitive area. For someone of twenty-four, it was a very exciting venture."

Sam's eyes reflected his understanding. "I'd like to go somewhere like that someday."

"Perhaps you will. So, that was one reason." Again he paused, finding it harder to go on. "But, I also thought it might be good for your mother to go abroad to a new place, meet new people, get away from…any bad influences."

"Bad influences?"

"Sometimes we are around people who aren't good for us. Your mother liked to go to parties, but sometimes her choice of friends wasn't so good. Your mother was the kind of person who could be so happy one moment, but she could also get very sad at other times." He took a deep breath, praying for strength. "She wasn't always happy living in London, as we did then, so I thought maybe a new climate, a place where there's always lots of sunshine, new faces and all kinds of exotic things to see like elephants and—" he smiled at Sam "—snake charmers, that a place like this might lift her spirits…and perhaps help her to love me more," he ended quietly.

Sam was worrying his lip again. "When you left me with Grandfather and Aunt Bobbie, did that mean you didn't love me enough?"

He turned stricken eyes to his son. "I loved you when you were first born. You were such a tiny, little thing, like a little miracle from God. I would hold you in my arms and just watch you sleep. Everything about you was so perfect. I couldn't believe two people could produce such an amazing little boy."

Luke swallowed, continuing. "I loved you when you were a little tyke and just starting to walk. You'd cling to my trouser leg and smile up at me as if you had accomplished the biggest thing imaginable. Which you had, in my eyes."

Sam was looking at him as if Luke were opening up a whole new world to him, and Luke realized no one had ever told Sam about his earliest years.

"When your mother…left India, I didn't know what to do." Luke looked away from his son's clear-eyed gaze. A ladybug was crawling along the edge of the bench. "If I'd kept you with me in India, you might have got sick and died. It's a harsh climate for Europeans." He smiled sadly. "You had a nice woman who used to take care of you." He didn't add that there were times Irene couldn't bear to look at her son. "She was your ayah. Her name was Farida. You used to say *Faida*."

"I don't remember." He sounded awestruck.

"No, you wouldn't. You were only two years old when your mother left."

"But that means she left me, too."

How could he explain this? "I don't think she quite knew what she was doing. I was angry at first, and hurt. But I've had a lot of time to think about it over the years. I don't think your mother was always in control of her feelings."

"I don't understand," Sam lamented.

Luke tried his best to explain. "When your mother was sad, she wouldn't be able to get out of bed for days. When she was angry, she could lash out and say things that afterward she was sorry about. But the intensity of her emotions went both ways. When she was happy, she was positively euphoric. That's why people liked her. She was the life of the party, as they say, and knew how to make those around her happy." He sighed heavily. "It was only those who lived close to her who knew the other side of her. I think it was a sort of sickness. I don't think she really could help herself."

Luke took a deep breath. "When your mother left me—left us—I think she was very unhappy and thought she could be happier somewhere else…with someone else."

Sam's eyes narrowed. "With someone else?"

Luke nodded.

"Who?"

"It doesn't matter now. It was so long ago. The point is, she had a very sad life. It was only a couple of years later that she was killed in that horrible accident." He struggled to find the right words. "The important thing is that I should have stayed with you…I shouldn't have given you up. But back then, I wasn't in very good shape to take care of anyone. I hardly knew how to take care of myself. I just threw myself into my work, and it wouldn't have been fair to you to only have an ayah take care of you, even if she did love you. She had her own children."

"So you sent me away," Sam said glumly.

"Yes…I thought that you'd be better off with your mother's family here in England." His voice cracked. "But I never stopped loving you, Sam."

"Then why didn't you ever come back to Sydenham? Didn't you want to visit me?"

Oh, dear God, please help Sam to forgive me. To Luke's amazement, there was no accusation, only bewilderment in his son's eyes. "I *should* have. I wish I had. I think I was scared to come back because of the memories it held for me."

"You mean about Mama?"

"Yes. It wasn't a good reason, I know that now. I was a coward and I'm sorry. I think, too, that I thought you would be better having Grandfather as your father, and Bobbie as your mother. I didn't want you to have to be divided between us."

Sam nodded. "That's what Aunt Bobbie told me."

Luke glanced at him in surprise. "What did she say?"

"When I first asked her why you'd never come back to see me, she said that maybe you were scared."

"Your aunt Bobbie can be very wise," he said softly.

They sat together for a long while listening to the birds chirp above them and to the muted sounds of the town around them.

"You should have married Aunt Bobbie."

Sam's sudden statement startled Luke. When he could think of nothing to say, Sam asked, "Why didn't you fall in love with her instead?"

He gave a slight laugh. At least he was able to answer that. "Well, for one thing, your aunt Bobbie was too young. She was just a girl still in pigtails when I first knew her and I was already a young man."

Sam kicked his feet back and forth, hitting the dirt under the bench. "Why did you fall in love with Mother?"

Luke tugged at an earlobe. "She was very beautiful."

After a moment of kicking at the earth, Sam said, "Aunt Bobbie is pretty."

Luke swallowed. "Yes…she is." Quite pretty, in fact. Something he'd never really noticed, too blinded by Irene's beauty.

Sam sighed. "When I grow up, I want to marry someone like Aunt Bobbie. She's my best friend and is always there when I need her."

Luke gazed at his son. "Yes…that's the kind of person one should marry."

"But I'm not going to get married till after I've gone to America and India and all kinds of places," Sam pronounced, jumping up from the bench.

Luke stood more slowly and stretched. "That sounds like a good plan. Now, how about some lunch? Then maybe we could visit Fotheringhay Castle outside the village. We could even take a picnic lunch up there."

Sam immediately perked up. "A castle?"

"There are only a few ruins left, but it's a pretty sight by the river. It's where Mary Queen of Scots was executed, so it can serve as a history lesson as well. You can tell your Mr. Southbridge and Aunt Bobbie about it when you return home, so they'll see you haven't neglected your lessons while you've been away."

Sam was already walking toward the gate. "Let's go. I'm hungry!"

"So am I. Maybe we can rent some fishing poles and do some fishing on the river after our picnic lunch."

"I've never been fishing."

"You haven't? Well, it's certainly time you went."

Feeling as if a great burden had been removed from his shoulders, Luke followed his son out of the graveyard.

At the end of the weekend, Luke stood with his son at a newsstand in the train station in Oundle, looking at the books and periodicals before their trip back to London.

"See anything you'd like?"

Sam picked up a book. "This one."

He glanced at the title. *The Children of the New Forest.* "That was a favorite of mine, too, at your age. Let me pay for it and a newspaper and we can go out to the platform to await our train."

He counted out the money at the register. The man smiled as he wrapped up the book. "Oh, don't bother," Luke said. "He's going to read it on the train."

"Very well, sir," he said, handing the book to Sam. "You just have to cut the pages." He met Luke's eyes. "If you or your father has a sharp knife. Mind your fingers, though."

"Yes, sir," replied Sam, taking the book and looking up at Luke. "My father has a pocketknife, don't you?"

"Yes," he said, patting his pocket. He turned his attention to the clerk, who handed him his change.

"There you go, sir. Have a good trip back with your son. He's a handsome lad."

"Thank you."

He walked away from the stand with Sam, the words still ringing in his ears. *Your son. If you or your father has a sharp knife. He's a handsome lad.*

This was what should be normal in his life—going places with his son and receiving matter-of-fact compliments on his offspring. This was what he had forfeited.

Later, sitting in the train compartment across from Sam, he observed his son, who sat reading his new book.

It had been a good holiday—one that had gone by much too quickly. They had toured Luke's old school and taken a few hikes in the fields and forest surrounding the town. Sam had asked him so many questions about Luke's youth, his schooldays and his time in India and America. Luke in turn had learned a lot about his son.

He now knew that Sam's favorite dinner was sausage pie the way "Cook made it." And that his least favorite was devilled kidneys, though he didn't mind steak and kidney pie. And his favorite dessert was raspberry cake, which Aunt Bobbie always made in the summertime when the raspberries were ripe.

His favorite book was *Robinson Crusoe*. And he'd recently fancied a girl who sat across the nave from him at morning prayers.

Now, as Luke looked at his son's golden head bowed over his book, he thought of all the years he'd given up of knowing his son and watching him grow up. All because of his own selfishness and a series of unfortunate events.

His thoughts returned to Bobbie, as they had throughout the few days away. He told himself once more that that sudden moment of awareness between the two of them had been an isolated incident. Things would be firmly back to normal once he returned.

He'd always be grateful to Bobbie for filling Irene's role as mother to Sam. But that was all. Yet the closer they drew to London, the stronger the pull he felt to get home.

Home. The word startled him. Since when had he begun to consider the house in Sydenham home? The image of Bobbie kneeling in her garden kept coming back to him. It felt so right…coming back to a home… to the kind a woman whose face lit up when her eyes met his. He tried to extinguish that last thought but it kept recurring.

It wasn't about Bobbie! He shook his head, as if the physical gesture would rid his mind of the thought. It was about what he'd missed all these years—a home, a wife and a son.

These past few days with Sam had shown him that perhaps it wasn't too late to have a relationship with his son.

But did it mean he had to stay in England? Luke watched the passing scenery through the soot-stained train window, his mouth a grim line. The thought still didn't sit well with him.

Thanks to his late father-in-law, Luke had already lost enough years of his son's life. How could Robert Gardner dare think he could make up for the past by including Luke in his will—almost forcing him to accept its conditions even from beyond the grave?

Was America the answer? The green fields, pastures and meadows rolled by as Luke considered the idea. Sam had brought it up more than once. He didn't seem adverse to traveling there. On the contrary, he seemed excited about going across the ocean.

How would Bobbie feel about an extended stay? She'd taken care of Sam all these years. Didn't that give her a say in his future?

Luke shifted in his seat, uncomfortable with the notion. He knew he had given up all rights to his son. Yet now that he'd come back, he didn't want to lose another moment of Sam's life, knowing how few years were left before he became a young man and struck out on his own.

Sam was old enough, too, to have some say in his

immediate future. Would Bobbie deny him the chance to be with his father for a few years before he had to leave for college?

Chapter Thirteen

Bobbie tried not to anticipate Sam and Luke's home-coming on the day they were scheduled to return. After all, she had no idea what time they would arrive. For all she knew, it wouldn't be till midnight. Yet, Luke knew that Sam had lessons the next day and that he himself had to be on the project site. Thankfully, there had been no further mishaps in the tunnel, but his presence had been sorely missed by the crew and her alike.

Bobbie sighed, leaning her chin on her elbow at her father's desk in his study, where she'd spent most of the weekend. The tunnel plans and documents were scattered over its mahogany surface.

The firm had kept remarkably on schedule consider-ing the sudden loss of her father. And that was in large part thanks to Luke and all of the experience he brought to the project. She kept telling herself not to come to depend on his input, but the fact remained undeniable—he had been a lifesaver to them.

She leaned back in her father's old chair now, hear-ing its familiar creak. Sitting at his desk in his study the first time had been difficult. Just as his desk at the office, she'd thought of it as sacred to him. But as the weeks went by, she realized that she needed to have access to her father's papers, since her mother seemed incapable of taking over the household accounts. And Bobbie needed a place to go over work she brought home from the office. Her father's study was the most suitable area.

But now it gave Bobbie a companionable feeling to be among his familiar things—the leather-bound account books, green blotter, black inkwell and steel-nibbed pen, and prism paperweight. And most of all, the scent... tobacco, leather and that indefinable smell that was the whole mixture of the room, all reminding her so vividly of her father.

She started when she heard the sound of carriage wheels. Could Luke and Sam have arrived? It wasn't quite teatime. Jumping up from the chair, Bobbie hurried from the room and ran to the front parlor, where she could peer through a filmy lace curtain.

Yes, a hansom cab had stopped. A few moments later, she glimpsed Sam and Luke, clutching their valises, coming up the path.

Should she run into the corridor and be there to greet them? Whenever Sam was away from home for any reason—not that it happened often—she wouldn't hesitate. But Luke's presence stopped her.

Chiding herself for being silly, she straightened her shoulders and turned toward the door, but stopped at a wall mirror. Quickly she pinched her pale cheeks and straightened her spectacles. She patted her hair, tucking in a stray curl or two into her chignon. Her fingers were already ink-stained. She peered down at her blouse, hoping it was still intact. Thankfully, it was clean, though a button dangled loosely from its thread. She'd have to fix that, but not now.

As she stepped into the dim hallway, the front door was opening, bringing the murmur of male voices. Bobbie pasted on a bright smile and quickened her step.

Sam's face lit up at the sight of her. Almost afraid of looking at Luke, yet unable not to, she flashed him a quick smile over Sam's head. Luke returned it, a genuine look of gladness in his light-colored eyes.

Her own smile wobbled a bit. How good it felt to have him back. The house had seemed so empty without the two of them. But she'd missed having a man, someone to share the burden of home, family and business with. "You're back."

She gave Sam a brief hug, knowing at thirteen he only submitted to outward displays of affection out of politeness. Before he began squirming in her arms, she let him go with a final pat. He smelled good, her little boy. Already, he had passed her height by a couple of inches. Would he be as tall as his father?

Her eyes returned to Luke. "How was your trip?"

"It was stupendous," Sam answered before Luke could respond. "We saw the castle where Mary Queen of Scots was put to death and the church where Papa was christened and all of my relatives buried in the churchyard. We went fishing along the banks of the Nene and ate hot-cross buns and hiked loads!"

She forced herself to exclaim, her gaze going from her nephew to Luke and back again. "Oh, my, how lovely. Goodness…you did all that!" What fun the two must have had together. Sam was calling him "Papa" now with no hesitancy. *Dear Lord, thank You for bringing this about.*

"Are you hungry? It's just about time for tea. You must be tired."

"I'm not tired at all. Papa bought me a book to read on the train." He held it up for her. "And I started it, but then I fell asleep, so I had a nap."

"Can't say the same for myself." Luke spoke up behind his son with a lopsided grin, which brought a flutter to Bobbie's heart.

"But I could eat a horse," Sam put in.

Bobbie raised her eyebrows at Luke in inquiry.

"Perhaps not quite a horse." He draped a hand across his son's shoulders, which gave Bobbie a start. They must have made progress indeed if Luke felt comfortable showing a physical sign of affection like that. "I asked him if he wanted to get a bite to eat in the city, but he preferred coming straight home."

She turned gratified eyes toward Sam. "Oh, well, I think we can prepare you an early tea. Why don't we go into the kitchen and I'll see what I can rustle up? Cook's gone out, but I know she baked a ginger cake especially for you."

Sam turned to his father as they started down the hall. "You'll like Cook's ginger cake…."

Bobbie followed beside Luke. "So, it was a successful trip?"

He glanced sidelong at her with a nod. "I'll say so. I…I had no right to expect so much," he said in a low tone as Sam got ahead of them.

She forced herself to smile. "I'm glad. I'd prayed for such."

"Thank you." His eyes reflected his gratitude.

When they all sat around the kitchen table with plates heaped with bread, ham and cheese, thick slices of cake beside them, a tall glass of milk for Sam and cups of tea for themselves, Luke turned to Sam. "Now we have to think of something for your aunt Bobbie."

Sam's glance questioned him. "What do you mean?" he asked, after swallowing a bite of his sandwich.

"You had your outing. Now she should have a special day."

Bobbie folded her hands atop the table, trying to hide the anticipation she began to feel.

"You mean like an excursion to the zoo or a museum?" Sam inquired.

Luke grinned, shifting his attention to Bobbie. "Yes, something like that. I was thinking more along the lines of a visit to the university."

Sam set down his sandwich. "The university. Whatever for?"

Bobbie's hands tightened around each other. Luke hadn't forgotten.

"To visit the engineering school."

Sam glanced at the two of them, a crescent of milk over his mouth. "You mean where Grandfather wanted me to study?"

Bobbie handed him his napkin. "Wipe your mouth, dear."

"That's right." Luke rubbed his own napkin between his fingertips, his eyes on Sam. "What would you think of your aunt becoming an engineer?"

Sam scrubbed his mouth, his round-eyed gaze on her. "An engineer? B-but she's a—you're a…lady, Aunt Bobbie."

She felt torn inside between the shock in Sam's eyes and her long buried desire to do the work her father had done. "Is that such a ridiculous notion?"

Sam swallowed visibly, clearly at a loss. "I didn't know women could be engineers."

"There aren't many, that's true," Luke said. "But it's not impossible. You know, women are doing more and more things every day that people thought they could never do."

Sam brow furrowed. "Why do you want to be an engineer?"

Before Bobbie could formulate a reply, Luke smiled. "Why do you want to play the piano?"

Sam's glance went immediately to his father's. "Because I like playing the piano." Understanding dawned in his eyes as he turned back to Bobbie. "Is that the reason? Do you really like engineering so much, Aunt Bobbie?"

She nodded. "I always have. Ever since I was a little girl, I wanted to do what Grandfather did. I liked studying mathematics and tinkering with things." She smiled nostalgically. "Once in a great while, he'd take me to see what he was working on, the way we took you down the tunnel. I'd get so thrilled when I'd see a bridge being built or a railroad tunnel through a mountain."

Sam's face had gradually grown more serious.

"What is it, dear?"

He toyed with his sandwich. "I wish I felt that way about engineering."

"What do you mean?"

"I mean, I don't get excited when I look at bridges and things, the way you sound." He slumped in his chair, his voice glum.

She reached over and patted his hand. "You're still young. You're not expected to know how you're going to feel about your work."

His blue eyes met hers. "But you did." He turned to Luke and his voice brightened a bit. "But you didn't, did you?"

"Not entirely. But I did always like to build things.

And like your aunt, I was always fonder of mathematics and science than I was of literature and the classics."

Sam pursed his lips. "What if I'm the opposite? I like books, especially history books more than I like mathematics, even though Aunt Bobbie teaches me and she's a good teacher. But most of all, I like music."

Luke smiled at him. "I wouldn't worry too much about it. Nobody said you have to follow in your grandfather's footsteps and be an engineer. You have plenty of time to find out what you'd like to do with your life. Maybe you'll be a piano player and write musicals like Mr. Arthur Sullivan."

Sam's mouth relaxed into a wide smile and his eyes lightened. "Do you really think I could write pieces like Mr. Sullivan?"

He shrugged, turning to Bobbie. "I don't know, but I wouldn't be surprised. What do you think?"

How could Luke put her on the spot like that? She'd never imagined Sam being anything but an engineer. All he'd heard about his whole life was being an engineer. Being a musician was something one did in one's spare time. What about her father's wishes? He'd always expected Sam to take over the firm one day. Didn't his will make it clear? Her eyes narrowed on Luke, her exasperation increasing. Luke knew very well the conditions of her father's will. Was he deliberately undermining them by encouraging Sam to choose an impractical profession?

She cleared her throat, selecting her words carefully. "I think you're very talented, Sam. You have a great gift for music. But as your father said, there are many years before you have to make any decisions. You'll go to university and discover all kinds of interesting things to study, far more than you've studied here at home."

Luke set his plate away from him. "So, speaking of university, don't you think your aunt Bobbie ought to visit the University of London and discover if maybe she can study engineering? After all, your grandfather left her the firm, and she needs to know a lot about engineering if she wants to run it."

Again, she restrained her frustration. Father had left the firm to Luke as well, but he made it sound as if only she would be responsible for it. She fumed inwardly, unable to express any of her thoughts aloud.

"Yes, that's true." Now that he had it settled in his mind, Sam seemed to find the idea perfectly acceptable. "Will you take her, Papa?"

"If she'd like." Luke turned to her. "I was thinking we could visit one afternoon later this week. I have a few acquaintances who are professors there. They could give you some insight into the program, and maybe put you in contact with some young ladies who are students there. What do you think?"

He left her little choice or time to think about it. She wasn't used to making decisions on the spot—at least not such life-changing ones. She wasn't at all sure she would be able to undertake a rigorous course of study. Perhaps she wouldn't need it at all to run the firm—not if Luke was there to help her run it.

But would he be there?

She took a deep breath, fearing the day she'd have to go it alone. "Yes…I suppose we could go…just to visit. Thank you."

Luke slapped the tabletop with his hands. "Good. That's settled then." He seemed almost relieved, and she wondered how long he had been thinking about this. And why. "Now, Sam, tell your aunt about Oundle Grammar School."

Bobbie forced a smile to her lips as she tried to focus on the new topic. "Oundle School?"

"Yes, it's the school where Papa boarded. It's terrific. I visited all the buildings and met some professors and some of the boys who attend…."

Bobbie felt her calm slipping, wondering if this was another maneuver of Luke's. Was this why he had taken Sam to visit his village and why he was so interested in having her go to university? To take Sam away from her?

Friday afternoon, as he'd promised, Luke accompanied Bobbie to the University College campus of the University of London. In the intervening days, he had written to his professor friends and received their replies. He had only told them that he was bringing a prospective student, saying nothing that she was female. He wanted to ensure that Bobbie would receive a warm reception and be shown all cooperation.

He wondered why she had expressed little excitement or interest in the visit during the week. She'd even tried to beg off, saying he needn't trouble himself after his busy weekend away. "Nonsense. I'd like to see my old school chums in any case."

"Oh. But there's a lot at the office—"

"I thought we were well caught up since my brief absence. Apropos, I think it's a good idea to begin interviewing candidates for a general manager. You need someone you can trust to oversee things when you can't be there or in the office."

She had clamped her mouth shut as if she'd wanted to argue then finally said only, "Very well. You can see to it, if you wish."

He'd taken her at her word, and early the next morning had arranged for some advertisements to go into the paper. He'd also sent along some inquiries to colleagues he knew who might recommend the right individual for the position.

He wasn't going to wait until the last minute to make sure everything was left in order at Gardner and Quimby before he went back to America.

Now, he alighted with Bobbie from the omnibus and walked around Bloomsbury Square. The trees had the pale green of leaves just unfurling. A cherry tree was a mass of pink blooms. Daffodils poked out everywhere at the edges of the black, wrought-iron fence and bases of the thick tree trunks. Their bright yellow heads bobbed in the sunshine, creating a splash of color against the green grass of the square. Luke had always liked this neighborhood with its Georgian buildings flanked by the imposing buildings of the University of London, the British Museum and the British Library.

"My friend gave me the address to his office." He consulted the street name again. "I believe it's down here." He took Bobbie lightly by the arm and guided her across the broad avenue to a side street.

She hadn't said much on the way here, and he glanced down at her now, wondering what she was thinking. He hoped she wouldn't be intimidated by the male-dominated profession. She'd proven herself quite apt at handling the men at her father's firm, but the world of academia might prove more daunting.

They knocked on a black-painted door of a narrow brick building with a window box at each window. A clerk opened for them and ushered them into the professor's study after Luke presented his card.

"Luke!" Charlie Fitzhugh held out his hand, a genial

smile on his lips, and the two shook hands warmly. "Good to see you, old man."

"Likewise. It's been some years." Charlie hadn't changed much from his university days, except for a more mature face. His hair was still brown, and he still wore a mustache. He was dressed in a tweed suit. After the first keen look at him, Charlie turned with an expression of friendly interest to Bobbie. "And this is Mrs. Travis, I presume?"

Bobbie's cheeks deepened in color. Luke realized how it must appear since Charlie wasn't expecting a female student. He should have explained in his note. He cleared his throat, feeling awkward. "No—this is my…sister-in-law, Miss Roberta Gardner, the late Robert Gardner's younger daughter."

Charlie didn't appear at all embarrassed by his mistaken assumption. "So, this is your prospective student." His eyes twinkled as if appreciating a joke played on him. "You sly fox. Robert Gardner's daughter. Well, well…I am pleased to meet you." He held out his hand. "I'm so sorry for your recent loss. It was a blow to the entire profession, believe me."

Bobbie appeared touched by his heartfelt words. She took his hand in hers with a shy smile. "Thank you. We have felt his loss profoundly. It was…so sudden."

"I understand." He released her hand, though his gaze remained on her as he gestured them to a sofa. "Please, won't you have a seat? I'll ring for some tea."

They murmured their thanks as they sat in the book-lined study. Two windows flanked by bookcases gave onto the square. It would be quite a pretty view in summer when the trees were fully in leaf.

When they were seated, Charlie returned and sat at his walnut desk, crossing his legs. He smiled at Luke.

"So, the prodigal has finally decided to grace our shores again. I've heard good things about you—working on projects from coast to coast in America, haven't you? Apparently you did some consulting on the Brooklyn Bridge?"

Luke nodded.

"I should like to see that marvel."

"It's not such a long journey on a steamer."

"Perhaps one of these days." Charlie gestured to the files and papers on his desk. "If I can ever see a way clear of all this."

Luke stretched out his legs in front of him. "It's probably high time you escaped that mound of paper and visited a real building site."

The two chuckled, falling easily into the type of banter they used to enjoy at college, as if more than a decade hadn't gone by.

The same clerk who had opened the door for them brought in tea and served them each a cup. When he had left, Charlie rubbed his moustache, ignoring the cup and saucer on his desk. "So, what may I do for you, Miss Gardner?"

At her hesitant look, Luke replied, "Whatever you would for any prospective student. I was thinking a tour of the campus, an introduction to a few colleagues, and perhaps some advice on pursuing a course in civil engineering." Before Charlie could express any reservations, Luke added, "You'll see she already has some experience, since she has taken over Gardner's firm."

Charlie's eyes widened. "Ah, that is something. You realize, Miss Gardner, there are very few female students."

"Yes." Bobbie looked quite intimidated already, her hands clasped around the teacup on her lap.

"But the college did begin granting degrees a couple of years back, isn't that so?" Luke put in.

"Yes," Charlie answered carefully, his gaze still on Bobbie.

Luke continued. "Miss Gardner has inherited her father's firm. She has always wanted to study engineering, as a matter of fact, but that has never been possible, for a variety of reasons. Now, however, it seems not only opportune, but also necessary, if she is to successfully oversee her father's firm."

Bobbie seemed about to say something, her eyes on him. Afraid she would mention that he, too, had part ownership of the firm, he hurried on. "I thought perhaps if she could look in on some classes, she might see that it's not such an unrealistic dream to study civil engineering."

Charles had listened patiently, his fingers smoothing down his moustache. Now, he smiled at Bobbie. "Well, I admit to being surprised that such an attractive young lady would want to study this very difficult subject, but now that Luke has explained it—and knowing you are Robert Gardner's offspring—I can see the sense to it. Actually, today is an excellent day to visit. Classes are in session. As soon as we finish our tea, I'll take you 'round to a few."

They chatted awhile longer—Luke and Charlie bringing each other up to date on some of the things that had transpired in their lives since leaving Oxford. Luke didn't talk of his marriage and thankfully, Charlie was too tactful to ask. He noticed that Charlie didn't wear a wedding ring, either.

As they got up to leave, Charlie made a point of escorting Bobbie out of the office. When they stood back on the pavement, he took her elbow and motioned farther down the square. "We'll start there. It's an introductory course. I believe we have one female enrolled at present, actually. I hope you are not easily flustered, Miss Gardner. I'm sure more than one young student's attention will wander from the lecture when he sees you."

"I don't want to cause a disturbance, Professor Fitzhugh."

Charlie grinned, leading her down the sidewalk, Luke trailing behind them. "Don't worry about that. On a spring day like today, I'm sure they will be thankful of anything to distract them from a dry physics lecture."

Luke followed them, trying to ignore his irritation at his friend's attentiveness to Bobbie. He remembered now Charlie's way with the ladies. He didn't want him flirting with Bobbie. It wouldn't be right—and he didn't want someone toying with her. She was too fine a person.

Chapter Fourteen

Bobbie's head was in a whirl by the time Professor Fitzhugh, who kept insisting she call him "Charlie," finished taking them all around the engineering school. She'd been to lecture halls and classrooms, the blackboards behind the professors full of mathematical equations, and to laboratories where students were building things to demonstrate physical principles.

With the exception of one, all the students she'd seen were males, young men who'd stared at her curiously. She felt like one of the stone dinosaur statues on the grounds of the Crystal Palace.

On the one hand, it was all she'd ever dreamed of—to be able to sit and listen to lectures on the mechanics of tension and torsion. Most of what she'd managed to listen to sounded like Greek, but she knew if she could begin, she would be able to grasp the material.

And, oh, how it would help her to continue her father's work.

On the other hand, her shoulders slumped just thinking of the challenge. Would she have to prove herself to all those males before they accepted her as just another student? More than one professor had given her a decidedly rude stare, as if to say how dare she interrupt their important work?

She wanted to laugh. If they only knew she was part owner of one of the city's most prominent civil engineering firms.

That reminded her of another disconcerting thing. She glanced sidelong at Luke, who was declining Professor Fitzhugh's offer of lunch.

Why had he made it sound as if she was the sole owner of her father's firm? It wasn't the first time he'd done that.

She pressed her lips together, impatient to be alone with Luke to ask him about this. But Professor Fitzhugh turned to her now, and she forced herself to smile and take the hand he held out to her. "Thank you, again, for the tour. It was most informative."

"The pleasure was all mine." He chuckled, pressing her hand. "At least you got me out of my stuffy office on such a lovely day. But please, Miss Gardener, don't hesitate to stop in or drop me a line if I can be of any assistance in your future plans. If you apply soon, I'm sure you can enter the autumn term."

She nodded slowly, unwilling to commit herself to anything, her thoughts too much in a jumble. "W-would I have to take any sort of entrance examination?"

He nodded, his face turning serious. "Yes, but if you're as qualified as Luke says, and if, indeed, you are already heading up the late Mr. Gardner's firm, that should be no problem at all for you. In fact, I can give you some textbooks to study."

They thanked him once again. Luke promised to come to dinner one evening and then they left.

At the corner, Luke paused and turned to her. "What about an outing?"

Bobbie stared at Luke, unsure of his meaning. "An outing? Didn't we just have one?"

He grinned, looking suddenly quite boyish, a shock of honey brown hair slanted over his forehead. "That was business. Now, it's time for pleasure." When she still looked puzzled, he added, "You are always taking Sam on outings. How long since you did something purely for your own enjoyment? Or, since someone took you on an excursion?"

She found herself blushing and found it hard to look away. The bright sunshine brought a more intense green to his eyes. "I—I don't remember." *How long?* Since Graham had taken her to a pantomime or a walk along the Embankment? But she didn't want to bring that up now.

Luke looked up at the blue sky. "Well, I think today would be a very appropriate day." His gaze returned to hers. "What about a garden?" He gestured to the square behind them. "I noticed the flowers when we walked by this morning. I bet Kensington or Kew would have a lovely display. We can buy some meat patties at a shop and eat them outdoors."

He couldn't have chosen a more delightful idea. "I wonder if the tulips are out at Kensington yet?" She murmured, tilting her head. "They always make a pretty display."

"Well, shall we go see?"

She opened the watch pinned to her jacket. "Oh, I don't know…we've probably taken too much time already. We should get back to the office, and I need to check Sam's lessons later…."

He took her by the arm, a gesture that never failed to make her feel cherished and protected, and began walking once again. "Everything was running quite on schedule this morning at the site. If anything untoward should happen, I think Melville can handle things today. In any case, we shall stop by the office on our way home."

He left her no room to object further, although she felt guilty going off like this, telling no one, almost as if she were running off from school for the day. But she said nothing more, as the idea of spending a few hours in Luke's sole company, out on a beautiful spring day in a garden, was too good an opportunity to pass up.

On their way to Kensington, in the close confines of a hansom cab, Luke turned to her. "So, what do you think of becoming a full-fledged engineer?"

His face was so close to hers it was difficult to form a coherent thought, much less one about so important a topic. Her light veil did little to hide her gaze from his. "It—it sounds almost too good to be true. I don't know if I could do it."

"It wouldn't be easy." Just a mere hint of mustache and beard shadowed the skin around his slim lips, which were serious as he replied. "It would take a whole-hearted commitment. I found it difficult as a young man of eighteen with no other cares in the world. You are a woman responsible for a household and a business."

His words reminded her of all that rested on her shoulders. She sighed, leaning back against the seat.

"I didn't mean to discourage you. I think you ought to undertake this course of study. You owe it to yourself to follow the profession you've always dreamed of—as well as to your father, who entrusted the company to you."

She swallowed, fearful of saying the next words. "And to you."

He looked out the side window at the passing street.

"Mine is a temporary stewardship, I told you that from the beginning." His words were gentle yet firm. Then he turned back to her, his tone solemn. "Yours is a vested interest. Your father founded and built up one of the first engineering firms into an internationally known company of some prestige. You've always wanted to practice engineering. Don't let conventions or supposed responsibilities keep you from that. Your mother is not well, it's true, but you can find good help for her during the daytime hours." He smiled faintly. "She is far from elderly. I wouldn't be surprised if someday she were to marry again."

Bobbie let out a disbelieving laugh. "Marry again? Oh, no! Not Mother."

He chuckled. "Perhaps you can't see it, you are too close to her. But she is quite a handsome woman for her age. I've seen the way Mr. Southbridge looks at her. I think he's quite fond of her, though he might be too timid to ever let his affections be known."

Bobbie's mouth fell open. "Mr. Southbridge, you must be joking!" Not the old rector who had known the family for years, dined at their table since she was a little girl, been friends with her father. Her cheeks colored at the very thought.

Luke shrugged. "Have it your way. But I'll wager before the year is up, you'll have a few gentlemen callers coming 'round to pay their respects to your mother."

As she was struggling to envision this picture, he added in a serious tone, "And if you enroll at the University College, I'll further predict that you'll have a half-dozen engineering students lining up at your door to offer to help you with your studies."

Her cheeks were flaming by the time the meaning of his words sank in. He was looking at her so closely, and she found there was nowhere to look but downward, at his fine lips and chin. Her next thought was to wonder what his lips would feel like on hers. "That's utter… nonsense," she tried to protest, but the words came out only in a whisper, her thoughts too incoherent. "Those boys looked barely out of grammar school. I'm an old lady in their eyes."

"I think you underrate yourself," he said softly. "Besides, Charlie took you to the freshman classes. There are upperclassmen…and professors. Charlie was tripping over himself to be charming to you—and he's a confirmed bachelor since I've known him."

Her gaze flew up to his, amazed that he had noticed Professor Fitzhugh's attentiveness. "Don't say such things! He was being perfectly proper and took time out from his busy schedule to show me around, even though it seemed he still wasn't quite accustomed to the idea of a female engineer."

Luke chuckled. "Until he found out whose daughter you were."

Her brow furrowed, forgetting her discomfiture for a second. "Do you think it will always be like that? I won't be taken seriously until they find out my name and connection to my father? And then will they just be in awe of his name?"

He shrugged, his shoulder touching hers in the small space, and making her aware once more of his proximity. "You'll probably encounter that in your first years. But I have no doubt you'll prove yourself in time. Your colleagues will end up respecting you for who you are and what you contribute to the field."

Her eyes gazed into his and she forgot all else. "Th… thank you. Your faith in me means a lot to me."

He only inclined his chin a fraction. "But it won't be

easy, as I said, and it will require your full dedication for some years."

Before she could reply to that sobering statement, they arrived at the park. Luke helped her alight and paid the driver, then guided her through the tall, wrought-iron gates to the wide lawns and tree-lined avenues enclosed within the fence.

Bobbie looked around her with a satisfied sigh. "I haven't been here in some time, since we have such a lovely park close to home. I'd forgotten how beautiful it is."

They left the street noises behind and walked deeper into the enclosed area.

"Let's find a bench where we can eat our lunch. If I recall, the nicest gardens are closer to the palace."

He must have come with Irene. After all, they had lived in London for a few years when they were first married. "Oh, yes, the Dutch-style ones originally commissioned by Queen Mary," Bobbie murmured.

She breathed in the sharp scent of boxwood as they stepped into one of the walled gardens, then stopped at the lovely sight before them. There was a pretty rectangle of green grass in the center of the garden. Rows of tulips stood straight and tall around the perimeters of the garden, against the dark green clipped hedges. A wide swath of purple grape hyacinth edged the stone pathway. Pink and purple hyacinths filled the air with their sweet scent.

Bobbie took a step forward. "I love tulips. I think they're my favorite part of spring. They're so bold in their colors."

They walked closer to the bright display. "It's a lovely spot," Luke agreed. "You'd almost think you'd left the city behind."

"Mmm-hmm."

They found a bench and sat down to eat. After she'd taken a few bites of her English pastry, she glanced at him curiously. "Do you do any gardening?" What was his life like?

His lips tilted upwardly at one side. "No, I confess I've done very little. In India, the climate was so different and of course, everything was done by a hired man. The vegetation was lush and the flowers exotic, but somehow, they weren't as pleasing as an English garden, at least to me." He paused, his look pensive. "My mother was quite a gardener."

"I never met your mother…except at your wedding."

"Yes…she didn't like coming to London."

"And what about in America? You didn't have a garden?"

He shook his head. "I've moved around quite a bit in America, so I haven't settled in any place to really call home. I keep a flat in New York and rent a room whenever I take on a project in another city." He shrugged, brushing away the crumbs from his fingers. "I enjoy the city parks when I can. Those are my garden."

She said nothing but her heart went out to him. He had no home and probably hadn't since Irene had left him. "You've never thought of marrying again." She spoke the words without thinking then regretted them as she saw his shuttered expression.

He rubbed a temple, as if the very thought were painful to him. "No."

The simple word told her the subject was closed. When they finished eating they resumed walking over the square paving stones, but the flowers no longer pleasured her as they had. How she wished she could offer him the comfort he needed, but clearly, he had shut off all hopes of matrimonial happiness since Irene had left him.

"When your time of mourning has passed, you ought to wear colorful frocks, flowery things."

Bobbie blinked at Luke's words. It was the second time he'd mentioned her mourning clothes. She stopped, feeling flustered that he'd noticed her appearance in such a seemingly unflattering way. "Pardon me?"

His momentary displeasure seemed to have vanished and he grinned at her. "Since you've grown up, all I've seen you in is black. You are no dowager widow. You are still a young woman with a life ahead of you. You'd look lovely in blues and greens…I don't know…a whole palette of colors as we see here." His hand swept across the flowerbeds.

Her cheeks felt warm beneath his smile. "I don't know…somehow I don't think that's the garb that will be most appropriate in a physics laboratory."

He chuckled. "You're absolutely correct. For your classes at the university, feel free to wear black for the entire course of study."

What did he mean by that? "I don't mean to act frivolously there, I can assure you."

"No, but you will prove a distraction enough in black with your hair in a tight roll."

Her hand went to her chignon. Did he find it unbecoming? Feeling awkward, she stepped away from him, pretending to study a section of garden.

"Oh!" She flinched, as Luke's shadow told her he had come up behind her. She laughed nervously. "I didn't hear you there."

"I'm sorry, I didn't mean to offend you with my words."

He stood close to her, too close, she could hardly breathe. "You d-didn't, not at all."

"I was just being the protective older brother. I'm afraid you're going to face not only a rigorous academic program, but you'll also have a lot of unwanted male attention."

She raised her eyes to him, finding the expression in his so somber she wanted to reassure him. "You're not m-my older brother." Once again, the words coming out of her mouth were not the ones she'd intended to say.

Instead of replying, he sighed.

She bit her lip. Why had she said such a foolish thing? He was her former brother-in-law. Of course he saw her as his younger sister. She clenched her fingers in consternation.

The next second she drew in her breath. Was it her imagination or had he leaned his head a fraction closer to hers?

He still said nothing. His eyes were no longer on hers but lower. The next second she could no longer deny that his face was indeed moving closer to hers. Was he going to kiss her?

She swallowed, sensing—but finding it impossible to believe—that he might indeed kiss her. In the instant before he closed the gap between them, she drew in a breath, smelling the scent of soap on his skin, and then she felt the soft touch of his lips on hers.

Was he mad? What was he doing?

These thoughts flashed through Luke's mind as he lowered his head and touched Bobbie's slightly parted lips.

But the foremost thought, what drove him beyond

reason, was the overwhelming desire—and need—to kiss her.

Oh…the moment his lips touched hers, he was lost. Her mouth was warm and inviting. Her lips tasted like spring. She didn't pull away, as he half hoped she would, shocked, horrified that her former brother-in-law, a man who'd only seen her as a baby sister, was kissing her.

No, she seemed to draw closer. She inhaled, as if she, too, were breathing him in the way he was her. Gently, as if afraid she would break, he placed his hands at her waist. Even as he wanted to do more, a part of him—that iron will he'd exerted for so long over himself—held him back.

He would not succumb to this madness. For madness was what it was.

And yet, he couldn't draw back—not yet.

The scent of hyacinths surrounded him, mingling with whatever faint perfume Bobbie wore. Her waist was small, though he felt no corset, just the soft material of her gown.

No, he couldn't do this! With every reserve of strength, he withdrew his lips from hers and eased back. Her eyelids fluttered open and she looked up at him, dazed. Her hands rested on his forearms. How he wanted to take her in his arms and kiss her till neither knew what was what.

But he dropped his hands from her waist and stepped back. "I—I beg your pardon. I shouldn't have done that."

He felt ashamed by her puzzled gaze behind her spectacles. The next instant she turned her back to him, taking some steps away from him. "Why did you?"

Her question was so direct it left him without an answer. Why did a man kiss a woman? Wasn't it obvious? He studied her, trying to gauge her tone. She sounded so matter-of-fact, like a scientist analyzing an event as she adjusted her hat. He'd expected something more.

He himself was shaken…more than he ever dreamed possible. He'd never felt this way since Irene, and he'd blamed his callow youth for that infatuation.

How could he have kissed Irene's little sister? Never mind that Irene had been dead these past six years. In Luke's mind, Bobbie would always be his young sister-in-law, someone to respect and honor in that relationship.

He observed her straight stance. "I don't know—" He fingered the brim of his top hat in his hands. "You looked so lovely there against the flowerbeds. Too much sun, I suppose. I beg your forgiveness." He tried to inject a measure of levity in his tone to reassure her she didn't have anything to fear from him.

"I see." They were the same stiff words she used when replying to his ideas about Sam.

A second later, she turned to face him. "Shall we continue to explore the gardens?" The words were said with a smile, but it didn't seem to reach her eyes.

He felt like a clumsy fool. "Yes, of course." Why couldn't he have controlled his impulses? The good friendship he enjoyed with Bobbie would now be marred. Just when things between him and Sam had improved and he needed Bobbie, his only ally in the Gardner family.

Bobbie kept her smile in place even though she had to bite her bottom inner lip to keep from bawling like a baby. She wanted to plead a headache and go home, but her pride forced her to continue with the outing.

Was she like a child to Luke, needing to be entertained like Sam? Hadn't he seen that she was a woman—a full-grown woman when he'd kissed her?

She stumbled as it occurred to her that she was older now than her sister when she'd died.

Luke's hand came to her elbow. "Careful there."

Praying for a steady voice, she finally managed, "It was just a tuft of grass. Why don't we go to the orangery?"

"That sounds like a good idea."

They walked in silence, a silence that continued strained for the remainder of their walk, broken only by an occasional, "Oh, how lovely…look at the robins… these trees must be a hundred years old…"

Finally, they were once more in a hansom on their way back to the office. Neither said anything. Bobbie stared out her side, praying for strength and control. Strength and control. *Please God, don't let me break down in front of him. Please, Lord, grant me Your strength…please, please, please…*

Finding nothing out of the ordinary at the office, Bobbie told Luke that she needed to get back home to check on Sam's lessons, and Luke seemed almost glad that she was going. He told her he'd be home in time for dinner.

She sat in the train car, gazing out the window unseeing…her mind reliving that moment when she knew Luke was going to kiss her. It was as if suspended in time, she was made aware that all her dreams and yearnings since girlhood were now going to be fulfilled.

His gaze had shifted from her eyes to her lips and then his face had moved closer to hers. She couldn't help but notice the curve of his lashes before her own gaze moved down to his lips. An instant later his face had blocked out the sunshine, her eyelids had shut and she'd breathed in the scent of him—that dear, masculine scent of him that made her head spin and her knees grow weak. Unlike her father, he didn't smell of tobacco. He had never smoked to her knowledge. The subtle scent of his shaving soap drifted to her nostrils.

And unlike most men of her acquaintance, he was clean-shaven, not even sporting a moustache. Her fingertips tingled to reach up and feel his smooth cheeks and jaw. But the next second he bent down and her heart leapt to her throat as Luke's soft, warm lips touched hers, fusing their mouths perfectly together. Her lips had already been parted in breathless anticipation and now they opened slightly more.

Then she felt his hands span her waist as if he could read her mind and knew she needed some support to keep from falling against him.

And before she had a chance to reach up and draw him closer, it was over.

She touched her lips now with the tips of her gloved fingers. How could a person be so changed from one moment to the next? For she knew she'd never be the same person again. No matter how much she and Luke tried to pretend this had never happened, she was irrevocably altered.

Why had he stopped? Why had he apologized to her as if he'd committed an unpardonable act? The questions spun around and around in her mind as the train clattered along on its tracks, alternating with her memory of the kiss. She could focus on nothing else but those two things.

Like an automaton, she descended the train at her stop and then took a cab, feeling her legs would not be able to carry her the mile walk home.

Everything seemed quiet at home. Gretchen, the parlormaid, greeted her with a cheery smile when she entered the house.

"Is Sam about?"

"I think he's up at his desk since he had his lunch."

"Thank you." Slowly, feeling as if she would shatter at the slightest pressure, she removed her gloves and unpinned her hat, setting them aside. She patted her hair, more out of habit than any real consciousness of her actions.

"I think I'll lie down a little bit. I seem to have a bit of a headache." For the first time in her recollection, she was using the time-honored excuse of every woman, the one she'd always disdained. How many unpleasant things had her mother and sister avoided by lying down in a darkened room pleading a headache?

"Oh, dear, would you like me to bring you a cup of tea?"

"No, no. I'll be fine. Just a bit too much sun."

Gretchen tsk-tsked. "You have to be careful, with spring coming on so fast, we forget. You must take a parasol with you next time."

"Yes…yes, I must. I seem to have forgotten mine." Because she had thought they were going to a business meeting, not for a stroll in the park. She moved toward the staircase. "I'll be only lying down a few moments. Don't tell anyone. It's nothing serious. I'll be up to see Sam in a little bit."

"Mum's the word." She smiled, continuing her dusting. "Have a good lie-down."

"Thank you, I shall." Bobbie grasped the newel post as if she were scaling a mountain and made her way up the stairs, to the pinnacle of her room.

At last.

The door clicked shut behind her and she was left alone, silence surrounding her.

She removed her jacket and set it on a chair then sat on the edge of her bed and took up the buttonhook for her shoes. Finally, she was able to seek the solace of her bed. She curled up on her side, cradling her pillow.

Oh, dear Lord, why did Luke kiss me? Why did he open up an unimagined world only to snatch it away? Why did I respond? Why did he draw back?

The more she asked the Lord for answers, the greater her sadness and despair grew. Her eyes filled with tears and spilled onto her cheeks. She took off her spectacles and buried her face in her pillow, letting the sobs come.

Her shoulders shook though she tried to muffle all sound into her pillow. She felt unloved and alone; she wept for the loss of her father, for the mother she'd never been able to turn to; for the widening gap she sensed between herself and Sam since Luke's return; for all the weight of responsibility she'd had to assume since her father had passed away.

Why did you have to leave us so soon, Papa? she cried silently. He was the only one in her family who had understood any part of her—and even he had seen so little beneath the surface. Bobbie was just the one who could be relied upon. Good old dependable Bobbie, who never fussed but went about her business doing what needed to be done. Growing up, all the family's attention had been taken by Irene, her ups and downs, her tantrums and her joys. And then the pride and joy had become Sam.

Bobbie had not begrudged Sam any of that; he'd been the center of her life as well. He'd filled the empty space after she'd turned down poor Graham.

But now, even Sam's affection seemed to be drifting. It was only right, she scolded herself, wiping her eyes with her handkerchief, and asking the Lord's forgiveness for her moment of weakness. But why did everything have to hurt so much?

And why did Luke have to come into her life only to remind her how out of her reach he was? It was cruel— too cruel—to tease her like that. To pretend she was someone attractive when all she was was Irene's plain, younger sister.

She wept until she felt spent, then she lay there telling herself she must get up and wash away all remnants of tears and go see what Sam was about. Soon, Luke would be home, and she wouldn't show by a hint that this afternoon had affected her in the least.

Only pride and God's grace had helped her this afternoon. She'd held herself so rigidly her back and shoulder muscles ached.

She wiped her eyes once more and blew her nose, but still didn't have the energy to rise.

She had no idea how much time had elapsed when a soft knock sounded on her door. Her eyes flew open. What if it was Luke? A second later, she realized how silly that notion was. He wouldn't come to her room. "Wh-who is it?" Her voice sounded shaky.

"It's Sam."

"Oh, yes, come in." She scrambled off the bed and went to her dresser to arrange her hair. She looked a fright. Too late to bathe her face in cool water. She could only pat her wayward strands of hair into place, though she really needed to take the pins out and begin all over.

She turned around with a bright smile as Sam entered

the room. "I was just coming up to see you, but I must have fallen asleep."

Sam's eyes frowned. "But you never take a nap in the day. Are you feeling all right, Aunt Bobbie?"

She forced a laugh. "Me? Right as ever. I must have felt a little tired with my trip into town."

He stepped closer to her, his frown deepening. "Have you been crying?"

"Wha—no—not really," she amended, not wanting to lie. "Just a little."

"What's the matter, Aunt Bobbie? Is something wrong?"

He sounded so concerned, she realized how careful she must be to reassure him. He'd just lost his grandfather and could easily be frightened if he thought she was feeling ill. She gave another laugh. "Oh, no! It's just sometimes I get a little sad."

"About grandfather?"

She nodded vigorously. That much was true, at least. "Yes, I miss him terribly."

He nodded slowly in understanding, his hands in his pockets. "I miss him, too." After a bit, he added, "I'm glad Papa's here."

"Yes." There, she'd said it in a natural voice, her expression giving nothing away. Seeing how young he suddenly looked to her, she put her arms around him and hugged him. "I'm glad you've got to know him again and can call him 'Papa.'"

When they drew apart again, Sam looked at her. "He said he doesn't mind that I used to call Grandfather that. He said he understands and that it was right."

She said nothing, unsure if she would be able to speak, her throat felt so tight.

"But I'm glad he's my papa again now even though I still miss Grandfather, too."

"Of course you do. But I'm glad you have your father back. It's the way it ought to be."

"Do you think I…might go with him to America?"

Her tenuous composure almost gave way. "I don't know…someday, I suppose." She went to the bed and busied herself with smoothing out the covers and setting the pillow back in place.

Sam sighed. "I hope I may soon."

Chapter Fifteen

That night, Luke deliberately stayed in London until dinner time. He spent most of the intervening hours down in the tunnel overseeing the men. The more he worked alongside Melville, the foreman, the more he thought the man would make a good manager. Bobbie would need someone dependable, trustworthy and honest once Luke removed himself from the firm. It would help if it were someone who was already with the firm and had worked with Robert Gardner.

Luke had already received a few letters from engineers eager to join the firm of Gardner and Quimby. He hadn't yet shown them to Bobbie. He had them folded, still in their envelopes, in his desk drawer. Why he waited, he wasn't sure.

Cowardly, that's why, he thought to himself in disgust as he changed for dinner. As cowardly as he'd behaved this afternoon in Kensington Gardens. As cowardly as he'd been all these years when he'd avoided England.

The thought stopped him short.

He studied himself in the mirror as he brushed his hair before descending for dinner. His reflection revealed a man entering the latter half of his third decade. His hair hadn't started to thin yet, at least not anywhere noticeable, nor turned gray. But that would commence in the next few years. He kept his body trim, mainly through the work he did. He wasn't the type to sit at his desk for hours but preferred spending his days on the project site once the construction began.

Was he a man his son could be proud of?

For all his domineering ways, Robert Gardner had left behind a solid legacy. Both his daughter and grandson missed him sorely.

Could Luke say the same for himself, should he disappear from the face of the earth tomorrow?

Turning away from these thoughts, he set down the brush and gave his dinner jacket a final tug. Time to face Bobbie and Mrs. Gardner now. His former mother-in-law was beginning to show a little more vivacity but dinners were still not the part of the day Luke looked forward to.

And tonight he must face Bobbie again. He'd berated himself the whole afternoon for having kissed her. A moment of weakness, that was what it had been—nothing more. She'd behaved so calmly and aloofly the rest of the time that he'd managed to convince himself it had not affected her as it had him. He wouldn't have blamed her if she'd been deeply offended. He deserved a slap in the face.

He managed to still the small yearning in his heart to hold her in his arms and kiss her again.

No! He wouldn't even contemplate it.

His thoughts lifted at the thought of seeing Sam. His son would greet him with a smile, as he had each evening since their return from Oundle. He really should plan another weekend away for the two of them.

Away from Bobbie.

* * *

Bobbie sat in the drawing room pretending to study her embroidery. Sam had played a piece for them on the piano after dinner and now sat with his father on the settee talking with him. They were both in animated conversation.

Her mother sat with Mr. Southbridge on the settee opposite. Bobbie sat by herself in an armchair. She tied her silk thread off and snipped it. Then she rummaged through her basket looking for another color.

"Scotland might be a bit cool yet. What about Cornwall? Have you ever been there?" Luke asked.

Sam shook his head. "No. I haven't, have I, Aunt Bobbie?"

Bobbie picked out a purple skein of thread and looked across at the two. "No, you've only been as far as Southampton, once when you were quite younger."

"Yes, we went to visit some friends of mine," Mrs. Gardner put in. "Don't you remember the seaside? You were a little tyke." She turned to Bobbie. "How old was he then, dear?"

Bobbie threaded the thick embroidery needle. "Let me see, it was when you had lost your front tooth, so you must have been about seven or eight."

Luke watched her, the way he had all evening whenever she dared look his way. He had been very polite and attentive, though not seeking out her company in any way. She had tried not to feel hurt. What had she expected from someone who had apologized for kissing her, as if he regretted it the moment he'd done it? He turned back to Sam as soon as her eyes met his. "That must have been some event. Do you remember it?"

Sam grinned now, showing a very nice, straight row of teeth. "Yes."

But his grandmother cut him off. "Do we ever! It was my birthday." She turned to the rector. "I had planned a party. You were invited, do you recall?"

Mr. Southbridge chuckled. "I'd have to think back."

"Well, that noon day, young Sam bit down on something and let out a yell. It must have loosened his tooth."

"It had been loose for a few days," Bobbie explained, remembering that day as if it had been yesterday. "But whatever he bit on dislodged it to the point that we knew it had to come out."

"But young Sam wasn't going to let anyone touch his tooth," Mrs. Gardner said. "No matter how much Bobbie or I coaxed him to the contrary, he wouldn't let anyone near. We tried everything, and here I was preparing things for my party."

Bobbie could see Sam didn't like this part of the story. He was looking down at his lap, his fingers fiddling with a cushion. She interrupted her mother. "But all's well that ends well. By five o'clock, just before the guests were set to arrive, Sam opened his mouth for me. Before he knew what had happened, I plucked his tooth right out."

Luke looked from Bobbie to his son. "Did you know what was coming?"

Sam shook his head. "I don't remember it too much. I know she fooled me. She said she just wanted to look at it. The next thing I felt a little pain and then I had a big space."

"Which tooth was it?"

Sam pointed to one of his front teeth.

Bobbie smiled. "He was so proud of himself that evening. He showed everyone the gap in his mouth."

"Oh, yes, I do recall that birthday dinner now," the

rector said with a chuckle. "What a young boy you were and how much you've grown."

"I guess you can thank your aunt Bobbie for saving the day."

Bobbie felt herself blushing from Luke's words and probing gaze.

"But at first I was angry with her for fooling me."

"He didn't know whether to laugh or cry when he realized what I had done." She cleared her throat, taking up her embroidery hoop once more. "But now Sam is practically a young man and rarely scared of anything."

"That's right," Sam said immediately. "I never cry anymore. Except of course when Grandfather died." He looked suddenly pensive.

Luke reached out and squeezed his shoulder. "It's perfectly natural to cry when you've lost a loved one."

Sam swallowed and looked up at his father. Bobbie could see the bond they'd developed over such a short time. Her heart ached with the sense of loss for her little boy.

"Do you think we can go on another trip then?" he asked, his momentary sadness dispelled.

"I don't see why not." Luke's glance encompassed both the rector and Bobbie. "Of course, we'll have to ask permission of your two tutors. What do you think?"

"I think it's a capital idea," Mr. Southbridge put in at once, leaving Bobbie to be the only voice of dissent.

She pushed her needle into the linen and tried to think how to say something without sounding like the killjoy. "Well, he did miss a couple of days of lessons scarcely a week ago. When did you plan to go away on this…trip?" she asked, faltering under Luke's direct gaze.

Luke sat back against the settee, rubbing his jaw in consideration. "I hadn't really thought about it. It depends on the progress of the tunnel, of course, but I was there this afternoon, and things seem on schedule, if not a little ahead."

She concentrated on another stitch. Her hyacinth was looking quite nice. "Where did you plan to go?"

He glanced at Sam. "Well, what about Cornwall then? I had some acquaintances there whom I could look up. But I kind of like the idea of wandering around wherever our fancy takes us. We could visit the coast, a few castles, maybe the tin mines…"

"That sounds like an adventure. When may we go?" Sam turned to Bobbie, his eyes alight with excitement.

How could she refuse him? A part of her yearned to go off with them. How much fun it sounded to be off to new places with no itinerary to follow. The few times she'd been traveling with her mother and father, rigorous preparations had to be made, lists kept, the best hotels contacted. And then loads of things had to be packed. By the time they were off, she was exhausted. How different Luke's style of traveling was.

She met his look of inquiry as he waited for her reply. Did he see the longing in her eyes? She turned away quickly. "We'll see, Sam," was all she said, hating herself for the typical grown-up person's response she used to abhor as a child. "I shall have to check your lesson schedule. And it mustn't be before your piano recital."

"Oh, no," Mr. Southbridge agreed, "that is an important event. You'll want to do your best now that your father is here."

Sam's attention turned to his father.

"But after that, I don't see why you shouldn't have a little time off, eh, Bobbie?" The rector winked at her.

With an effort, she returned his smile. "Perhaps."

Toward the end of the week, Luke thanked himself that things seemed to have returned to normal between him and Bobbie. He spent most of the day at one of the building sites, while she spent mornings in the office and afternoons with Sam at his lessons. Sometimes their paths crossed either at the office or down in a tunnel. He'd make sure at these times to bring her up to date, pointing out the progress at the site and she would do the same with anything at the office. But they both kept their conversation strictly on business.

Most often, however, they didn't see each other until dinner and in the evening hours. It was always in the company of Sam and Mrs. Gardner, and sometimes the rector. Luke found himself being overly polite, as if Bobbie were some fragile porcelain to be handled with care. But she didn't seem to notice. She seemed to have retreated into some kind of shell, treating him with distant courtesy. At these times, their conversation had mostly to do with Sam.

Luke was relieved that he and Bobbie were rarely alone, without seeming to have contrived it. On the surface they behaved as they always had.

If he missed Bobbie's easy friendship, there was little he could do to regain it. Their kiss had changed everything. He could not castigate himself enough for it, but nothing could undo it.

He had a hard enough struggle keeping himself from wishing to repeat it. Lying in bed at night, his thoughts would take flight and he'd imagine taking her into his arms and kissing her until they both forgot everything else—the past and future.

This afternoon, when Luke returned to the office from the tunnel site, he was surprised to hear voices coming from Bobbie's office. She usually left by noontime.

Now, he approached her office door with curiosity more than anything. He entered after a light knock and found her talking with one of the clerks. When she saw him, a look of relief seemed to cross her features. She didn't smile but gave him a nod before turning back to the clerk. "All right, John. I'll let you know tomorrow."

"Very well, miss. Have a good evening."

"You, too." With a brief smile, she bid the man goodnight, then turned her attention to Luke as he approached her desk. He still couldn't accustom himself to seeing her behind Gardner's desk. It always seemed to dwarf her. Yet at the same time, it served to remind him of who she was: the daughter of the late Robert Gardner, owner of a large engineering firm.

He smiled. "I didn't expect to see you here this late. Is something wrong?"

Nodding grimly, she held up a sheaf of papers. "I've had a notice from the railroad president. There's a new hitch."

He frowned and leaned forward in his chair. "But I just came from the site. Everything seemed fine."

Her eyes looked dark, her pupils large behind the spectacles. "The firm that was to manufacture the cable cars has gone bankrupt."

Bobbie gazed at Luke. Never had she felt such relief at having someone to turn to who could help share the load. No matter how distant he had seemed since he had kissed her, deep down she knew she could count on him.

Luke seemed to understand at once the gravity of the news. He held out his hand to receive the papers she gave him. "That leaves the project in a bit of a pickle, doesn't it? Without a cable system, there are few if any options left for the type of locomotion needed."

"Yes. A steam engine is impossible in such a narrow space." She sighed deeply. Things had been going along so well on this front. "The railroad had an awful time merely convincing the government to issue it a permit to attempt this underground. No rail has ever been run this deeply."

She wearily ran a hand through her hair. She must look a fright by now but it mattered little. "The fact that the only other underground tunnel, the Tower subway, was so short-lived, did not work in our favor. And that was not nearly as deep."

"It used a cable system?"

"Yes, but it only transported twelve passengers at a time. It was more like an underground omnibus, and now the tunnel is only used for pedestrians. Our two tunnels are for trains to transport passengers into the city all day long."

"What about electric?"

She pursed her lips. "It had been considered but finally discarded. Remember, there's such a steep grade between the Thames and the station at King William Street. Could we have the kind of power needed to pull a load upward?"

"It might work. There are a few short lines in America and here in England that use electricity."

"But it's never been used underground."

"We'd have to experiment. In many ways electric

engines seem ideal for this. It's a short haul and the increased traction of an electric engine should work in our favor. Why don't we see the railway officials tomorrow and discuss this idea further?"

She didn't have any better solutions, so she nodded. "Very well. Let's hope and pray it proves an adequate solution."

Their meeting with the railway company had gone well. Luke agreed to work with their engineers on experimenting with electrical locomotives. Luke found the prospect an exciting one since only a few electric railways existed in the world—a couple in America and the others in Great Britain. Nothing as yet had ever been attempted underground.

If they could successfully use electric power for underground locomotives, Luke envisioned a whole network of underground tunnels under large cities, moving commuters to and fro with speed and efficiency, thereby unclogging the current congestion on city streets. He'd tried to convey his enthusiasm about this challenging endeavor to Bobbie, hoping to allay her worries over the future of the project.

He returned home late the next afternoon. After quickly freshening up, he went in search of his son, wanting to spend a little time with him before having to change for dinner. When he didn't find Sam in his room, he descended the stairs to the drawing room, although he hadn't heard the piano.

Only Bobbie sat in an armchair by the bay window. He almost backed out again, but she looked up, and he was captivated. There was a vulnerability to the gentle slope of her neck. The afternoon sunshine highlighted the coppery tints in her dark hair. He smiled self-consciously. "H-hello. I was—uh—looking for Sam."

She laid down her embroidery. "He had a piano lesson this afternoon."

He frowned, taking a few more steps into the room. "I thought his lesson was on Tuesdays."

"Yes. But with his recital drawing near, his teacher is holding rehearsals almost every afternoon."

"Yes, that makes sense. He's taken on an ambitious work." Feeling foolish standing there as if he didn't know whether he was coming or going, Luke walked farther into the room. He gestured toward the settee. "Do you mind?"

Her eyes widened. "What? No, of course not." Then she bowed her head over her embroidery.

Why hadn't he just excused himself and left the room? Seeing the newspaper folded on the tea table, he picked it up with an excessive sense of relief and took it with him to the settee. But after unfolding it and glancing at the front page, he couldn't focus enough to attempt an article. He lowered it enough to ask, "Is this recital with other performers?"

Bobbie looked up from her work. "Oh, yes. This teacher has quite a few students. I think a dozen will be playing. He's very much in demand so all these students are quite talented."

"Where is it to be held?"

"At the church next Saturday afternoon."

"Yes, of course. Sam did mention the day."

A few awkward moments passed. Why didn't he feel uncomfortable talking business with her, but now that it came to personal matters, he felt like a bumbling schoolboy?

"The annual Handel festival begins at the Crystal

Palace in June. That's little more than a month away. I usually take Sam to those concerts on Saturday afternoons. Mother goes with us when she feels inclined."

He nodded. "Perhaps we can all go."

"I think you would enjoy them. They attract world-renowned performers. To hear the choir is a magnificent experience. There is a great organ in the main transept of the palace."

"I'm sure they must attract quite a crowd," he said, feeling as if they were strangers making conversation in a waiting room.

"I read that a chorus of four thousand will perform Handel's *Israel in Egypt* oratorio this year."

He whistled. "That sounds quite impressive."

He would probably still be in England in June, he calculated, with this latest setback. His eyes drifted over to Bobbie, who was nibbling her bottom lip, her fingers stilled on her needlework.

"Is something on your mind?" he asked gently.

She looked down at her embroidery hoop. "I—I was wondering if you were planning to be here in late June— when the festival is held."

The quietly worded question threw him. He took his time refolding the newspaper. "I believe so," he finally answered slowly, not wanting to commit himself. "I will, of course, see how the idea with the electric locomotive works. If it's successful, then I foresee no great stumbling blocks to the continuation of the project."

Her dark eyelashes fluttered upward. "You've been very helpful with this idea. I was so glad you could come with me to the railway company. Without my father there anymore, I'm not sure how they would have received me by myself." Her words were uttered in a breathless voice.

He found himself unable to look away from her. The warmth and gratitude in her eyes was not only reaffirming, but it was something more. Something he had never received from her sister, Irene. He felt Bobbie understood and appreciated who he was, not only as an engineer, but also as a man. The thought unsettled him.

He cleared his throat. "I didn't do anything any engineer worth his salt wouldn't have done. I'm glad I could be here at this time. It would have been difficult for anyone to fill your father's shoes—man or woman— but you are definitely proving worthy as your father's successor."

He read relief in the look she gave him. She laid aside her work. "I couldn't have done it without you. You have also proven yourself worthy. I've seen the way the men treat you. You're very respected here in London, although you've worked most of your life abroad."

He didn't know what to say. He wanted to be annoyed and say he didn't need to prove his worth as Gardner's successor; it was the last thing he wanted. Yet, the admiration in her eyes and tone gave him a sense of satisfaction he'd never quite experienced before. He gave a shaky laugh. "Engineering is a small world, I suppose. We keep abreast of the things being built in other countries. Innovations are looked at closely and, if successful, are quickly adopted."

"Yes." She grimaced. "Which is what will happen with this electric train notion."

"Are you concerned about it?"

She pursed her lips, considering, and he found himself remembering their kiss…again. There were moments when he actually managed to forget it. Moments when they were working together, discussing railways and tunnel construction and he almost forgot she was a woman and saw her only as a fellow engineer. Which was why he much preferred to see her at the site or in the office and avoided her at home.

But then, no matter where they were, there were moments when she would do something—tuck a strand of hair behind her ear or indicate a line on a blueprint with her slim fingertip—and her femininity and close proximity would hit him full force and he'd remember that kiss as if it had just taken place.

And all he wanted to do was take her in his arms again—except this time, there would be no holding back. He knew it deep in the marrow of his bones. Which is why he didn't trust himself around her alone.

She finally spoke, clearly oblivious to where his thoughts had been in the previous seconds. "Since you are behind this idea, I feel a lot more secure in pursuing it. Although I shudder to think what will happen if it should fail. Brunel's first tunnel under the Thames was a financial disaster, and the Tower tunnel closed after three months. What will happen if that should prove the fate of this venture?" She raised troubled eyes to him, and he wished to reassure her with more than just words.

He wished he could kiss her eyelids, taking the worry from her gaze then travel down her soft cheeks. "Ahem!" He clasped his knees and strove to keep his thoughts on the topic. "I don't think you'll fail."

"But it's never been done before."

"But a lot of innovations have been done with electric rails in the last decade. Just think, this could be the turning point for use of electric locomotion for commuter railways."

"Oh, I hope so, I truly do!" She paused as if she wanted to ask him something more.

"What is it?"

"Doesn't it make you feel good to be a part of this?"

"Of course it does."

"Does…it help you forget that you're not working for my father's firm anymore, but for your own?"

That was a much more difficult question to answer. "I don't think I can ever separate it from your father," he began slowly. "It was his—he founded it. It represents him."

She sighed but said nothing more and bent over her embroidery once again.

He thought it best to change the subject. "I'm looking forward to Sam's recital. He has certainly been practicing a lot for a young boy. It seems strange not to hear the piano this afternoon."

"Yes, he's very dedicated."

"Do you ever think he'll follow his musical bent instead of engineering?"

She looked up at that. "What do you mean?"

He pressed a crease into his trouser leg. "I mean, you recall the terms of your father's will. He made it a condition that Sam take over one day."

Bobbie didn't seem to find anything unusual in that. "It's just always been assumed…. After all, Father was constantly talking to him about engineering and about how he would eventually succeed him. Once in a while he took him to see a project or pointed out bridges and railroads that others had built."

Luke remained unconvinced. "What if someday when he has finished his studies, Sam decides he hasn't the inclination to be an engineer?"

She frowned. "Has he talked to you about this?"

"No. I hardly think he knows himself what he wants to do when he grows up. My point is that he should have all doors open and not be funneled into only one, no matter how attractive it sounds."

She didn't say anything, but pursed her lips again, looking down at her embroidery.

He felt the conversation had once again deteriorated and he didn't know how to get it on a better track. Perhaps it was better if they were at odds. It helped his own self-control at any rate.

But it didn't feel right to be on opposite sides with Bobbie.

Chapter Sixteen

Bobbie sat in one of the pews near the front of the church. Luke sat on one side of her, her mother on the other, Mr. Southbridge on her mother's far side. Bobbie had to fight her awareness of Luke sitting so near.

It was the afternoon of the piano recital. They had listened to the performances of the younger children and now waited anxiously for Sam's recital. She felt more nervous for him than any of the mothers present, she believed, glancing about her. At least most of them could relax and enjoy the rest of the performance, since their children had already played their pieces.

Her glance crossed Luke's and he smiled. "Nervous?" he asked, as if reading her mind. At her small nod, he leaned toward her, whispering in her ear. "So am I."

She shivered at his proximity. His hand lay atop his thigh. It was such an attractive, manly hand. Her own hand rested inches from his own. If she moved it over to his, would he turn his over and take hers? How she longed for that warm hand clasp. What would it be like to have the reassurance and protection of a godly, upright man? A soul mate.

Was there such a thing? She had long ago stopped

praying for such a person. She glanced over at her mother. Although she'd had a long marriage to Bobbie's father, Bobbie wondered sometimes how compatible the two had been. Her father had spent most of his time at his job, her mother with her social circle. Her friends had seemed to bore her father, who spent his time at home reading his engineering journals in his office.

Ever since Luke had kissed Bobbie, she'd felt a wall between them, a wall which had increased since the talk the other night about Sam's future.

Why did the thought that Sam might not follow in his father's and grandfather's profession bother her? It had honestly never occurred to her. As a young boy, Sam had always seemed interested in hearing of his father's work. Like any boy, he enjoyed building things with his blocks and playing with his train set.

Later, he'd transferred his fascination with his father's profession to interest in all that his grandfather did. Bobbie had encouraged that interest, believing it was the strongest way to forge the link with his absent father. Of course, her own love of the profession had only added to her desire to foster this interest.

Had her interest in engineering prevented her from seeing Sam's lack of interest? She had tortured herself with this question for the past few nights. She's also had to fight her annoyance that in the few weeks Luke had reentered Sam's life, he'd already gained the boy's confidence enough to be privy to his deepest thoughts.

As Sam entered his adolescent years, he confided less and less in her. She understood that it was a natural process. A boy on the verge of becoming a young man didn't run to his mother—or in this case his aunt—with every internal thought. She was glad he had a father to turn to now.

But it still hurt to know how easily he'd turned to a virtual stranger, a man who had not given him a thought in over a decade.

She gave a slight shake of her head to dispel these contrary thoughts. Thank goodness, the young pianist who'd been playing just finished her piece. Bobbie joined the rest of the audience in their applause, though she had scarcely heard the music.

Good, now Sam would play. The young girl curtsied and walked off the makeshift stage set up in the crossing of the sanctuary interior.

Bobbie held her breath as she watched Sam step up to the wooden stage, which had been covered in carpeting. He faced the audience, looking all grown up and yet very young in his new black broadcloth suit, his blond hair darkened by the Macassar oil his grandmother had insisted on combing it with to keep it smooth.

"Courage," Luke whispered in her ear before sitting back again. For an instant, Bobbie felt as if she were like the other couples in the church. She was Sam's mother, and Luke her husband, the two of them there to champion their son and applaud his accomplishment. But she shook aside the foolish fantasy.

Sam bowed once as the audience fell silent then turned and sat on the piano bench.

All was quiet as he leaned over the keys a moment as if in meditation.

Bobbie prayed silently that the Lord would guide his hands.

Then Sam's fingers touched the ivories and the first notes rang out. It was a well-known piece, Beethoven's *Für Elise,* but it took a skillful and sensitive performer to deliver it with the kind of emotion and lightness it deserved.

Bobbie was swept away by the heartbreaking notes. Even though she'd heard him practice it countless times, it felt as if this afternoon she were hearing it anew, with a pathos she had not heard in Sam's playing before now.

His fingers seemed to barely touch the keys in the opening movement. They bore down more firmly in the second part and tripped like lightning as the notes sped up, then slowed once more to the soft, haunting melody.

Bobbie forgot all else but the music. Her breath evened out as she realized her nephew would carry it off. She rested her back against the pew, the tension draining out of her.

When the piece was ended, she couldn't help glancing at Luke, and found him looking at her with a smile in the depths of his green eyes. "Congratulations," he whispered to her then turned back as they applauded with all their hearts.

After the recital, everyone gathered in the church basement for refreshments. The vicar of the church went to every performer with his beaming smile, congratulating them one by one. He ended with Sam.

"Well, my boy, you did it again."

Sam smiled shyly, clearly pleased.

"Mind you, I had no doubts, but I know how daunting a stage can be, even when one has rehearsed something over and over again in private."

"Is it like that with your sermons, sir?"

Mrs. Gardner looked shocked. "I'm sure not. Goodness, child, you mustn't compare yourself to a man of God."

"Oh, no, Sam is absolutely right to compare himself to anyone who performs in public." He chuckled. "I wouldn't want to call my sermons performances, but yes, to answer your question, I was shaking in my shoes the first times I had to stand behind the pulpit. It gets easier with time. And, of course, I rely on the Lord's anointing. Without His direction, my sermons would fall flat, no matter how well rehearsed."

"You did us all proud," Mr. Southbridge added when the vicar had moved away. "You didn't miss a note. It shows all your hours of practice weren't in vain."

Luke clapped a hand over his son's shoulders. "Well done, Sam."

Sam grinned at his father. "I was nervous. For a second, when I stared at the keys, my mind went completely blank."

Luke chuckled. "That's understandable. I think we can always remember a moment like that in our lives." He glanced at Bobbie. "But I know for certain that someone was praying hard for you."

Bobbie blushed under his warm gaze.

"Thank you, Aunt Bobbie. I know God listened to your prayers." He turned to his father. "Were you praying for me, too?"

Luke's gaze didn't falter from his son's. "Yes, I was," he said quietly. Then his look rose above his son's head to meet hers again in silent communication.

She swallowed and was able to give him a small smile in response. For a moment, all barriers seemed to fall between the two of them. Then other people came up to congratulate Sam, and their brief connection dissipated.

Her mother had arranged another tea party at home for Sam's close family and friends, so they soon departed the church. A few great-aunts and uncles and their offspring, second and third cousins to Sam, who had attended the recital, stopped by.

It was the first party at the house since her father had passed away. Bobbie was glad her mother was showing interest in life again. Yet a part of Bobbie felt fresh grief over her father's absence. Life marched on, and it didn't seem right in a way.

"You would have been proud of Sam," she whispered, as if to her father. Luke's words about Sam's future returned to her. Hopefully, everything would sort itself out in good time. Sam had many years of schooling ahead of him before he had to make any decisions.

That brought more heaviness to her heart. Would Luke renew his desire to send Sam away to school? He hadn't mentioned the topic lately, their attention having been taken up with things at the tunnel.

"You must be so pleased with Sam."

Bobbie turned to a second cousin, putting on a bright smile. "Oh, my, yes. He is very talented...."

It seemed hours later, though it had only been at most a few, when the last guest left. Bobbie felt exhausted, perhaps because she had been up since dawn. Sighing wearily, she asked Gretchen for a tea tray in the drawing room, then made her way there to see if anything needed straightening up. Invariably, Aunt Rose left a shawl or Great-Uncle Theodore his monocle. She entered the room to find both Sam and Luke sitting on the settee side by side, their long legs stretched out before them. They smiled at her as she entered.

"There you are," Luke said. "We wondered where you'd gone off to."

"I helped Mother to her room. She was quite done

in. It's her first effort at entertaining, you know, since Father passed away."

Luke nodded. "It was brave of her."

"Yes." Bobbie stood at loose ends, near the settee, unsure where to take a seat. "I've rung for some tea, if that should appeal to you."

"Very much. What about you, Sam, care to wet your whistle?"

Sam laughed at his father's slang. "Sure."

"Why don't you sit down and take a rest?" Luke indicated an armchair close by. "You must also be done in. After all, you were the main hostess."

With a look of gratitude, she picked her embroidery off a small side table and took the chair.

Gretchen brought in the tea tray. Luke took it from her and set it down on the low table. Bobbie leaned forward to pour.

They drank in companionable silence for a while. Then Sam turned to Luke. "Now that my recital is over, may we talk about our trip again?"

"Certainly." He glanced at Bobbie. "We had a bit of a situation at your grandfather's firm, but I think things will turn out all right."

"What happened?"

Luke proceeded to explain. Bobbie watched the interplay, curious for signs of Sam's lack of interest. But the boy seemed as interested as he always had in the engineering firm. In fact, he asked a number of questions, and seemed excited about the possibility of using electric locomotives for the first time deep underground.

"When will you know if it works?"

"We won't know for sure until we lay the track down in the tunnel and test an engine. Of course, we're doing it aboveground now."

The conversation turned back to their planned trip to Cornwall. Bobbie tried not to feel left out. It would only be for a few days. They would be back in no time. In the meantime, perhaps she could give further thought to the idea of enrolling at the college in the autumn. She hadn't broached the subject with her mother yet. She dreaded the expected response, which would range from shock to ridicule…and possibly end with her mother's urging her to get married. She hadn't done that for a few years, probably because she thought Bobbie was long past marriageable age….

Her attention was jerked back to the conversation when Sam asked her, "Do you think I might go to America, Aunt Bobbie?"

Her heart sank. She'd hoped that topic wouldn't come up again. She glanced at Luke. Why couldn't he satisfy himself with one outing at a time? Wasn't Cornwall far enough for now?

"I…don't know…dear. There are your lessons to think of, and your piano, of course."

"But Papa says I can do all those in America, isn't that right, sir?" He turned eagerly to Luke.

"That's right, son," he answered quietly, his eyes on Bobbie.

Bobbie stood her ground. "Why should you have to interrupt your studies when you have everything you need here? Perhaps for a holiday next summer—"

"But, Aunt Bobbie, I didn't mean for a holiday. I meant to live with Papa."

Bobbie let her embroidery hoop fall to her lap. "Live in America…?" When had the two of them cooked up this scheme?

Silence fell. Luke appeared calm, but Sam looked scared, as if he'd said something wrong. She certainly didn't want him to feel scared by her shocked reaction. "Well, I don't know, Sam. I've never considered your moving to America. I—I'd have to give it some thought. As would your grandmother." She cleared her throat, trying to find a way to gently explain to a thirteen-year-old why his idea was completely preposterous.

Sam's bottom lip jutted out and he slumped back on the settee, staring down at his cup. "I don't know why I couldn't go. He's my Papa."

"We'll discuss it later," she said quietly, not trusting herself to look at Luke, for fear he'd see the anger in her eyes. How dare he build castles in the air for his son—a boy she'd brought up—before even breathing a word to her about it! Didn't he have the least understanding of what she and her family had done for his son over the last eleven years?

She picked up her embroidery and stared down at it, raising the needle and running it deliberately into the linen, all the while hearing a pulse throb at her temples.

"Sam, when you finish your tea, why don't you excuse your aunt and me. Perhaps I can tell her a little more about our idea?"

"Yes, sir." Sam gulped down his tea and set the cup and saucer down on the tray. Bobbie concentrated on her stitches all the while, only watching his actions out of the corner of her eye and hearing the sounds. "May I be excused, Aunt Bobbie?"

"Yes, dear." She forced a smile to her lips.

When he'd left the room, she still didn't trust herself to look at Luke.

"Are you angry?"

She swallowed. Carefully, she set the linen back on

her lap and finally locked eyes with him. "Should I be?" she asked in a measured, brittle voice.

He gave a slight shrug of one shoulder. "I'm not sure, but I sense that you are."

She pursed her lips, tilting her head to one side. Finally, trusting herself to speak, and praying for the right words, she took a deep breath. "When, precisely, were you going to discuss this…this idea of taking Sam to America?"

"Soon." He leaned forward and set his cup and saucer down. "Believe it or not, it's only just come up between Sam and me recently." He held up his hands in front of him as if warding something off. "I haven't encouraged it, no matter what you may think."

She wasn't sure whether or not she believed him.

"But when he brought it up, I certainly wasn't going to discourage the idea."

"When did he first bring it up?"

He thought. "During our trip to Oundle."

"I see."

"He opened up quite a bit," he explained.

Of course he did. Which boy wouldn't when a long-lost father waltzed in and took him places and fulfilled his every boyhood fantasy? But what would the day-to-day reality be like?

When she remained silent, he continued. "I didn't press him for anything. I felt privileged—and infinitely grateful—when he seemed disposed to talk. He asked me a lot about America." Luke shrugged. "It probably sounded more exciting than it was. But I tried to paint a realistic picture of my life and travels there. He began by expressing a desire in coming to visit me, and I suppose it has developed into wanting to live with me. It's natural for a boy to want to be with his father."

"Yes, I understand that." Her voice sounded clipped.

He exhaled deeply. "I hope you understand."

"Oh, yes, I do."

He didn't reply to the acerbic tone but rubbed a hand over his jaw with a sigh. After a moment, he said quietly, "I also told Sam a bit about his mother."

She stared at him in sudden fear. "About Irene? What did you say about her?" Sam knew nothing of the reality of his mother and what she'd done.

"Nothing but the truth."

Her anxiety grew. "How could you? Sam thinks his mother was an angel—"

"I only gave him a very superficial account—and a very sympathetic picture, I should say, of his mother. But I tried to broaden his understanding a bit about why I haven't been here for him over the years."

When Bobbie could think of nothing to say, too shocked still by this revelation, he continued. "Sam is thirteen. He deserves to know something of the past. I'll tell him more as he gets older, if he expresses an interest."

"I think you are taking a great risk in doing so. He thinks his mother loved him very much and died in his childhood."

"I have no interest in shattering his picture of his mother. I explained to him that Irene suffered in her own right—that some people can't adjust to things the way others can."

"You painted her as having some kind of mental illness—" Her voice rose, and she could feel herself losing control.

"Didn't she?" he shot back.

She was left speechless, her knuckles gripping the embroidery hoop. "B-but why reveal this to Sam? And how can you presume to take Sam away from the only home he has known?"

Luke let out an angry laugh. "Do you think I would be incapable of taking over Sam's upbringing?"

Bobbie's deepest fear since Luke's return was unfolding before her, and she was helpless to stop it. She set the embroidery hoop aside and clasped her hands tightly in her lap, trying desperately to achieve a tone of wisdom and self-control. "I have known Sam since he was two years old. I've seen his fear when both his mother and father abandoned him. I was the lap he could always climb onto."

She sucked in a deep breath to still the trembling in her voice. "I'm not saying you can't get to know your son and have a satisfactory relationship with him. Nothing makes me happier. But it's one thing to come into Sam's life again and take him on a few outings. It's quite another to presume to take him thousands of miles from the only home and family he's ever known and assume the task of parenting all by yourself."

Luke rose as if unable to listen to her lecture. He stepped away from the settee, shoving his hands into his pockets. "Look, I don't think this is the time for us to get into this. You're tired."

She stood. "I'm not too tired to discuss my nephew's future carefully and thoughtfully. I won't sit by while you cook up some farfetched notion of taking him away and then present it to Mother and me after you've already sold Sam on it. Whether you intended to or not, you're positioning us as the villains if we are to now show any opposition to your scheme—"

He stared at her. "Listen to yourself. You make it sound as if I'm stealing away your child. He's old enough to have some say in his life. He's not a little boy anymore for you to hold on to."

Her voice rose. "I'm not 'holding on to' him."

He gave a short, derisive laugh. "You can't even stand the notion of having him go away to school, which, as you remember, is the other thing we did in Oundle. I showed him my old school and told him all kinds of stories about my school days. He met some of the professors and other students. I wasn't 'conspiring' against you, but I think it's high time he understand he has options." He sighed angrily. "What kind of youth is he going to have here with two women and an old rector who comes a few mornings a week? My goodness, he needs to be in the company of boys his age."

"I never said I wouldn't consider sending him off to school. But I won't be railroaded into something just because you think you know what is best for Sam—"

"And I won't be coerced into succumbing to your point of view. I'm tired of submitting to the Gardner will just because it's stronger—"

"This has nothing to do with the 'Gardner' will—" Her eyes widened. "Or, does it? Are you taking out your resentment toward Father against me?"

He pointed his finger at her. "I could ask you whether you're not holding on to Sam because you've poured your whole life into him, thwarting and sublimating all your other desires and dreams in order to please your father. Are you afraid to let Sam go because he represents the only lineage you have left and you want to force him into your father's legacy?"

She gasped. How dare he? All she'd ever done was accept Sam into her life when Luke abandoned him.

Before she could respond, Luke leaned closer. "If

that's the case, I will take Sam as far away from you as I have to."

Without another word, he turned and marched from the room.

Chapter Seventeen

Luke trudged along the path, Sam a few steps behind him. The slate-strewn trail lay high atop a cliff facing west to the sea. The field to their right was dotted with gorse, the landscape covered with its yellow blossoms as far as the eye could see. Scattered here and there were pink and white flowering crabapple trees, bent away from the prevailing sea winds. An abandoned mine shaft stood in the distance, overgrown grasses obscuring the heavy pieces of timber boarding up its entrance.

He glanced back at his son, who usually didn't lag behind. "Are you winded?"

"Yes, a bit."

Luke slowed his steps to allow him to catch up. Indeed, he was puffing more than normal. They'd had a good three days on the Cornish coast, hiking trails by the sea and visiting a variety of sights. The weather had been warm and sunny.

"We're almost there." Luke pointed down below them to the sandy cove where their inn lay nestled at the foot of the cliff. "Just the climb down, and then we can enjoy some hot tea and pasties. How does that sound?"

Sam only nodded. Luke gave him a sharp glance, as

the boy usually responded with much more enthusiasm at the mention of refreshment and food after a long hike in the bracing sea air. He ruffled his son's hair. "Tired?"

Sam glanced at him. "My head hurts a little." He rubbed his temple. "I don't know why. I don't usually get headaches."

Luke stopped and looked more closely at him. He didn't wear his usual smile. Luke touched his forehead. Despite the cool air, it felt a little warm. "Hmm. Maybe you got a touch of sun. Why don't you lie down when we get back?"

"Yes, I think I shall."

They said no more on the steep path down to the cove, keeping a sharp eye on where they placed their feet.

"Here we are," Luke said in relief, putting his arm around Sam as they walked up the steps to the terrace of the white plastered inn, which had stood there for a couple of centuries.

"Afternoon, Mr. Travis, Sam," the owner said from behind the bar in the taproom when they entered the inn. "Had a good walk?"

"Yes, we did. Might we have some tea and pasties brought up to the room? Sam's not feeling quite himself."

The older gentleman looked at Sam with immediate concern. "Oh, that's a shame. Well, we'll fix you right up with a cup o' tea."

They climbed the narrow wooden steps up to their cozy room. It faced the front with two windows overlooking the sea. The afternoon sun sent long rays into the room across the bedspreads.

Luke pulled down the covers off one. "Come on, take your shoes off and get in."

The boy complied and immediately closed his eyes. "Would you like me to draw the curtains some?"

"Yes, please. The light bothers my eyes."

Luke drew the thin lacy undercurtains across the windows. Perhaps it was the headache that was causing the sensitivity to light.

By the time the tea tray arrived, Sam was asleep. Not wanting to disturb him, Luke sat by himself at one of the windows, pushing aside one of the filmy curtains only far enough to enjoy the view, and sipped his tea.

Despite the enjoyable weekend, he had had an uncomfortable feeling the entire time. No matter how much he tried to shut it out, he couldn't forget the stricken look in Bobbie's eyes that his threatening words had caused her. He'd hurt the person he least wanted to hurt, the one he owed the most to.

By the following day, they'd hardly spoken to each other, and those were formally polite words only, more for the benefit of those around them.

Luke glanced back at his son's sleeping profile. Sam's benefit more than anyone else's.

That's when he'd decided to leave for Cornwall with Sam for a few days. If Sam wanted to come with him to America, then the more time they spent in each other's company, the better. Sam would have to decide if he truly wanted to live with his father.

Luke turned back to watching the sea. He never tired of it, from its changeable colors of blue or green and its endless motion and expanse. Today, it was an inky blue with a bit of chop from the whitecaps visible now and again topping the waves. What would Bobbie have thought of this trip?

More than once over the last few days he'd thought how nice it would have been to have her along, sort of a family outing for the three of them.

But it wouldn't be proper to be traveling alone with her, only a thirteen-year-old boy as chaperon. And Bobbie wouldn't feel able to leave her mother by herself, though Luke couldn't see that Mrs. Gardner was so helpless. She had a wide circle of friends who stopped in almost every day.

Luke sighed, rubbing his temple as he allowed the endless sound of the waves to soothe him. It was pointless to think of these things now after the angry words he and Bobbie had exchanged.

Why had he said such an awful thing to Bobbie? He'd never take Sam away from her like that. For a second, he'd felt the kind of acrimony and frustration he used to feel toward Irene.

It was what he had dreaded most, the reason why he'd avoided any relationship with a woman after Irene. To see love turn to bitterness and hostility.

He covered his eyes with his hand. How could he have felt anything like that toward Bobbie, his friend and ally?

Whatever it was that drew him toward her, would it eventually degenerate into recriminations and accusations as it had with Irene?

He kneaded his forehead, unable to bear the thought.

No, he concluded, he would never let that happen. He preferred having Bobbie at arms' length than risk that kind of anger.

He would apologize to Bobbie when he returned. And then he would ask her to allow him to take Sam with him to America. If it didn't work out, then he'd promise to bring Sam back. In any case, Sam would probably return when it was time for college.

Bobbie would adjust once she was enrolled in the engineering program at the college. Yes, that would be best for her. She would thrive, Luke was certain of it.

She would meet some nice engineering student and eventually marry. His hand formed a fist at the thought, but logic told him it was likely.

Yet, why had she never married before now?

With her father's firm to run, it was perhaps best that she had never married. Otherwise, she would be settled down with children and likely a husband who would object to her having any other responsibilities.

Bobbie had so much more to offer. He'd seen her intelligence and imagination during their work at the firm. She was willing to take on anything that any man was; she almost thought like a man, he thought at times, when approaching engineering problems. She just lacked some of the formal skills, although she had had more schooling than most young ladies he knew.

Luke sighed. A pity her life had gone the way it had. Her parents had been mainly to blame, but then so had he, hadn't he, by saddling her with Sam?

Luke had come round full circle in his ruminations. Without Sam, where would Bobbie's life be? Yet, to hear her and see her with his son, Luke felt as if he would be robbing her of life itself if he took Sam away from her.

His tea had grown cold. He tipped the cup back, draining the last dregs. The pasties lay uneaten. He had lost his appetite. He rose slowly, stretching the kinks from his back, and approached Sam's bedside.

The boy's face was flushed and his forehead felt hotter.

His eyelids fluttered opened. "I don't feel well, Papa."

"I'm sorry, son." He squeezed his shoulder. "I'll call a doctor and he'll give you something to take for your head. You'll be better soon, you'll see."

Sam definitely had a fever. Luke didn't like this. He rubbed his jaw, considering what to do. He knew little of children. All he knew was that fevers could turn deadly. He'd suffered enough chills and fevers in his youth and survived by God's grace, but he wasn't taking any chances with his only son. Best call for a doctor immediately.

The physician was a typical country doctor, elderly and genial. "Well, what have we here, young man? I heard you were ailing." He examined Sam's eyes and throat and listened to his chest. After some minutes, he removed the stethoscope from his ears and turned to Luke.

"Well?"

"Well, he's definitely a sick young man." His glance met Sam's again. "You'll have to stay in bed for a while. No running along the cliffs for a bit."

Sam nodded. He had complained of a sore throat as well.

"Come along and we'll order him some hot toddies. Mrs. Munson is a good soul. She's brought up seven of her own and seen every childhood ailment imaginable."

Once outside of the room, the doctor looked more serious. He questioned Luke about Sam's childhood illnesses and Luke had to plead ignorance. "I—I didn't bring him up. I've been out of the country most of his life. His aunt and my late wife's family have been his godparents."

"I see. Well, from the looks of it, it could be a bad cold—possibly influenza, though there haven't been any cases around here recently—but my guess is it's actually—" he paused, his light blue eyes holding Luke's gaze "—a case of measles."

"Measles?" The word filled him with dread. When would Sam have been exposed to measles? "How could that be?"

The doctor shrugged. "He must have been in contact with someone. It's very contagious. I've seen a few cases recently but it could have been anywhere."

"How serious would that be?"

"I don't want to distress you, but it's a serious illness. He'll need plenty of bed rest. I'll stop by and check on him later this evening. Don't be alarmed if his fever should rise in the evenings. Give him plenty of fluids. I'll leave a powder for him."

"When will we know for certain?"

"In a few days if a rash breaks out. But his eyes are red-rimmed, which is classic with measles, and there's a bit of a rash inside his mouth, which you see in some cases." He spoke calmly but his tone was grave. "You'll notice the rash first on his face and back. Keep the curtain drawn. The biggest danger is to his eyes. They'll be sensitive for a while against the light."

"Yes." He thought of their hours in the bright sunlight that afternoon. What if Sam should lose his sight?

The doctor gazed at him over his spectacles. "Have you had them yourself?"

Luke blinked. "Me? Oh—yes, ages ago, as a young boy." He barely remembered. He'd been much younger than Sam.

"Good. Then you'll not be at risk." He hefted his black bag and turned away. "I'll inform Mrs. Munson and tell her to bring up a pitcher of water and some hot tea for the both of you."

Later that night, as the doctor had predicted, Sam's condition deteriorated. He thrashed about for a while, clearly uncomfortable. But it was more alarming when he say still, as if too tired to move. "I hurt all over," he whimpered.

"I know, son." Luke could only rub his forehead gently, cajoling him to take a few sips of water or tea every so often.

"I want Aunt Bobbie," Sam moaned into the pillow. "She'd make it go away."

Luke's hand stilled. Bobbie might not be able to make the measles go away, but her presence would bring relief to both of them. The hard knot of fear and worry eased a bit in Luke's chest. "I'll telegraph your aunt. She'll be here soon, you'll see."

Bobbie sat in the office on the Saturday, looking over Luke's latest reports on the electric locomotive trials. She tried to focus on the words, and not on his handwriting and the fact that he had penned these words. She'd preferred coming into the office today rather than sit home moping and thinking of the fun Luke and Sam must be having and how with each outing Luke was taking Sam farther and farther away from her.

The building seemed empty today even though some offices were filled with people working. She swiveled her chair around, looking out the dirty window to the street below. The city was as busy as usual, however. Life seemed to go on everywhere except in her own life.

Oh, dear Lord, help me let Sam go. Help me do what is best for him even if it means relinquishing him to Luke. America is so far across the ocean. Will I ever see him again?

Her eyes filled with tears and she didn't bother wiping them away as the view of the buildings outside her window blurred. She imagined Sam a tall young man, broad-shouldered with one side of his mouth tilted up in a smile like his father's, the edges of his eyes crinkled in suppressed humor.

Oh, please, erase these feelings I have for Luke. I know they're not right. I know I should be long over them. Oh…why did he have to come back and resurrect them? She moaned, leaning her head into her palm.

She started at the sound of a knock on the door. The office was closed on Saturdays even though the crew still worked at the tunnel site. She straightened, fumbling for her handkerchief and blowing her nose, swiveling her chair back around to face the door. "Yes? Come in."

A young man peeped in. "Pardon me, Miss Gardner?"

She nodded. "Yes."

"Telegram for you, miss."

"Oh." What could it be? She stood and quickly searched about for her handbag, taking out a coin, which she handed to the messenger when he gave her the envelope. "Thank you."

"Good day to you, miss."

"Yes, the same to you," she answered, her mind already on the envelope in her hands.

She opened it and scanned the few words, remembering the last telegram she'd received. It had been from Luke, announcing his return.

Her eyes glanced to the end of this telegram. It was also from Luke. Her alarm increased a hundredfold in an instant.

Sam measles Please come Trevaunance Cove Inn Trevaunance Luke.

"Oh, dear God," she whispered, "not the measles." However, deep in her heart she feared it was true. For Sam had never yet had the measles. She knew how deadly they were. Oh, where had he caught them? Perhaps if he'd stayed home, he'd have been safe.

As these thoughts whirled through her mind, she was already closing the portfolios on her desk and picking up her handbag and jacket.

She must think. First, home to pack a few travel clothes, then head to Paddington Station and catch the next train to Truro. Was there any local line to Trevaunance Cove? She'd have to check the map, not quite sure where it was, the western or southern coast of Cornwall. Oh, Luke and his lack of a concrete itinerary! Didn't he know that traveling with a child was different than drifting around as a single man?

She fumed as she hailed a hansom to take her to the London Bridge station.

What was she going to tell her mother? Oh, dear, she couldn't hide the fact that something was wrong. Mrs. Gardner would want to know why she was taking off for Cornwall. She'd have to find someone to look after her mother for a few days…or even a couple of weeks.

It might take that long for Sam to recover from an attack of measles. She wouldn't think about any worse possibilities. And his eyes! Was Luke aware of all the dangers? Had he consulted a doctor? She prayed for wisdom for him. She prayed for her nephew.

Thankfully, there was a train going toward Sydenham soon after she arrived at the station. During the ride back, she alternated between praying and jotting things on a list as they came to her. So many things that she must do before leaving…

She didn't arrive in Cornwall at the village of St. Agnes until midafternoon the next day. There had been no local train after Truro and she'd had to take a carriage. From St. Agnes, she hired a dogcart to take her the last few miles to the tiny fishing village of Trevaunance Cove.

Exhausted, hungry and worried sick, she stood before the whitewashed building facing her, with only a passing glance at the scenic surroundings.

"Good afternoon," she told the middle-aged woman who sat behind the bar in the taproom when she entered. A few people sat at tables covered with red gingham cloths in the low-beamed room.

"Oh, hello, Mrs.—"

"Miss Gardner."

The woman's face lit up. "Oh, Miss Gardner. Mr. Travis is expecting you. Come, let me take you right up. I've prepared a room for you." She looked around the taproom, lowering her voice, as she stood and came around the bar. "The poor lad, he's quite ill. I know you'll want to go to him right away."

They climbed a dark, narrow staircase. "Is he getting proper medical attention?"

"Most definitely. Mr. Travis had Dr. Morris see him day before yesterday, as soon as he noted the boy a bit feverish. He came again in the evening when the boy seemed worse." She turned at the top of the staircase. "Pronounced it measles, though the lad hasn't broken out any yet. But the doctor said he's seen a few cases. I don't want to noise it about. People get so worried. We'd have a panic."

"I understand." Bobbie continued following her as the woman led her to a guest room door.

"I'm not worried meself, nursed all seven of my younguns through them. Must've 'ad them meself ages ago."

They arrived in front of a door. "Here you go, miss. Why don't you freshen up? I've made the room up this morning. There's water in your pitcher. Mr. Travis is next door—" she gestured with her chin to the room adjoining hers "—with poor Sam."

"Thank you, Mrs. Munson."

Hardly noticing the small room, Bobbie set her valise down and quickly took off her hat and veil, her only interest washing her face and hands and going to the next room as soon as possible.

Finally, she stood in front of the door and knocked softly.

Luke opened immediately, a look of relief visible on his face at the sight of her. A great weight lifted from Bobbie's shoulders at the realization that there was no residual anger in his expression.

"Bobbie. Thank God you're here." He ushered her in, keeping his voice low. "You received my cable, I take it?"

"Yes, yes. How is he?" She was already glancing toward the bed.

He led her to Sam's side. "Not well."

"Oh, poor dear," she whispered, leaning over Sam and touching his forehead.

He opened his eyes. "Aunt Bobbie!" he whispered, his voice sounding congested. His nostrils were red as if runny.

His skin was hot and dry. She smiled at him, hiding her worry. "Yes, I'm here. I heard you were having so much fun, I decided to come see for myself."

"My head hurts."

"Yes, I know, dear. You just close your eyes and try to sleep."

Thankfully, the curtains were shut tight and the room in semidarkness. She straightened and looked across the bed at Luke.

"Why don't we go into the corridor a moment and I'll bring you up-to-date," he said.

"Very well."

Without a word, she followed him out. When he closed the door softly behind him, she asked, "How did this happen?"

He shook his head and sighed. In the daylight, she noted the fatigue in his face. He hadn't shaved and dark blond bristles covered his jaw and chin. His eyes looked bloodshot. "I don't know. He was fine. We hiked and did a lot of sightseeing. He ate well and was in good spirits up until late afternoon the day before yesterday. That's when he seemed a bit fatigued. It wasn't like him." He scrubbed a hand across his face. "As soon as we returned here, he lay down, and that's when I noticed he was warmer than usual. I thought he might have had a bit too much sun, but I summoned a doctor in any case."

"I'm glad you did. He's usually very healthy." She bit her lip. "The doctor is sure it's measles?"

"He won't be certain until Sam breaks out in a rash, which won't be for another day or so. But Dr. Morris has seen a few cases in the last few weeks, so he suspects it."

She looked away. "How dreadful. Sam has had whooping cough and mumps as a child and a few colds and fevers, but has never been exposed to measles until now."

"I swear I wouldn't have brought him if I thought I'd put him at such risk. It has been such pleasant weather. We were in the outdoors, breathing sea air. He's scarcely been around other children." He gave a laugh of disbelief. "Who would have thought I'd expose him to a deadly disease in these surroundings?" He raked a hand through his hair and she could see the desperation he felt.

On impulse, she reached out and touched his forearm. "It's not your fault. It could have happened anywhere. Perhaps it was even in Sydenham." She looked pensive. "Maybe at the recital. There were so many children there."

His eyes expressed his gratitude. "I suppose so, but if I hadn't brought him now, who knows? At least he'd be at home in his own bed." He sighed heavily and she saw the pain and guilt on his face. "If anything should happen to him, I'll never forgive myself."

She tightened her hold on him, longing to reach for him and comfort him. "Nothing will happen to him. He's strong and healthy and is receiving good care." She rubbed his arm up and down, as if to impart her faith and hope to him. "The Lord is merciful. I know He'll see Sam through this."

Luke nodded, his gaze never leaving hers. "I'm sorry for the words I spoke to you. They were completely unfounded and uncalled for. I would never take Sam away from you."

The two stared into each other's eyes for several seconds. Bobbie's throat tightened and all she could do was nod.

He took a deep breath. "Thank you for coming so quickly. Is everything all right at home?"

"Yes." She knew he meant her mother. "Mother is fine. I sent messages to the rector and Mrs. Allston. They are sure to look in on her. Everything is fine at the firm as well. I left Mr. Melville in charge." She gestured at him. "You were right. He is quite a reliable foreman."

He nodded, but it was clear his mind wasn't on the firm. "By the way, have you had measles before?"

"Yes. When I was ten."

"Thank goodness for that. So, you'll be at no risk."

She smiled slightly. "I remember being covered in a rash and itching awfully. It was summertime. But mother was adamant. She threatened to tie my hands behind me and said I'd be the ugliest little girl all scarred over if I dared so much as touch my face."

He smiled and her own widened in response. Then as if they both remembered the gravity of the situation, their glances went to the door, their smiles evaporating. "Let me sit with him awhile," she said. "You look exhausted. Do you have another room you could use to get some sleep?"

He shook his head. "But I'll go down to the desk now and arrange another room. Did you find yours satisfactory?"

"To be honest, I scarcely noticed. But I'm sure it will be fine. Well, if you'll excuse me, I'll go to Sam."

He nodded and they parted. "I'll have some tea sent up for you."

She watched him only a few seconds as he walked

down the corridor toward the staircase. Had he meant what he said about not taking Sam away from her?

She remembered the intensity in his gaze when they had looked at each other. And knew that she could trust him.

Once again, she felt as if she was in a partnership with him—and that she could face anything with Luke at her side. This realization filled her heart with hope and strengthened her resolve to nurse her nephew back to health.

She opened the door softly and entered the room. She took the seat at the bedside, the chair Luke had occupied till recently. Too tired to busy herself with anything like her embroidery or a book, she simply sat there and prayed.

Chapter Eighteen

Luke had never been so glad to see anyone as he had Bobbie when she'd shown up five days earlier. The weight of guilt he'd been carrying had lifted at both her encouraging words and the lack of condemnation in her eyes. It was at that moment that he'd realized he couldn't—and wouldn't—take Sam away from her and had felt compelled to tell her so.

She had stayed by Sam's side constantly, only leaving to sleep a few hours, when he literally took her by the arm and dragged her away. Now, they took turns, he the night watch and she the day.

Sam had suffered from fever and congestion, but thankfully, his fever finally passed, although his body was now covered by small red bumps. He lay propped up on pillows while Luke read to him. He'd picked up a copy of *Treasure Island* in a local bookshop on a brief foray outside. Now that Sam's fever was over, the greater challenge would be to keep him amused.

"Tired?" he asked Sam with a smile.

"A little, but don't stop reading."

"Very well." He looked back down at the page,

seeking his place. "We're still at the Admiral Benbow Inn."

"It sounds like this inn."

"Yes, it could be a place just like this. The story opens on a coastal town in southwest England, except a century ago, when there was much more pirate activity."

Sam hugged one of his pillows, his eyes shining. "Will they find a treasure?"

"I'm sure they will. They will probably go off to the Caribbean to the islands, which were a hotbed of pirate activity back then."

Bobbie entered the room, holding a tray in her hands. Luke laid down the book on the bed and quickly went to relieve her of it.

She smiled at him. "Oh, thank you. I just brought you two a snack."

He returned the smile, always feeling better when she was around. He looked down at the tray. "Biscuits and milk, just the thing for reading an adventure story."

"The pot of tea is for us," she added.

They settled back down and Luke continued reading, conscious of Bobbie on the other side of the bed with her embroidery. Now that Sam was out of the woods, Luke didn't have to stay up nights, and he and Bobbie were in each other's company more and more each day.

He realized how restful her presence was—and how right it felt. How he longed for the time when he could tell her so. The question was, did she feel anything for him? He thought about their kiss a lot and hoped neither time nor their differences had diminished what he'd sensed in her that day.

These last few days had shown him Bobbie's true nature and character. He'd sensed it but until living with her and watching her take care of his son, he'd never really understood how much love she was capable of. She had revealed to Luke what true love was—sacrificial and giving, as she put aside her own needs to care for the child she loved.

He'd taken her guardianship of his son for granted all these years, and he would always regret the way he'd belittled her devotion and accused her of using Sam for her own means.

Each day he grew more impatient to be able to express to her all that was in his heart—all that the Lord had shown him over the course of Sam's illness.

All Luke was waiting for was for Sam to feel a little bit better. He picked up the copy of *Treasure Island* again and continued reading, telling himself to be patient.

With each day's improvement, Sam grew more restless, until finally by the eighth day, the doctor pronounced it safe enough for him to sit outside on the terrace for a short period of time. Luke continued reading to him. By that time, all three were engrossed in the story and looked forward to its continuation.

That evening, after saying good-night to Sam, Luke asked Bobbie if she wanted to take a walk on the beach. She looked at him, uncertainty in her eyes. "Do you think he'll be all right if we leave the inn?"

"I'll tell Mrs. Munson. We'll be within calling distance."

"Very well."

She wrapped her shawl around her shoulders as they made their way down the inn steps to the hard-packed sand edging the cove. She gave a small laugh. "I've hardly stepped outside since I arrived. It's so beautiful here."

He wanted to say how beautiful she looked. The soft

breeze caught the tendrils of hair around her face and whipped them gently across her pink cheeks. He had to clench his hand to keep from reaching out to them.

The steady sound of waves filled the air. There were a few people still about, strolling along in the twilight.

Luke wanted to take her arm but instead he thrust his hands in his pockets. "Yes, it is."

She had her arms folded in front of her against her chest.

"Cold?"

She shook her head. "It's very pleasant. Quite warmer here than in Kent."

"Yes, it's due to the ocean current. There are even palm trees in parts of Cornwall."

"Yes, though I can scarcely imagine it. I've seen so little of the area. Even the train trip here was a blur."

He smiled at her, remembered how he'd wished she had been along with them on the outing. "We'll need to remedy that now that Sam is on the mend."

"I don't know…we probably need to get back as soon as possible. I left in such a hurry." She glanced at him, concern in her eyes. "Do you think Sam will be well enough to manage the journey back soon?"

"We'll have to consult the doctor. I don't want to rush it." Part of him longed to stay here in Cornwall, just the three of them.

"Oh, no, of course not."

He frowned. "If you'd like to go on ahead, I can stay on here until the doctor's sure that he is completely recovered." He didn't want her to leave, but wanted to put her mind at ease about the project.

"Oh, no… I mean, if it comes to that, I can stay with him and you could go back."

He looked at her steadily, trying to read her mood.

"I would prefer that the two of us stay with him until we feel he can travel safely."

She didn't look away from him, and he began to hope that she was as conscious as he of something between them. As if they were the only two people on the short stretch of beach. "Bob—"

"I—"

They both smiled self-consciously. He drew in a steadying breath. "I'm sorry. Go ahead."

She shook her head. "Nothing…nothing important. Please, you first."

He puffed out his cheeks and let out a breath as he looked seaward, his hands forming fists in his pockets. Not since he was a young man had he felt so unsure of himself around a lady. "I just wanted to ask your forgiveness."

"My forgiveness?" Her voice expressed astonishment. "Whatever for? If it's about Sam, I told you, there is nothing to forgive. And thank the Lord, he is going to make a complete recovery."

He didn't reply right away. They reached a rocky promontory of sorts at one end of the cove. The waves lapped against the dark boulders. He perched one foot on a rock, uncertain how to begin.

"What is it, Luke?" Her voice came to him softly.

"I—" It was harder than he'd anticipated. He began again. "I've had a lot of time to think while Sam's been laid up."

"Yes, I suppose we both have."

He finally turned to her. "When I told you I wanted to take Sam with me back to America, I think deep down I wanted to punish you."

He heard her soft gasp and it pained him that he must

confess these ugly things to her. "Punish me? What for?" she whispered.

"For all you've been to Sam."

She looked down, her inky-black eyelashes covering her eyes. "I've told you before I only did what anyone in my place would have done. It was my pleasure and delight to help raise Sam."

"But it only showed me all the more everything I failed to be."

"Oh, Luke, no."

"I think I've always blamed you in some degree." At her quick look of shock, he finally took his hands out of his pockets, making a gesture. "Oh, not like your father, or even your mother. But I didn't want to see all you'd done for me. I didn't want to have to be grateful to you. Because…then I would have to admit my own shortcomings where Sam was concerned…where my position in your father's firm was concerned."

She drew in her breath at the last words. "Oh, Luke, you weren't at fault with my father. I was young then, but I know how Father could be. I know you had to break with him and take Irene away."

He passed a hand through his hair, looking out at the darkening sea once more. "Did I? I've asked myself that so many times that it's become a litany. Would it have been better for Irene to be here closer to her family? Would things have ended differently?"

"We'll never know. What I do know is that you can't keep taking the blame for Irene's behavior. If you two had stayed in London, Irene would probably have run off with someone there." Bobbie sighed with regret. "My sister was destined never to be happy where she was. No one individual could fill her longings."

Luke had turned to look at Bobbie as she spoke. Now, he listened in wonder at her wisdom.

"There is only one who can fill us in that way and that is our Lord and Savior. It might not seem possible to you," she said with a nervous laugh, "but I was once dissatisfied with my life. But I came to know the Lord in a way that brought me contentment and…joy." She tilted her head. "I don't think Irene ever knew what joy was about. I pray and can only trust that she knew it sometime at the end. And that she knows it now."

They were silent for some minutes, each lost in thought, listening to the ebb and flow of the waves. Luke breathed in deeply of the sea air, feeling cleansed and lightened.

He looked at her profile. "You are so different from Irene."

She glanced at him and he read fear and concern in her eyes. "Am I?" she whispered.

He cleared his throat. "That day when…when I said such awful things to you—"

She reached out a hand. "Oh, Luke, you don't have to—"

"No, please, let me finish what I have to say."

She nodded, her eyes wide behind her spectacles.

He looked down at the sand at his feet and dug a small hole with the toe of his boot. "It was as if my worst nightmares were coming true."

"How?" she breathed.

"After Irene left me, I never wanted to…to love another woman again. I thought that if love meant the kind of bitterness and anger—and ultimately betrayal— that I had lived through with Irene, it wasn't for me. I'd never risk it again."

He cleared his throat again. "When I came back here

and began to get to know you, Bobbie, as…as a woman, and admire whom you had become, I fought what I was beginning to feel for you. I didn't want to feel it." He risked a glance at her.

"But I couldn't. Everything about you drew me. Your love for Sam, for your mother, your dedication to your father's firm and all he stood for. You are a beautiful, intelligent woman whose heart overflows with love for those around you."

Her eyes were suddenly filled with tears. He found it hard to speak himself for a moment. When he was able to, he continued. "When…when we had such a sharp disagreement over Sam, I thought that it was happening once again. The anger and hatred were beginning. What was beautiful in you…was being destroyed because of me. I wasn't capable of love—"

She was shaking her head vehemently. "No, Luke, oh, no."

The tears slipped from her eyes. He reached out and wiped one away with his thumb. "Please don't cry. I never want to make you cry. I'd rather go away—"

She covered the hand he had on her face with her own and held it there, the warmth of her palm sustaining him. "Luke, you don't have to be afraid of anger or disagreement w-with me. I would have let you have Sam. I'd never hold him back for myself. I—I know he's not mine to keep." She was struggling for the words, the tears beginning to flow. "Don't you know I prayed all these years for you to b-be reunited with him?"

He cupped her cheek with his palm. "You've shown me what true love is with your generosity and sacrifice."

She smiled through her tears. "Please don't put me on some kind of pedestal. I'm just an ordinary woman."

"You are no ordinary woman, Roberta Gardner," he said, handing her his handkerchief. She took it from him and turned away from him a little, wiping her face and blowing her nose.

When she faced him once more, she seemed more composed, her hands clasped in front of her.

He chuckled. "Who would have thought that girl with the messy pigtails who dropped cake on my head would prove to be such a wise, young woman."

She gave him a lopsided smile. "I thank you for the kind words, except you flatter me by calling me 'young.' You'd better amend it to 'such a wise old spinster.'"

He snorted at her description. "If you're a spinster, then I'm a doddering old man."

"Hah! You're a man in your prime. Every lady within a radius of a hundred miles of Sydenham is just waiting for Mother to be out of mourning so that they can hope for an invitation to a sociable in order to meet you."

"You are hallucinating. I'm about the worst prospect a woman could hope for. I failed at one marriage, have been a cranky old bachelor for over a decade, with no home, nothing but a rolling stone."

They stood staring at one another until once again, the atmosphere became charged between them. "A woman would be mad to want to join her life to mine," he said in a low, hoarse tone, his heart thudding in his chest.

"Does this mean you...you still believe in love?"

He held her gaze, reaching out a forefinger and pushing aside a stray strand that had blown across her forehead. "It means I believe if there's anyone's love I can believe in, it's yours, Bobbie, if you dare to risk it with mine."

They stared at each other some seconds longer. Her

lips parted and her eyes filled with wonder. "I think I have been in love with you since that day I first met you in my parents' garden."

He let out a laugh of sheer relief. "You cannot possibly be serious."

She smiled tremulously. "It was a childish idolatry, I'll admit, but the admiration and respect…and love never completely went away." She moistened her lips, looking down for a second. "Even when I tried to love another. I knew it was a mistake, and that's why I had to break my engagement to Graham. Even though I knew there would never be anything between us—" she stared back up at him "—even when I knew my feelings were wrong, and that they'd never be returned, I couldn't help it." She sighed softly. "That's why it was so easy to welcome Sam and take care of him. Not that I didn't love my nephew for himself, but he also represented a little part of you…the only part of you I'd ever have."

He had not removed his finger from her face, and with each word, he drew his hand closer until he cupped her cheek once again with his palm. "And now, do any of those feelings remain for an old, damaged widower?"

"Oh, Luke—"

Not allowing her to finish, he bent his head and once again touched his lips to her, breathing in the essence of her. "Oh, dear Bobbie, can you still love me?"

"You know the answer to that," she replied against his lips, drawing her arms up around his neck as if to anchor him before he had a chance to draw away again. "My feelings have never changed, only deepened."

"I love you, dear, sweet Bobbie, and will try with all of my being to show you that love for the rest of my life," he whispered, the last shackles of the past breaking away with his declaration.

Her eyes looked deeply into his. "I trust that love and will honor you with the same kind of love for all of my days."

He smiled at her and saw the response in her gaze before leaning back down and kissing her once more.

Afterward, they walked arm in arm back to the inn. Bobbie struggled with something that had been niggling in the back of her mind since Luke had told her he loved her. "Do you think Sam will mind?"

He tightened his hold on her shoulders. "About us? I should think not."

She glanced over at him and found him grinning in the lamplight from the inn's porch. "What makes you so sure?"

"He told me so himself not too long ago."

She raised her eyebrows. "He told you? When was that?"

"On one of our many man-to-man talks on our outings. I believe it was way back in Oundle."

She stopped in mid-stride. "You already talked about this as far back as that?"

"Well, I didn't. Sam brought it up. He asked me why I had never married you. I was as shocked as you look now and asked him why he had thought it. He said we seemed so good together."

Her fears eased. "Perhaps Sam is the wise one in the family."

He chuckled, a low-throated sound that never failed to send a thrill down to her toes. "Perhaps. The Gardner and Travis wisdoms combined."

"A very good combination, I would say."

He leaned down to kiss the tip of her nose. "The best."

Epilogue

November 10, 1890

Bobbie and Luke stood side by side, with Sam on Luke's other side, among the small select crowd down in the bowels of Prince William Station. A bright blue ribbon was strung across the platform separating them from the rail tracks. A brand-new engine with two cars attached to it waited behind it.

The Prince of Wales beamed as the magnesium flashlamps ignited, allowing the photographers to catch his image. With a final flourish, to the sound of the brass band behind them, he cut the ribbon. Cheers and applause went up.

The engine began to hum, the electric rails beneath it emitting a different sound to the usual hissing and puffing of steam. One by one, the railway officials, civil engineers and other dignitaries invited for the occasion followed the prince aboard the small train for its maiden voyage.

As the train began to move out of the station, Luke took Bobbie's hand as the two sat on the long bench along one side of the narrow train car. He glanced at Bobbie, then Sam. "Ready?"

"As I'll ever be," Bobbie replied with a smile. Everyone cheered once again as the train left the station. Bobbie sat back with a sigh, her hand still firmly held in Luke's, and sent a prayer of thanksgiving heavenward. The project was a success after three years in the building and many before that in the planning. She thought of her father. How happy he would have been. Maybe he was smiling down from heaven.

Luke leaned toward her. "Well, Mme. President, are you satisfied with the first run of the City and South London Underground Railway?"

She smiled into his twinkling green eyes. "Yes, Mr. Chief Engineer and Copresident, very satisfied."

"You look very pretty, today, I must say."

She warmed under his admiring gaze. She was wearing a sapphire blue gown, specially made for the occasion—and with enough give at the waist for the coming months. As if reading her mind, Luke squeezed her hand with a glance at her waist. "How is our other member doing?"

She patted her growing waistline. "A few kicks when we started, which I'm sure signaled her approval." She didn't know why she called the child in her belly a "she." Only time would tell if her instincts were correct. Whatever the child, son or daughter, Bobbie would welcome it with joy and gratitude. She glanced across at Sam, who seemed fascinated by the ride. Her love for her first "son" would never diminish no matter how many children the Lord blessed her and Luke with.

They'd been married over a year now. Bobbie had enrolled at the University of London that autumn—at Luke's insistence. She was in her second year now and didn't know how she would manage once the baby arrived. But Luke told her not to fret. He would be by her side and help her in any way possible, as long as she fulfilled her dream and continued working at his side at the engineering firm of Gardner & Travis.

Bobbie sighed happily as the train gathered speed through the dark tunnel so far underground. Who would have thought that at the age of thirty, all her dreams would come true?

She glanced sidelong at Luke. She was the beloved wife of a man whom she'd only come to love and admire more deeply since they'd wed. She looked the other way toward Sam. She was the mother of a fine young man and soon to be mother of a child of her own and Luke's. She gazed ahead at the darkness whizzing by. And she was an engineer, doing the work she'd always longed to do, carrying forward her father's legacy.

* * * * *

Dear Reader,

The more I read about the Victorian era, the more impressed I am by the accomplishments of the civil engineers of the Industrial Revolution. The nineteenth century is full of great building projects—railroads, steamships, tunnels and bridges. In London, this era brought the underground subway, the sewer system and bridges spanning the Thames. It was the age of engineering, when it grew from a trade into a highly regarded profession. The great names, Bazalgette, Brunel, Stephenson, live on in the monuments they left behind in London and throughout the United Kingdom and the world.

By the end of the century, the field also included a few intrepid women, who left their stamp on the profession. In this spirit, I wanted to tell a story of one such engineer…and a woman who shared his passion. The story of the City and South London Railway underground rail is based on fact, though my characters are fictional. Any errors are mine alone.

Please let me know what you thought of Luke and Bobbie's story. You can email me at cutler207@hotmail.com or write to: General Delivery, Cutler, ME 04626.

Blessings,

QUESTIONS FOR DISCUSSION

1. Luke was hurt by Bobbie's sister. How does this affect his view of Bobbie and her family?

2. How does Luke receive the news of his joint inheritance from his late father-in-law? Why isn't he grateful?

3. How does Bobbie receive the news of this inheritance?

4. Luke doesn't know how to approach his adolescent son. How does Bobbie's intervention help him learn to become a father again?

5. Although Bobbie has prayed for a reunion between father and son all these years, how does Sam's admiration of his father make her feel? Does she feel left out at times?

6. How does Luke see Bobbie's care of his son? When does he begin to chafe at her authority over his son?

7. How does Luke's gratitude gradually shift to seeing Bobbie as a woman in her own right? What strengths does Bobbie have that her sister didn't have?

8. What is different about Luke's attraction to Bobbie from what he felt for her sister? How does age and

life experience change one's concept of romantic love?

9. Was Luke right in staying away so long? Why did he? Can circumstances and people sometimes hamper our decisions regarding those we love?

10. How is the late Mr. Gardner's legacy a godsend for Luke? Does Luke begin to see this? How does Luke's involvement in the engineering project bring him closer to Bobbie? How is he different from Bobbie's father in encouraging her talents?

11. The Gardner family has assumed that Sam will follow in his grandfather and father's footsteps of becoming an engineer. But Luke begins to open up the possibility that perhaps Sam's talents lie elsewhere. How can Luke, as an outsider, see things about his son that someone closer, such as Bobbie, can't see?

12. How does Bobbie deal with her resentment over Luke's involvement with his son?

13. Why is Luke so afraid of committing himself to remaining in England and exploring his feelings for Bobbie?

14. Why does it take something drastic to open Luke's eyes to the importance of Bobbie in his son's life still?

15. A child of thirteen can be very thoughtless. When Sam turns wholeheartedly to his newfound father,

he seems to take his surrogate mother for granted. How does his illness show him he still needs her?

16. What spiritual lesson does each one of them, both Bobbie and Luke, learn by the story's end?

HISTORICAL

TITLES AVAILABLE NEXT MONTH

Available April 12, 2011

YUKON WEDDING
Alaskan Brides
Allie Pleiter

THE LAWMAN CLAIMS HIS BRIDE
Charity House
Renee Ryan

AT THE CAPTAIN'S COMMAND
Louise M. Gouge

THE SHERIFF'S SWEETHEART
Brides of Simpson Creek
Laurie Kingery

LIHCNM0311

REQUEST YOUR FREE BOOKS!

2 FREE INSPIRATIONAL NOVELS
PLUS 2
FREE
MYSTERY GIFTS

Love Inspired.

HISTORICAL
INSPIRATIONAL HISTORICAL ROMANCE

LIHII

*When David Foster comes across an unconscious woman
on his friends' doorstep, she evokes his natural born
instinct to take care of her.*

*Read on for a sneak peek of A BABY BY EASTER
by Lois Richer, available April, only from Love Inspired.*

"You could marry Davy, Susannah. He would look after
you. He looks after me." Darla's bright voice dropped. "He
had a girlfriend. They were going to get married, but she
didn't want me. She wanted Davy to send me away."

David almost groaned. How had his sister found out?
He'd been so careful—

"I'm sure your brother is very nice, Darla. And I'm glad
he's taking care of you. But I don't want to marry him. I
don't want to marry anyone," Susannah said. "I only came
to Connie's to see if I could stay here for a while."

"But Davy needs someone to love him. Somebody else
but me." Darla's face crumpled, the way it always did before she lost her temper. David was about to step forward
when Susannah reached out and hugged his sister.

"Thank you for offering, Darla. You're very generous. I
think your brother is lucky to have you love him." Susannah
brushed the bangs from Darla's sad face. "If I end up staying with Connie, I promise I'll see you lots. We could go to
that playground you talked about."

Susannah's foster sister Connie breezed into the room.
"I'm so glad to see you, Suze. But you're ill." She leaned
back to study the circles of red now dotting Susannah's
cheeks. "You're very pale. I think you need to see a doctor."

"I'm pregnant." The words burst out of Susannah in a
rush. Then she lifted her head and looked David straight in
the eye, as if awaiting his condemnation.

SHLIEXP0411R

But it wasn't condemnation David felt. It was hurt. He'd prayed so long, so hard, for a family, a wife, a child. And he'd lost all chance of that—not once, but twice.

How could God deny him the longing of his heart, yet give this ill woman a child she was in no way prepared to care for?

Although David has given up on his dream of having a family, will he offer to help Susannah in her time of need? Find out in A BABY BY EASTER, available April, only from Love Inspired.